Asher Black

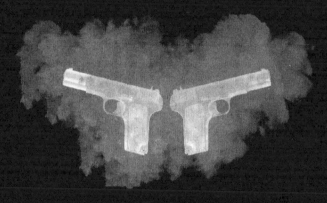

PARKER S. HUNTINGTON

Copyright © 2017 by Parker S. Huntington

All rights reserved.

No part of this book may be reproduced in any form or by any electronic or mechanical means, including information storage and retrieval systems, without written permission from the author, except for the use of brief quotations in a book review.

The characters and events in this book are purely a work of fiction. Names, places, characters, and plots are a product of the author's imagination. Any similarities to real person, living or dead, is coincidental and not intended by the author.

MORE BOOKS

Asher Black
Niccolaio Andretti
Ranieri Andretti (#2.5)
Bastiano Romano
Damiano De Luca (#3.5)
Renata Vitali (#3.75)
Marco Camerino
Rafaello Rossi
Lucy Black

He was supposed to kill me...

I had done the unthinkable.
I called the cops on him,
on his family,
but he let me live.

We became friends...
and then, we fell in love.

AUTHOR'S NOTE

Beloved Readers,

Asher Black is my debut novel, and after years and years of dreaming of becoming a writer, I finally am one! This is a story that's near and dear to my heart, because, like Lucy, I've struggled with being courageous. In my life, my courage comes in the form of pursuing my dream of writing.

    I was supposed to become a doctor. I finished my pre-med requirements, did a boatload of medical volunteer work, and kissed a whole lot of biology professors' asses while under the impression that I'd need letter of recs. And to go from the prospect of a stable career to a make-it-or-break-it profession took a lot of cajones, which I didn't know I had until now.

    Yet, here I am—*writing*! I hope that, as you find what you want to be in life, you guys follow your dreams and not the dreams others have set for you. Find courage to pave your own path, and be the fearless people I know you all are.

xoxo,

The best kind of love starts with an unexpected hello.

— Unknown

*To my family: L, Chlo, & Bau.
& you, too, Elan.*

Courage
cour·age
ˈkərij/
Noun
The ability to do something that frightens one; strength in the face of pain or grief.

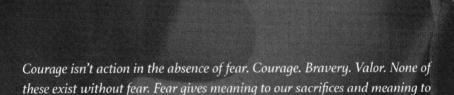

Courage isn't action in the absence of fear. Courage. Bravery. Valor. None of these exist without fear. Fear gives meaning to our sacrifices and meaning to our victories.

Being afraid doesn't make you a coward, just like being fearless doesn't make you brave. Don't be ashamed of your fears. Be grateful for your courage in spite of them.

Face your fears. Gather the audacity to confront them. Be brave, and above all, find the courage to follow your heart.

We were made to be courageous.

PROLOGUE

> Above all,
> be the heroine of your life,
> not the victim.
> Nora Ephron

*I*f you knew calamity would bring peace, would you endure the bad for the good?

Fortune cookies had a tendency of making you scratch your head. This particular one tasted like an omen, and the harsh aftertaste lingered on my tongue as the bus made its way into the city.

I cracked the next one open, not bothering to brush the crumbs off my lap as they fell like scattered raindrops onto my sweats.

The act of living is a leap of faith. What's one more?

Horrible advice—if you could even call it that. Leaps of faith drive you off hundred-foot cliffs, and you can't survive that. Ask anyone who has.

Exactly.

They don't exist.

I devoured the bullshit fortune cookie in two bites, cursed my dinky food budget when a jagged edge of cookie scraped the roof of my mouth, and cracked open the next cookie.

The best kind of love starts with an unexpected hello.

Lovely. Panda Express could go from philosophical to Hallmark-style advice to bullshit romance, yet they couldn't offer me anything more filling than three fortune cookies and two sips of soup for under five bucks. This was how I knew I was back in America.

There was enough bad advice in the world to go around, but somehow it always felt centered here. Where life liked to kick my ass, then do it again just for laughs. I crumbled the three fortunes and shoved them to the bottom of my book bag.

Didn't even think twice about the words.

But I should have.

Maybe then, I would have been prepared for Asher Black.

Maybe then, I would have been safe in my dorm instead of hiding in a safe room as a gun battle raged nearby.

Maybe then, my heart would still be mine.

CHAPTER ONE

*It takes courage to grow up
and become who you really are.*
E. E. Cummings

The only thing running through my mind as we make our way to the bar is: *this place used to be a strip club.* Now, it's a trendy nightclub that caters to New York's elite and whoever is lucky enough to be allowed entrance. Tonight, that includes Aimee and me. How we got in, I have no idea, though I suspect it has something to do with Aimee.

At almost six feet tall, she has the body of a model and the looks to boot. She's a small town girl from a rural part of America, but looking at her, you wouldn't know. Dressed in a tiny sequined dress and sky high heels, she appears every bit the big city girl she pretends to be. With every step we take, I can see men eyeing her in lust and women staring at her in envy.

"I heard this place used to be a strip club," says Aimee, echoing my thoughts.

Aimee and I just met today. We're both juniors at Wilton University. She's my new roommate in Vaserley Hall, one of the upperclassmen dorm buildings at Wilton. As far as I know, we're also the only transfers in our hall.

Whereas I completed my breadth requirements online while volunteering internationally, Aimee went to the local community college in her hometown, eventually saving up enough money to pay the remainder of what her scholarship at Wilton doesn't cover.

We're both new to the area, and not even minutes after meeting me, Aimee suggested that we go to Rogue, the hottest club in New York. Earlier, she told me that the small town she grew up in was too isolated, and she was excited to become a New Yorker as quickly as possible. I believe her. She already looks the part, and I could have sworn that earlier she asked me to "pass the watta bottle, dahling."

I slide a sidelong glance at her, wondering what she's hiding behind her glamorous façade. I understand the desire to abandon roots better than most, but I usually do so by running from place to place, never settling down. I can already tell that Aimee, on the other hand, is choosing to become a different person entirely.

It's alarming to watch.

"But, like, a high end one," Aimee continues.

A surprised laugh tears through my throat. "A high end strip club? Do those even exist?"

I've always thought of strip clubs as seedy places, but as I look around, I can envision Rogue as a classy strip club. Even if those words together feel like an oxymoron.

There are dancers hanging from human-sized birdcages overhead. They're dressed in stylish, little black dresses, but I imagine that back in Rogue's strip club days, the dancers above used to wear absolutely nothing.

The bars enclosing the cages are black and shaped into webs of intricate, beautiful gothic designs. Instead of a covered bottom, the bases of the cages are made from thick glass, allowing the club patrons to see completely into the cages from below. I hope the dancers are wearing underwear, but I keep my head down just in case.

The rest of the nightclub has a modern gothic aesthetic that gives the place a noir and forbidden vibe. It makes me feel like I shouldn't be there, but I'm lucky to be. There are grand chandeliers that hang above the cages. The walls are painted a matte black, and the floors are concrete with a shiny, black epoxy finishing.

Above the chandeliers and suspended cages, the ceiling is a pure white, contrasting starkly with the blackness of the rest of the club.

The bar area, too, is a clean white painted over intricate, wooden fixtures. There are several tables cut into the wall throughout the club and hidden by rich, velvet red curtains that hang from the high ceilings and brush down to the floor for ultimate privacy.

A VIP level is also above us, partially covering the high ceilings on one side of the club. It has a balcony view that overlooks the rest of the club, but as far as I can see into it, which isn't very far at all, there doesn't seem to be anyone up there.

"If a high end strip club exists, leave it to Asher Black to own it," a guy says, approaching us from the side just as we reach the bar.

I catch Aimee eyeing the guy with interest. He's attractive in a stereotypical way, but he isn't my type. While I prefer men of the tall, dark and handsome variety, this guy is only slightly above average height and has pale blonde hair. Like every other guy in the club, he's wearing dress slacks and a button down.

As cute as he is, he's the type that would blend in with a crowd, and after two years of traveling the globe and meeting so many diverse people, I need someone different to peak my interest. Someone intriguing. Mysterious, even.

I turn my head towards Aimee and mouth, "He's all yours."

Even before she grins at me, I already know that she's interested. On our Uber ride here, she confessed that she has a boy obsession. It was more like a warning, cautioning me to ignore her one track mind if it gets too crazy. I assured her that it's nothing I can't handle.

As a former foster kid, I've seen more than my fair share of crazy. Hell, I was given the sex talk by one of my foster mothers, a self-proclaimed asexual being who had been my foster mother for less than an hour before she proceeded to tell me how to stimulate a frenulum. On top of that, she was actually still a virgin.

I watch in amusement as Aimee looks at the guy again, her gaze scanning him with renewed interest. The guy flushes as she sidles up next to him. I wince when I notice that she's at least a full head taller than him in her heels.

She must have had a hard time finding guys her height in her small town's slim pickings. At 5'8", I'm a few inches shorter than her, and even I sometimes have difficulty finding men taller than me wherever I go. Call it vanity, but I have trouble dating men shorter than me.

"Zeke," the guy introduces himself.

He's still fidgeting self-consciously, but I don't blame him. Aimee is absolutely stunning, and her attention is completely on him. I can see how that would be unnerving for him.

"I'm Aimee." She points to herself. "And that's Lucy." She gestures to me with the same hand, before continuing, "So, who's Asher Black?"

Zeke's eyes widen comically. "He owns this club..." His voice trails off awkwardly. He looks like he wants to say more, but when his eyes glance up at the VIP area, he quickly averts them and shuts up. He looks almost... afraid.

Intrigued by Zeke's reaction, I turn my head in the direction of the VIP floor. It's a level above the main area of the club, so I can't see into the top, but there's a grand staircase leading up there. It's no more than a few feet away from where we're standing at the edge of the bar area, which means I have a close up view of the two guards that are stationed in front of the stairwell.

They're both wearing suits and have coiled earpieces on like the ones I've seen in movies. Their eyes are constantly scanning the club, always on alert. And earlier, when we walked past them on our way to the bar, I heard them speaking what I think was Italian.

I also notice there are guards stationed all over the club, pressed against the walls with their arms crossed and eyes vigilant. They, too, have the cool coiled earpieces. In fact, there are a lot of security guards at Rogue, and they're all decked out in high tech gear and super serious faces like they know what they're doing. It's pretty intimidating and very over the top.

One of the guards at the bottom of the stairwell briefly touches his earpiece. He says something to the other guard, and suddenly, both of them tighten their formation beside one another. A beautiful blonde woman approaches the two.

She's tall and thin with a willowy model's frame similar to

Aimee's. I wouldn't be shocked to learn that she *is* a model. Usually, I would be blown away by her beauty, but standing next to Aimee, I'm used to it. I can't help but watch, though, as she ascends the stairs with grace after ignoring both guards along the way. I wonder who she is.

Behind her, she's followed closely by a man. A soft gasp escapes my mouth. He's breathtaking. My eyes trace the defined edges of his jaw, entranced. He has a face that belongs on the big screen, but my intuition tells me he'll never agree to such exposure.

It's his eyes that convey this to me. They're intelligent but also guarded. From this distance, I can see how sharp and vividly blue they are. A punitive coldness exists within their depths, mimicking the dark expression on his face, which gives me the distinct impression that he doesn't want to be here.

I look away from his eyes, because the callousness in them is too much. Almost inhuman. I try to look away from him altogether, but I can't help myself.

I stare.

I don't even try to hide it.

I look at his dark hair, which is cropped closely at the sides but kept longer at the top. I look at the tailored suit he's wearing, which does nothing to hide his muscular physique. I even look at his feet, which are encased in sleek dress shoes that probably cost more than my monthly rent.

As he passes the guards, I notice that he's taller than both of them. He has to be at least six feet and two inches tall. I watch, captivated, as his eyes scan the crowd before they lock onto mine. They stay there for longer than normal, long enough for me to see them darken before he sweeps his eyes down the length of my body, lingering a beat too long on the partially exposed swells of my breasts. I think it's lust I see in his face, but it's gone almost instantly.

Like it wasn't even there.

Maybe I imagined it?

His attention returns to one of the guards, whose mouth is moving. They nod at one another before he passes by. He was there for less than ten seconds, but the whole thing took my breath away. I'm winded by the time he's up the staircase and out of my sight.

I catch a rough elbow into my side from Aimee. I rub the area below my ribs, massaging away the ache, and glower at her. "What was that for?"

"Where'd you go just now?" she asks. "You looked like you were deep in thought." A giggle slips past her blood red lips. "Smile. We're at a club. And not just any club. *The Rogue.*"

I sigh. "Nowhere." And then I lie, wanting to keep the lust I saw in Blue Eyes to myself. "I was just worried about the first day of classes tomorrow. Almost everyone else has the advantage of going to Wilton since their freshman year. It's intimidating."

Truthfully, I'm not actually worried. I've always been the kind of book smart that doesn't require effort, but I know that if I have to, I can always suck it up and study. And it's unlikely that it will come to that. But I lie anyway.

I'm driven by an irrational desire to keep my sighting of Blue Eyes a secret. Something about the way his eyes ran down my body so intimately—even from the distance of a few feet away— feels private, like it should just be kept between us. Is it against the girl code to see a hot guy and not point him out?

I wouldn't know.

Aimee's my only friend, girl or boy, and I've only just met her.

I don't dwell on that depressing thought, because Aimee is already scoffing. "Please. I've seen your schedule. You're in classes with names I can't even pronounce let alone understand."

That's true. My major at Wilton is Bioinformatics and Genomics. When I showed her my schedule, Aimee told me that the name of my major is enough to give her a headache. She's a business major, though, and I know that alone is an impressive feat.

Wilton has the best business program in the nation, even better than Wharton's. With an admissions rate below one percent, the admissions process is incredibly selective and includes a series of interviews that occur over the course of a year. For Aimee to have been admitted means she's not only brighter than most people but also well-spoken.

Naturally, the first thing she said to me was, "I need to get laid. Are you up for a round of club hopping? Or are you going to be one of those buzzkill roommates that hates my guts?"

I didn't want to be a buzzkill, so here I am. Plus, finding a no strings attached one night stand doesn't sound like such a bad idea. I haven't had sex in years. And judging by the way my body reacted to Blue Eyes, I'm long overdue for some special attention from a man.

Zeke whistles, reminding me that he's here. He has an impressed look plastered on his all-American, pretty boy face. "You two go to Wilton?"

Among the small pool of Ivy League schools, Wilton is at the top. The name comes with a lot of prestige. And of all the Ivy League schools, Wilton is the only one where donating a building can't buy your acceptance or gain you favor. Intellect is valued over money, a rarity in this world.

I can understand why Zeke is looking at Aimee with even more intrigue. He knew that she was pretty, but now he knows that she's smart.

Aimee nods before dismissing the topic. "Yes, but that's boring." She gives him a flirty grin. "Let's dance. I can barely hear you guys anyway."

She has a valid point. With how loud the music is, I'm impressed that we've been able to hold a conversation. I look between the two of them. Aimee's giving Zeke her bedroom eyes, and I know that if I follow them to the dance floor, I'll just be the third wheel.

No, thank you.

So, when Aimee turns to me and nods her head toward the dance floor, I shake my head. "I'm going to go to the restroom and then maybe find a cute guy to dance with."

Aimee nods in approval. "Text me when you're ready to leave."

I agree, even though we have yet to exchange numbers. And then they're off. I watch as Aimee leads Zeke toward the center of the dance floor, her hand holding tightly onto his. The crowd parts for her like she's royalty. She certainly looks like she's *somebody*.

I smile. I like Aimee. I really do. She's quirky, but quirky can be good. Plus, it's nice to meet someone who's confident but not cocky. Kind but not a pushover. Interested but not nosy. She's the baby bear to my Goldilocks—just right. I can already tell that she's going to make a great roommate and maybe even a friend someday.

I watch Aimee and Zeke for another moment. They were holding hands when they left me, but now they're pressed tightly against one another. Aimee looks happy and in her element, so I decide to leave her and Zeke alone for the rest of the night.

And then it's just me here, and I can't help but feel like, no matter where I go and who I meet, it'll always just be me.

CHAPTER TWO

*All our dreams can come true,
if we have the courage to pursue them.*
Walt Disney

"If I step outside for a minute, can I come back in afterwards?" I ask the man guarding the door to what I think is a side exit. I've been dancing in the club for almost an hour straight without a break. My feet ache, and I'm in dire need of fresh air.

He glances at me, roaming his eyes up and down the length of my body in a violating scrutiny. It's the same look the bouncer gave Aimee and me earlier, full of unrestrained judgment, contemplating whether or not we're good enough to be here.

To my relief, he nods. "Knock three times when you want to come back in."

As soon as I step outside, the cold New York air relieves the pain building in my temples. It's quieter out here, but I can still hear the music that's playing inside. What was initially hypnotic is now giving me a headache, making me desperate for the fresh air.

I press my back against the brick wall of the building, stopping to take in my surroundings. I'm in an alleyway, but the only entrance and exit is the door I just entered from—another security measure, no doubt. The narrow street has been blocked off on either side by mountainous brick walls. They're painted black, and Rogue's logo is stamped onto the center of each wall in white spray paint.

It's odd being in an alley that's not actually an alley—more like an outdoor room with asphalt for floors and the night sky as a ceiling. I'm grateful for the privacy the surrounding walls give, though, because a dark alley in New York City isn't exactly the safest place for a girl to be alone at night.

I jump in alarm when the doorway opens beside me. "Just another minute or so. I promise," I say, turning to face the bouncer.

Instead, I find the guy from earlier.

Blue Eyes.

He's staring at me with amusement in his face, so different from the coldness I witnessed earlier. "I think this will take longer than a minute."

My breath catches in my throat as I take in his words and the dark promises they hold. His eyes are devouring me, skimming the length of my body and holding me captive. I scare myself when I take an unconscious step in his direction, wanting to be closer to him. To touch his face, his body, wherever he'll let me.

I clench my fists, forcing myself to stop that ridiculous line of thought.

Now I understand what heroines in romance novels are feeling when they meet their alpha males. It's not insta-love. It's insta-*lust*, and it's so strong and overwhelming, it's easy to confuse the two. Lucky for me, I have my head screwed on tightly enough to realize that what I'm feeling is simply pure, unadulterated lust.

And it needs an outlet.

But this is a man that followed me into an alleyway. A man I neither know nor trust.

I level him with an accusatory glare. "Did you follow me out here?"

"Yes." There's no hesitation nor remorse in his voice, just a lingering truth that hangs boldly in the air. He eyes me warily as I take an instinctive step back, pressing myself against the wall again. "Tell me you don't want me here, and I'll leave. No questions asked."

I wonder if he's telling the truth. If he is, it would do wonders to ease my safety concerns. Because the truth is I *do* want him here. I want this. I want the promises of pleasure his eyes are giving me. I want to kiss those full lips. I want his hands to ravage me. I want everything.

So, I test him.

"I don't want you here," I lie, waiting to see if he'll leave.

He nods his head and turns around, rapping on the door three times—the signal to open up. I'm relieved to learn he was telling the truth. That I can have this night of pleasure without worrying for my safety.

When the door opens and the guard sticks his head out, I say, "Wait."

I mean it. I want this. I want *him*.

Call it instinct or insanity or probably a little bit of both, but I can already tell that, when he touches me, it'll be electrifying. Just from looking at him, I can see that this is a man who takes what he wants. Right now? It's me. Tomorrow? Who cares? That's not what one night stands are for.

Blue Eyes nods to the security guard, who closes the door again. He turns my way, and the fascinated look of approval on his face sends a shiver of delight down my spine. "You were testing me."

I nod. "I was."

He takes a step closer to me. "And if I hadn't passed?"

I hook a finger into his belt loop and pull him nearer. "We'd probably be in the same position, only I'd be lying to us both when I tell you I don't want this."

He places his hands against the wall on both sides of my head, caging me in. "And now?"

My left toe brushes against his ankle, trailing its way slowly up the length of his leg until it's hooked around his waist. I use it to push him forward until we're pressed tightly against one another.

"I don't have to lie. *I want this.*"

His lips are on mine before I can blink, his tongue fucking my mouth the way I hope he'll do to my body. I respond eagerly, my tongue brushing against his and savoring the distinct taste of spearmint and amaretto. It's a filthy kiss, harsh and violent and messy, filled with the sinister promises I can't wait for him to unleash on my needy body. It's unfathomable how much I want this, how much I've thirsted for this since my eyes connected with his and saw the desire lurking within their depths.

His lips move to the skin below my ear, sucking lightly before he bites down gently, sending a jolt of pain straight to the stiff peaks of my nipples. An animalistic groan escapes my mouth as his tongue flicks over the sensitive skin he bit, lapping away the delectable pain. His lips trail down my throat, meeting his hands at my breasts.

He pinches a nipple with one hand, while his mouth sucks roughly on the other pebbled bud through the thin fabric of my dress. My hands tangle themselves into his hair, pushing him lower, wanting him *there*. He lets me, chuckling at my lack of patience, while purposely trailing his fingers slowly along the length of my inner thighs in a teasing touch.

I groan, taking the leg that was wrapped around his waist and hooking it over his shoulder. The movement lifts the skirt of my dress higher, exposing more of my skin to the crisp fall air. He leans forward and digs his nose into my sensitive flesh, dipping it into my slit through the cotton fabric of my underwear.

Hooking my fingers into the elastic band of my panties, I shove them downward, too eager for the skin to skin contact to wait. The vibrations of his responding growl send my hips thrusting forward, forcing our lips to clash.

I cry out at the feel of his tongue, tracing the length of my mound. He takes one of my lips fully into his mouth, sucking softly, before releasing it. The pad of his thumb brushes against my clit, spreading the wetness from my opening onto it and rubbing in slow circles.

When his lips take over his thumb's position on my clit, I nearly lose myself. He swirls his tongue around it, teasing me with the slow pace. I'm panting by the time one of his fingers enters me, pumping into my body with ease. A second finger joins the first one, and I ride them both, savoring the feel of his warm mouth on my clit and his long fingers in my body. With each thrust of his tongue, I can feel myself reaching the edge, coming closer and closer to the release I desperately need.

This is it. This is the moment I've waited for for years. The end of my dry spell. The beginning of ecstasy. I'm so close to coming. I can feel it in the quickening of my heartbeat; the phantom taste of his tongue in my mouth, his lips against mine; and the scrape of my nails against the nape of his neck.

I moan loudly, my voice thick from pleasure. "I'm close. I'm close. I'm so close," I say, gasping between each breath.

He pulls back suddenly, and the loss of his warmth is replaced by the still coolness of the air. "Can it wait?" he asks, his tone sharp and demanding.

"W-what?" I ask, struggling to settle myself through the dense haze of lust.

It's unnavigable.

Is he...?

I look down at him, following his line of sight. He's still staring at my exposed flesh down *there*.

My jaw drops.

Did he just ask my vagina if it can wait? To come?

Because the answer is a resounding *no*. It's waited, like, two years to come on someone's hand that's not my own.

I reach down and tug my underwear up from its position on my knees. When it's properly protecting me, I quickly cover it with my dress, realizing belatedly how ugly nude, cotton underwear is. I might as well be wearing granny panties.

There's a resounding silence as I wait for him to stop staring at my now covered crotch. When I chance a glance down at his handsome face, I discover that he's not staring at me. He's staring into space—in the direction my ugly ass panties once were. I side step discretely, putting as much distance between us as possible.

He may be the hottest man I've ever seen, but I don't hook up with Crazy. Even if he comes with a mouth capable of inconceivable pleasures. My eyes dart to the door, wondering if I can make a quick escape without him realizing I'm leaving.

"Fine," he says, and I gather that he *isn't* talking to my girly bits.

He's talking into an earpiece. It's smaller than the coiled ones the guards are wearing. Whereas theirs are larger and wired, his is wireless and tiny, fitting entirely into his ear and camouflaged by its flesh-like color.

He stands up, straightens his suit, and barks, "I'll be there in a minute."

With that, he raps on the door three times and enters the club as soon as it opens, leaving me to gawk by myself, my dry spell still intact.

No apologies.

No goodbyes.

The douchebag doesn't even give me the courtesy of *looking* at me.

CHAPTER THREE

> *Courage is grace under pressure.*
> Ernest Hemingway

*I*t takes me a few debilitating moments to settle my rage.

Because, seriously, *who does that?*

He couldn't give me thirty more seconds?

I was so close!

I'm still angry when I realize how freshly fucked I look. My hair is sticking up in every direction, I'm fully flushed from head to toe, and I smell like the sex I almost but didn't have. I need to go to the restroom and deal with this before I find Aimee and hightail it out of this wretched place.

One thing's for sure: I'm never going to Rogue again.

I can meet Blue Eyes in Hell a hundred years from now, and it'll still be too soon. I know for certain that's where he's going, too. There's no doubt in my mind that there's a special place down there for men who leave women on the cusp of coming like that.

I knock on the door three times. I'm quick to snarl when the door swings open, and I'm met with the guard's amused smirk.

Fuck him.

Fuck Blue Eyes.

And fuck this stupid place.

I stomp my way to the bathroom, forcing myself to calm down.

Deep breaths.

In.

Out.

In.

Out.

In.

Out.

I repeat the mantra until I no longer feel like I'm on the verge of turning into a certain green monster with a genius level IQ.

When I reach the hallway that leads to the women's restroom, I pass a man with the blonde woman from earlier, the one that went up to the VIP level with Blue Eyes. They're too busy arguing to notice me.

In fact, they don't seem to see me at all, so I keep my head down and angle my face and body away from them, trying to mind my own business. That's Foster Care 101: keep your mouth shut, your head down, and your opinions to yourself. Passing by them, I realize that, even though two years have passed since I aged out, Foster Care 101 is still second nature to me.

Nevertheless, I'm able to catch a good look at the man before I turn away. Built like a heavyweight champion and dressed head to toe in black, he's super scary. Intimidating. The snake tattoos that dip below his shirt and wind up to his closely shaved head give me unwelcome goosebumps. They only add to his hard countenance.

A dreadful shiver runs through me, and I quickly duck into the women's restroom, eager to get away from the duo.

I'm calm by the time I'm done straightening myself out and twisting my hair into a messy ponytail. After I go to the restroom, I return to the sink, only to realize the arguing outside has gotten louder. I want to leave quietly, but the two have congregated even closer to the restroom door now. There's no way I can leave without drawing attention to myself, and my gut is telling me I should definitely not be drawing attention to myself.

There's a thud followed by a sharp cry. My breath hitches. I open the door just a crack and peak an eye outside. The scary guy has a gun in one hand and the girl's neck in the other. His body is flush against hers, pressing the rest of her onto the wall. Had he not been holding a gun in his hand, I would've classified their behavior as sexual.

But no, he's trying to intimidate her, and it's working... on me.

My jaw drops. Sure, they're in an empty hallway, but it's still a public place. There are so many eyes in the club, and the hallway has no doors. Anyone can pass by and see what's happening. With all the security positioned on the floor, I'm actually amazed they haven't been caught already. Is this guy not worried that someone can see him manhandling this girl? With a gun!

I push the door open a little bit more, being careful to remain silent and unseen. From this angle, I am able to see into the crowd at the club.

What the heck?

I'm shocked beyond disbelief. The two are in clear view of the crowd, but people are practically going out of their way to ignore them. And the people that do look glance away after less than a second as if they haven't seen anything.

My fists clench. This guy is scary, sure, but they're all cowards for not doing anything. But then again, so am I. I'm the one who's hiding in the restroom. I have to help her, but what can I do? He has a gun, for goodness' sake. *A gun.*

After my time spent traveling through third world countries, I've gotten used to weapons and danger. But this is *America*. The richest nation in the entire world. It's supposed to be safe here. I'm not supposed to be in a situation involving a gun on my first day back.

I close the bathroom door, doing my best to keep quiet. My heart is pounding as I debate my options. Obviously, I have to help the girl. But if I go out and fight him, it would just be putting us both at risk. My self-defense training consists of kicking a handsy teenage boy in the balls back in high school and literally nothing else. I can't beat a gun! I wouldn't even know where to start.

The security guards are also out of the question. Alerting them will require passing this guy. Again, *he has a gun*. I'm not a fool, and I don't have a death wish. I won't be playing hero today.

I remember my phone in my clutch. I can call the police and hope they get here in time. That's what I'm going to do. *It's the best option*, I reassure myself. I pull out my phone and dial 9-1-1, waiting with baited breath at the sound of the dial tone. I pull further back into the restroom to keep quiet.

"9-1-1. What is your emergency?" The operator's voice is deep and masculine, calm and strong.

It soothes me immensely.

I close my eyes, allowing his voice to give me strength for a brief moment. "Uh…" I hesitate, unsure of what to say. I've never called 9-1-1 before. "I'm in the bathroom at a club, and there's a guy out the door with a gun. He's choking a girl. What do I do?"

"First of all, ma'am, remain calm. Is the club crowded?"

"Yes," I say, struggling to keep the incredulity out of my voice.

Is he serious? This is a Friday night in a college area in the most populated city in the United States. Of course, it's crowded.

"What club are you at?"

"Rogue."

There's a staggered gasp on the line before the operator recovers. He says, albeit weakly, "And there's a male with a gun?"

"Yes."

I'm starting to get a bad feeling about this. Well, I already had a bad feeling, but that was mostly worry for the girl. Now, it's worry for me, too.

Am I stuck in the Twilight Zone?
If so, where's Bruce Willis?
And how the Hell do I get out?

The operator finally speaks again, "Are you sure you wish to report this?"

My jaw drops.

What? Really?

Are cops even allowed to ask that when someone reports that a scary guy has a gun in his hand and is strangling a woman? This is beyond odd. Is this a thing? Are guns considered foreplay in New York? *50 Shades of Grey* hasn't prepared me for this.

Oh, gosh.

What if I just interrupted kinky sex?

That'd make me no worse than Blue Eyes. And he's an asshole. I don't want to be an asshole. They're gross and ugly and smel—I force myself to stop my nervous mental rambling. It's one of my many bad habits.

I peak my head out again in time to see Scary Guy running his hands down the side of the girl's body. It's slow and sensual, but the gun is still there. Light reflects off of the trigger, winking at me in spite of its deadliness. It can go off at any second.

The uncertainty running through me passes from my system. I pull back into the restroom, assured that I'm doing the right thing. Plus, I was scared for the woman before, but now I'm increasingly uncomfortable with my role in this. I want to leave as soon as possible without being the primary witness to a murder, and the cops are still my best bet.

"Yes," I say firmly, leaving no room for doubt.

"Are you sure he's not a security guard?"

I remember the matching suits that all the guards around the club are wearing. In fitted dress slacks and a tailored, navy blue button down, this guy is dressed similarly to Zeke, only Zeke looks like a little boy compared to him. This guy is certainly built like the guards, but he isn't dressed like one.

"I don't think so," I say.

"Okay," the dispatcher acquiesces. "I have a patrol unit nearby. They'll be there in a few minutes. Please, wait on the line and stay put." He hesitates. "Whatever you do, don't draw any attention to yourself."

No shit.

I release a breath and along with it goes my anger. I'm being unnecessarily mean to this guy, even if my jabs are just in my head. Sarcasm may be my defense mechanism of choice, but it's not a very nice one.

A few minutes.

I can do that.

I can wait that long.

"Okay," I tell the operator.

I walk even further away from the door with the phone still pressed against my ear. But I walk back to the door almost immediately after, my curiosity getting the better of me.

I'm saving this girl, so I can spy on her, I reason.

With my eye positioned at the door's keyhole, I watch as the man starts patting her down with his free hand. His body is still flushed against hers, keeping her pressed into the wall. The girl has an indignant look on her face, and she appears to be more angry than scared. That's yet another thing to add to the long list of things about this situation that are strange.

Something is off here. I start to reconsider my decision. Maybe I've been too hasty in calling the police. I've been in a lot of dangerous regions over the past two years, so violence seemed like the most obvious conclusion to me. But now, judging by how the guy steps back with a mischievous grin quickly replacing his angry features, I know I've made a mistake.

I glance down at the phone in my hand. The operator is still on the line. *Fuck.* He sent a patrol unit, and they're already on their way. Is it too late to call the whole thing off? I debate my options for two more seconds before making another hasty decision.

I hang up on the police.

I end the call and wipe down the phone, removing all of my

fingerprints from it. It's an international prepaid phone that I bought a couple years ago in Mozambique. It's unlikely that they'll be able to trace it back to me.

I've never even made a call on it before. I had no one to call, and I only bought it for emergencies anyways. I've been meaning to get a new phone with a national provider, but my lazy ass hasn't gotten around to it yet. I'm glad for that now.

After flipping the phone over, I remove the battery and SIM card out of it. The battery goes into the trash, while the SIM card goes in one of the toilets. I take the phone—which I'm still holding up with a paper towel in order to keep my prints off it—and place it in the sink under a stream of water. I make sure that it's low enough that they can't hear the sound of the water from outside, though the odds of that happening are slim. The club is loud, after all.

I grab the wet phone and throw it in the trash. Then, I use the wet paper towel to wipe down anywhere I might have touched. I know I'm being paranoid. No way will the cops take the time to fingerprint a bathroom that has to have a lot of fingerprints everywhere just to identify me.

Whatever.

Better safe than sorry.

When I am done indulging my paranoia, I return to the keyhole in time to see a guy approaching. He's a dark shadow of leisurely movement until he comes closer and the light shines on his magnificent, stony face. I recognize it immediately.

It's *him*.

Blue Eyes.

Asshole.

Hell-bound.

Whatever his name is.

I still haven't decided what I want to call him.

How do you give a name to someone who has the power to tilt the earth on its axis? Because, surely, that's the only way I can possibly be feeling like this right now. Like the world is tumbling inward, and this man, who brought me to the brink of orgasm then left, is suddenly in the center of it.

Maybe I'm just crazy?

I don't know, but I do know that I'm also still angry. My first instinct is to push out the door and slap him silly, but I restrain myself.

Barely.

"You pat her down?" he asks immediately.

No hellos. No pretenses.

He only said four words, but I revel in the sound of his voice again. It's rough and masculine and sexy. I want to drown in it, and then I want him to resuscitate me with those full lips.

Look at me.

I'm in a sketchy situation and am still horny. What's even more embarrassing is, even after he left me hanging, *he's* the one that's making me horny. I need to take a page out of Aimee's book and get laid. All the way this time. I add that to my mental to do list after I get out of this situation.

The scary guy nods and says, "Yeah, boss."

Boss.

Scary Guy works for Blue Eyes?

I wonder what they do. From his stylish suit to his fancy watch, Blue Eyes looks like he's dripping in wealth. Whatever he does must be lucrative.

The girl rolls her eyes and crosses her arms. There's no indication that she was just being manhandled not even a minute ago. She doesn't even seem to care. Instead, there's a haughty air about her as she says, "Yes, Asher. Now, if you're done treating me like I'm the enemy, can we begin?"

Asher.

That's Blue Eyes' name.

I remember what Zeke said about an Asher Black owning the club. Is this him? If so, it makes sense. He has access to the VIP area and looks like he has a lot of money to spare. And no one in the club seems to care that his "employee" was manhandling this girl.

Damn it.

What have I done? I called the cops on what now appears to be a consensual business deal. Sure, a gun was involved, but everything looks fine and dandy now. Aimee is going to hate me. They're totally going to blacklist me from Rogue for this.

This is bound to be the end of my clubbing days. Now, I have to meet men on Tinder. I don't even have a phone that swipes.

Stupid, waterlogged flip phone.

And as if it can't get any worse, one of Asher's guards comes over and whispers something into his ear. Whatever he said makes Asher's body go rigid.

He turns to the other two, eyes full of exquisitely restrained wrath, and growls, "Who the fuck called the cops?"

No one answers him.

Asher straightens himself, and his mask is back in place in an instant. Calm but also icy. The frustration on his face is quickly pushed aside, and he begins to bark out orders.

"Bastian," he addresses Scary Guy, "take her out through the back. Don't draw any attention to yourselves. No one can see the two of you together."

He leaves abruptly after that, and his guards, the girl, and Scary Guy, who I now know is named Bastian, follow after him. I breathe a sigh of relief, happy to be alone.

CHAPTER FOUR

Courage is fear holding on a minute longer.
George S. Patton

I wait a few minutes before I leave the restroom. The music in the club has shut off already by the time I reenter the main area of the club, searching for Aimee. There are several police officers inside, clearing out the club. Some of the faces in the crowd show confusion, but in general, everyone looks excited, even though their night is being cut short by the cops.

It's bewildering.

But I can't dwell on it, because a pair of hands grab me. I jump, alarmed, already on edge from the hallway incident.

"Relax! It's just me." Aimee throws her head back and laughs. "We've been looking all over for you! The police are here, Lucy! This is so exciting."

Zeke nods behind her. "We should leave. We don't want to be caught in the crossfire."

Crossfire?

His words, like the rest of this bizarre night, strike me as odd.

I fold my arms across my chest, not budging when he tries to usher Aimee and I towards the door. "Crossfire. What do you mean by that?" I don't bother restraining the accusation tingeing my voice.

He sighs, and I see him glance at the door with a contemplative look, as if he's debating just leaving us here.

Don't even think about it, buddy.

Are all men assholes or is it just New Yorkers?

He turns back to me and gives me a disbelieving look. "This is the Rogue," he says like it explains everything.

I give him a blank look. "And?"

Aimee glances back and forth between us, a frown tugging on the edges of her red lips.

"And it belongs to the mafia," Zeke says, sighing *again*.

Am I just a pain in everyone's ass today?

And then I process what Zeke said.

The mafia?!

But he isn't done. "The Romano family, to be exact."

Oh.

Oh.

Oh, no.

The Romano family.

I grew up across the country and I've been gone for a couple years now, but even I know who the Romano family is. They're one of the five American crime families. The entire Northeast of the United States and parts of Canada are their territory. They're big time, and the idea of being in a club owned by the Romano family is absolutely frightening.

Can it be that The Hallway Incident is connected to the damn mafia?!

It's then that I know I have truly fucked up. I can't come back from this. I interfered with mob business. I can only hope that no one has seen me or cares enough to find me. I remember the fury on Asher's face, and the memory causes a shiver to ease its way down my spine.

I really need to get out of here. Now. And pray to every god in the universe that no one will find out that I called the cops on *the mafia*. The Romano family.

Oh, my God.

Everything makes sense now. The guards. Asher's money. The pat down. The gun. The people who ignored what was happening. Bastian. The 9-1-1 operator. The sheer amount of cops in here right now.

I eye the door like it's my salvation and nod. "Okay, let's get out of here."

I'm playing it cool on the outside as Zeke leads Aimee and me out of Rogue, pushing through the crammed crowd, but I'm dying on the inside. Literally. In my head, I'm replaying the million different ways this might end in my death like a morbid movie reel on repeat. I'm also mentally putting my affairs in order. But really, no one will miss me, and I have nothing of value to leave behind.

I grew up in the California foster care system, jumping from home to home before I aged out and left to volunteer around the world. No one even knows I'm in New York, except the school records and Aimee, who I've only just met today. The mob can easily dispose of me, and nobody will even blink an eye. That's a depressing thought.

By the time we reach the doors, I have assured myself at least a dozen times that no one saw me enter the hallway. That Bastian and the girl were too busy arguing to notice me. When we exit Rogue, a line of cop cars catches my eye. I curse, causing Aimee to send me a confused look. But I barely notice it. I'm too angry at the police operator for lying.

That asshole told me that a patrol car was coming.

One.

Not eight!

I can't believe I didn't think about it when I saw how many officers were in the club ushering people outside. I want to groan and put myself out of my misery before the Romano family can. I'm the reason why eight cop cars are here. No way will they be able to let this go.

There are actually only two officers outside, though. The rest are probably still in the nightclub, kicking people out and doing whatever it is they're doing. The two officers are talking to Asher, who is leaning against a police cruiser with a devil may care attitude sprawled across his indifferent face. If I didn't see how angry he was when he learned the cops had been called, I would have thought that nothing can faze him.

There's an eager crowd surrounding Asher and the officers. Some of them even have their smartphones out, recording the whole thing.

Aimee pulls Zeke and I to a stop, her round eyes fixated on Asher with a look of hunger in them. I frown. Can't she see that he's dangerous?

But even I have to admit that his shady mafia connections do nothing to dim my attraction to him. There's no denying how alluring this man is.

Even if he did leave me hanging...

Oh, no.

The realization cuts me deeply.

I hooked up with a mobster.

I watch as one of the officers' hand twitches near his weapon holster. Asher's eyes narrow at the action, and he straightens from his position against the police car. The movement comes off as a taunt.

I tense, preparing myself for a battle that I imagine Asher will win. But it doesn't come, because the officer's radio goes off. Through it, someone is saying something about two suspects fleeing out of the back entrance. I remember what Asher said to Bastian about going through the back and know instantly that it's Bastian and the girl.

Asher's body is no longer relaxed. He has a neutral look on his face, but I can see the tightening of his shoulders and the apprehensively coiled muscles of his neck. I wonder if anyone else can see it, but the officers have taken off toward the back of Rogue and with them goes most of the crowd.

If we stay any longer, it will only be us and Asher. That definitely cannot happen. I place a hand on Aimee's back and one on Zeke's, urging them both forward. We're practically running now.

"Dude! What's your problem?" Aimee is frowning. Her head is still turned in Asher's direction, a look of awe and lust written all over her face.

"Nothing. I just... It's the *mob*." I continue to push Zeke and Aimee until we are a comfortable distance from Rogue.

Aimee rolls her eyes. "Relax, Lucy! They have no idea we exist." Then, her eyes light up, and she squeals. "But ohmigosh, did you see that?! That was so cool. I love New York!" She sighs a contented sigh. "Best. Night. Ever."

Zeke rolls his eyes and calls an Uber for us, but I am too out of it to really pay attention to what is going on. I distantly see them exchanging numbers before Zeke leaves in his own cab. A car comes, and I'm ushered into it. Aimee and I are alone in the back of the car as the driver rounds the vehicle to his side, having just shut the door for us.

"Relax," she says again.

But I can't relax. Even when we arrive back to the dorms and I'm tucked into bed, I can't relax. As I go to close my eyes, I realize that my hands are bleeding. They've been curled into fists for the last half of the night. I clenched them so tightly, my nails pierced my skin, leaving crescent shaped grooves across my palms.

I never go to sleep that night.

CHAPTER FIVE

Man cannot discover new oceans unless he has the courage to lose sight of the shore.
André Gide

The following morning, nothing happens. I stay in bed all day, even when Aimee insists that I explore the city with her before classes start on Tuesday. The next day, nothing happens. And the next, until it's the first day of classes already, and still—nothing happens.

I go to class, but I can barely focus. I should be excited about my first day at Wilton. It's the top school in the nation, and I've worked my ass off to get here. But the thrill of a stellar education is overshadowed by my fear that I won't live long enough to complete it.

The day after my first day of school passes by uneventfully, too. I am still alive, which is nothing short of a miracle after messing with the Romano family. Nothing out of the ordinary happens. I go to class like I should and even receive an interview request from the campus coffee shop, which I applied to online before moving to New York.

And the next day is normal again. I go to my classes. I even do well in the interview and get the job. Days pass, and eventually, I am finally able to breathe normally. The fear of death subsides, but I still remember that night. From the hookup to the police call, it's pinned to the back of my mind, but at least I'm able to move on with my life. A part of me starts to consider that they'll leave me alone. That the

It's a naïve thought that I have no business thinking.

It's a month after the incident, and I'm about to leave work at the coffee shop. I shove my little green apron into my employee locker and sling my leather backpack over my shoulder. It was a splurge from my first paycheck, along with a brand new iPhone to replace the cheap flip phone I lost to the Hallway Incident. Hell, I've even downloaded the Tinder app, however I haven't created an account yet. When I do, though, I know what my number one swipe right criteria will be—no mobsters.

I'm not paying attention as I exit the break room and bump into someone, spilling the coffee I'm holding all over me. I curse, though I'm grateful the coffee is iced not hot.

"Watch where you're going."

I know that voice.

It's painfully familiar.

Minka Reynolds lives in my hall. She and Aimee have butted heads since the beginning of the school year, so as Aimee's roommate and friend, I'm an enemy by default. And I'm getting sick of it.

I can't pass by her or her snooty friends without them sneering at my clothes or my hair or whatever they decide to make fun of that day. It's grinding on my nerves, but I've been telling myself that, if I ignore them, they'll stop.

I'm wrong.

They haven't stopped.

If anything, it has only gotten worse.

And when I look up at Minka and see the look on her face, I know that she bumped into me on purpose. There's a satisfied smirk on her lips, and she's lifting a goading brow as if to say, "What are you going to do about it?"

Of course, I do nothing.

I sigh and turn around, returning to the break room. I may have started ignoring her jabs with the hopes that they would stop, but now it's too late. I'm too committed to staying quiet, and I feel trapped in my stupid plan. Like if I speak up now, it'll be a victory for her, a confirmation that she's pushed me to my breaking point when she hasn't.

So, the only other alternative is to act like I don't care.

After slamming the break room door on her face, I drain the rest of the coffee down the sink and toss the empty cup into the trash. Looking in the cheap full-length mirror that hangs behind the door, I assess the damage.

The coffee is completely soaking my hoodie. I'm glad I have a job and can now afford to buy another one, because it's completely ruined. I take it off and throw it away, too, knowing I won't be able to remove the stains from my Signature Mocha Prevent a Nap Frappe™ —who names this stuff?—with heavy whipping cream instead of milk, two pumps of hazelnut syrup, an extra shot, one and a half scoops of java chips, a caramel drizzle, and one stalk of vanilla bean blended in. Oh, and extra whipped cream.

Yes.

I'm one of those obnoxious drink orderers, but I make my own drinks, so who cares?

I feel naked in my silky spaghetti strapped camisole that dips low into my cleavage. It clearly looks like it belongs to a lingerie sleeping set. It actually *is* a part of the skimpy pajama set my last foster father gave me.

He's creepy, and I know that he only bought it for me so he could see my body in it, but I kept it anyways. Beggars can't be choosers. At the time, I didn't own a lot of clothes and needed whatever I could get my hands on.

I actually grew to love how it looks on me, so I've never tossed it, even though I probably should have. I mean, who keeps lingerie sleepwear bought for them by their unnerving foster dad? Apparently, I do. And I like it. The clothes, not my foster dad. I ran away from that guy as fast as my social worker would let me.

But I was wearing the camisole and panties this morning when I woke up late. I didn't even have time to change. I just threw on yesterday's hoodie and black skinny jeans and high tailed it to work as fast as I could.

Now, I'm regretting my decision, but the dorms are across campus, and I have less than five minutes to get to Dr. Rolland's lecture. There's no time to change if I want to make it to class on time. And I do. Dr. Rolland is a spit talker, so I have to get to class early if I want a seat outside the splash zone.

I leave through the back door in a rush, hoping to avoid Minka. I make a mental note to leave through the back door from now on. It's cowardly, but the last time I tried to be a hero, I ended up calling the cops on the mob. I still can't sleep comfortably at night. The bags under my eyes are a testament to that.

I was maybe an eight before the Hallway Incident, but now I'm more like a six. I catch a glimpse of my reflection on a window and wince. It's more like a five and a half. I look really exhausted. Between the stress of retaliation, my upper division coursework, and the long hours at the coffee shop, I have reason to be.

Miraculously, I arrive to class on time. The lecture is almost starting, so all of the good seats in the center and back rows are filled. As if my day can't get any worse, I have no choice today but to sit in the splash zone. I take a seat in the center of the front row. I'm sitting in the splash zone anyway, so I might as well get the best view of the board while I'm at it.

I jump in surprise when someone sits down next to me. I thought I was the last person in here. At maximum capacity, only one person has to sit in the splash zone. That's me, so who is this? I turn to whoever it is, ready to warn him or her about the splash zone, when I'm met with familiar blue eyes. I realize who it is immediately.

Asher Black.

Oh, God.

I feel the panic instantly kicking in.

Is he here to kill me?

I must have said that aloud, because the serious look on his face is replaced with one of amusement. It cuts through his frosty demeanor like the ultimate icebreaker but does nothing to ease my concern.

"Am I that scary?" he asks, a brow arching in doubt.

I swallow and nod.

If this was a cartoon, there would be an audible gulp coming from me.

His brow returns to its normal position. "Serves me right."

Asher's eyes darken, the icy blue transforming to navy in a heartbeat, and I see the hint of danger there. It's always been there, but the shadows accentuate it until I can't focus on anything else.

"In all honesty, I *was* here to..." His eyes dart around the room, probably looking for eavesdroppers.

It's a fruitless effort. We both know everyone will be paying attention as soon as they realize he's here.

He glares at someone and lowers his voice until I'm straining to hear it. "... *take care* of you."

I turn away from him, so he can't see the horror etched into my tired face. If there's one thing the gazillion mob movies and books I've watched and read during my post-Hallway Incident research has taught me, it's that "take care of" is code for:

I'll kill you and hide your body six feet under a construction site, where they'll build a Section 8 housing complex over you and won't find your body until fifty years later when some rich, Trump-wannabe billionaire buys the complex, evicts the poor, knocks it to the ground and builds an apartment tower over it.

He'll even further desecrate your memory by not allowing minorities to rent there.

Oh, and Shawn Spencer will come in to solve your murder case, so at least they'll figure out who did it, and it'll be funny.

Scratch that.

Psych was cancelled.

So, Reese and Harold will get your social security number from their AI machine, and they'll find your body and bring your killer to justice.

Scratch that, too.

Person of Interest was cancelled...

Why are all of my favorite shows always cancelled?!

I hate T.V. networks. They always cancel my favorite shows and leave me with a cliff hanger. What am I supposed to do with that? Write my own damn ending? Nobody has time for tha—

Fuck me, I'm rambling.

Actually, I'm *mentally* rambling, which is worse, because when I mentally ramble, I have a tendency to mouth the words I'm thinking. Like a damn loon. I'm glad I'm looking away from Asher, because if I don't die by his hand today, I'll definitely die from embarrassment.

Winded, I stop myself. Thinking of his words, I can feel a panic attack coming on. I can't breathe. I open my mouth to say something, but nothing comes out. How can he be so brazen? Coming into my class, sitting next to me, and all but telling me in public that he's here to kill me. Will he do it in public?

I eye the clock. It's 9:10 A.M. on the dot. Class is about to begin. I have 50 minutes to think this through before I have to leave. I don't even have to think about it to know that he'll be following me out of class. The knowledge causes another panic attack to begin, before I even have the chance to get rid of the last one.

I can feel Asher leaning towards me.

"Hey," he says, his tone surprisingly gentle but firm.

I can't look at him. It would just make this worse.

"Hey," he says again, but this time, he places his fingers on my chin and turns me to face him.

When I finally do, I want to turn away again. There's a crease in between his eyebrows that wasn't there before. It's a look of concern that seems out of place on his stony features, but I don't know if it's *for* me or *because of* me.

Probably the latter, because no way is Asher Black concerned on my behalf.

Right?

"Calm down, *Lucy*," he says, frightening me with his knowledge of my name. His voice is full of condescension and annoyance, which only confirms my theory. He's not concerned for me. "You're drawing attention to us, and you don't want to do that."

I take a shaky breath. "W-why shouldn't I?" I swallow, gathering the courage to speak again, even though my words are ridden with stutters. "G-give me one r-reason why I shouldn't s-scream."

The glare he throws me vanishes any hope that I'll be speaking again. "Don't even think about it. I tracked you here. I can track you anywhere, except next time, I won't be so nice."

He's right.

I don't doubt for a second that, with his resources, he can follow me anywhere. I Googled him after the incident at Rogue. I was unsurprised to learn that he's a big deal here in New York, not just in the underworld but also in the business world, where he owns a Fortune 500 company that has made him one of the wealthiest men in the city.

I couldn't find much on his illegal dealings, only some speculation and ridiculous tall tales that he has never been formally accused of. I was, however, able to find out quite a bit about his legal businesses, which are all controlled through his company, Black Enterprises.

I feel the shift in the air when people realize that Asher Black is here. Not only does he own a successful company, his possible mafia ties and gorgeous looks have made him a media darling. The paparazzi seem to follow his every move, and there are fan blogs all over the internet that post pictures of him all day long. I know without a doubt that the majority of people in this class know who he is, and this is a lecture hall of three hundred.

The classroom, which was previously silently waiting for Dr. Rolland, is now buzzing with whispers. I hear a few people get up, and from the corner of my eye, I see some girls walking down the steps and heading towards the front row. It's almost full now.

A pretty girl with big eyes and a sultry smile sits down next to Asher. He doesn't even glance her way. He's still looking at me with a slight frown on his face. I swallow, give him a nod to confirm that I won't be screaming, and look away.

Someone takes the seat next to me. It's one of Minka's lackeys. Her name might be something like Nelly or Nessy. She eyes Asher curiously, not even bothering to conceal her interest. It annoys me.

This guy probably wants to kill me, and she's looking at him like she wants to get hitched, have his babies, and be buried next to him. And not necessarily in that order.

It's the knowledge that Asher is probably going to kill me anyway that gives me the courage to say, "Why are you sitting next to me, Nelly? You don't even like me." I feel Asher shift in his seat next to me, but so long as I'm not staring at him, I still have the courage to speak.

Her jaw drops. She's probably dumbfounded that I'm actually saying something to her after a month of silently taking her torment. "It's Nella," she says stiffly. Her eyes shift to Asher. "And I was going to ask Asher if you were bothering him."

I almost snort. She's full of shit. No way did she not see that he was the one to approach me. It's a classroom tradition for everyone to see who has the misfortune of sitting in the splash zone. I don't believe for a second that she didn't see me here first. She probably even got a kick out of it, looking forward to seeing Dr. Rolland's spit fly my way for fifty minutes.

So, I finally call her out on her bullshit after a long month of tolerating it. "Bull." I cross my arms. "You saw me sitting here alone in the splash zone." I distantly hear Asher question the splash zone under his breath, but I ignore it. I'm on a roll, and even he can't break it. "You probably even thought it was funny. Then, you saw him," I nod in Asher's direction, "sit down and thought you would come over here all demure- and innocent-like to get into his pants." I take a profound breath, realizing that this can be an opportunity to get away. "Well, you're welcome to take my seat and try."

Her eyes widen in astonishment. This probably isn't the direction she thought I was headed. Hell, even I'm amazed with myself. I wanted to embarrass her. This is the perfect opportunity to do so, but getting away from Asher is far more important. My *life* is more important than these petty fights with Minka and her crew.

I grab my bag and move to leave. I am halfway out of my seat when an arm wraps around my waist and pulls me back into my chair. Asher shifts his arm so that it hangs loosely around my shoulders, his long fingers casually dipping into the side of my slinky camisole.

I am distinctly aware that I'm not wearing a bra. I know he can feel my rapid heartbeat and the light sheen of sweat that is coating the area of my neck in contact with his arm. Hell, I can even hear the quickening of my breath.

I feel like I'm his prey, a meek little animal that he can toy with before going in for the kill. And when he leans into my ear and whispers, "You didn't think it would be that easy, did you?" I know that I'm right.

He's amused.

The bastard is amused by my fear.

I try to shrug him off my shoulders, but his grip only tightens. His fingers are now digging into the side of my breast, bringing back memories of his hands and mouth on my nipples. It's strangely erotic but an unwanted assault nonetheless.

The fear and my stupid, stupid lust feels foreign together but also not entirely unpleasant.

It's official.

I am a dumbass.

My tombstone can read, "Here lies Dumbass: horny, lonely, and not entirely right in the head," and it won't be wrong at all.

Nella huffs and crosses her arms, eyeing the way his arm tightens around my shoulders with disdain. She can hate me all she wants. I'll be dead soon anyway. I eye the clock. Only two minutes have passed.

Damn.

I have to endure this for 48 more minutes, and now I am literally in my soon-to-be killer's arms.

No one is fazed when Dr. Rolland comes in, looking disheveled and wearing his coat inside out. Dr. Rolland teaches quantum mechanics and is always in his own world. He's undoubtedly a bright man, but his sheer brilliance is overshadowed by his inability to arrive to class on time and make eye contact with his students.

He's already starting his lecture on Heisenberg's Uncertainty Principle, and he hasn't even reached the front of the class. He doesn't even have the little lecture room microphone attached to his shirt yet. This is usually where I would strain to hear what he's saying, but with my death looming over me, I know I won't be paying attention to today's lecture.

Hell, it barely even amuses me when, in a grand act of karmic justice, Dr. Rolland opens his mouth and spit flies onto Nella's cheek.

Serves her right.

For the next half hour, Asher keeps his arm around my shoulders, holding me in place. I tried to get up earlier, when I thought he wasn't paying attention to me, but he only tightened his grip. It's almost painful now. I haven't tried again, even when his finger brushed against my nipple.

I'm still not sure if that was on purpose.

The worst part is that part of me is grateful that only this is happening. That I have—I glance at the clock—14 more minutes of guaranteed safety, even if I have to endure it with his fingers on the side of my breast. I'm comforted by the knowledge that he can't hurt me in a room full of witnesses, but really, I'm living on borrowed time.

The last month of life has been a generous gift. In the back of my mind, I know that. I'd be stupid to think otherwise. The Romano family is not to be trifled with. Far greater people than me have died trying.

The shallow, senseless part of me tells me to forget who Asher is. To acknowledge and accept that my life will soon be over. That part of me is encouraging me to just take a moment to enjoy the touch of a gorgeous man before it happens.

Even if that gorgeous man may eventually be my killer.

That's the part of me that hasn't gotten laid in years. *Years*. It's the part of me that remembers how it felt to have his finger in me, his tongue on my clit. It's also the part of me that's responsible for my hardened nipples, which are currently pointy peaks under my camisole.

It's then that Dr. Rolland decides to put his glasses on. His eyes take a moment to adjust before they focus.

Right.

On.

Me.

Or more specifically, my nipples.

He stares in alarm for an awkward moment before his eyes trail up to my face. His eyes aren't leery. They're just stunned. And then he sees the arm around my shoulders and follows it to its owner. I'm not taken aback when the clicker in his hand immediately drops to the floor.

This is mortifying. I have a mobster playing with my nipples in the middle of class, a professor who just stared at said nipples and is scared of said mobster, and 299 sets of eyes on me. 301 if you count Dr. Rolland's and Asher's.

I watch warily as Dr. Rolland picks up the clicker. His hands are shaky, as is his voice. He's rambling now about something Heisenberg is quoted to have said on his deathbed, but his words aren't really making any sense. I can feel the tension in the room, half sympathetic and half anticipating. Many of the students have eager looks on their faces, ready to see what Dr. Rolland will do.

He picks up a thick set of papers and scans through them. He's still rambling about Heisenberg, and his hands are still shaking. A sheet of paper slips from his fingers and slides across the floor, landing at my feet.

I look at Asher, hating myself for instinctively asking for permission to retrieve it. He gives me a pleased expression, which contrasts greatly with the aloofness of his eyes, and nods. And then, because I am clearly an idiot and don't want him to think he can control me, I stick my tongue out at him. It's quick, just a flash of a tongue lasting no longer than a quarter of a second, but still...

I. Stuck. My. Tongue. Out.

I'm a twenty year old woman, and I just stuck my tongue out at a mobster.

Of course, I did.

I'm mortified when I lean forward to grab the paper. Unable to help myself, I glance down at it. It's part of the class roster. My guess is that Dr. Rolland was searching for Asher's name on the list. He won't find it, but I hand the sheet back to Dr. Rolland anyway.

A part of me is even amused when Dr. Rolland, with his sweaty forehead and face red with fear, nods his head at the paper and continues on with the lecture. He pretended that Asher is enrolled in the class instead of kicking him out, which is university policy for lecture crashers, something that's actually surprisingly common at Wilton. Dr. Rolland is a horrible actor, and his reaction is an unnecessary reminder of the fear Asher garners in respectable people from all walks of life.

My amusement at Dr. Rolland's poor acting skills fades when

Asher's arm returns around my shoulders, a heavy reminder of what's to come. I stiffen when people around us start packing up their things. I glance at the clock. It's 10 A.M. on the dot. I can hear the death bells ringing, taunting me in the privacy of my own head.

I'm going to die.
I'm going to die.
I'm going to die.

CHAPTER SIX

*Courage is resistance to fear,
mastery of fear—not absence of fear.*
Mark Twain

When everyone else gets up, the girls that filled the front row linger, their eyes jumping from Asher to me. Nella even remains seated next to me until Asher stands up, swings my backpack around his broad shoulder and grabs my hand. As we get up and leave, over a dozen girls follow, Nella included.

I never thought I would be grateful to have Nella's company, but I am. It means that I have a witness. But at the sound of the high pitched giggles, Asher shoots a menacing glare at the girls behind us. They instantly scramble, quicker than I thought possible in their sky high heels. There go my witnesses.

Asher and I exit, hand in hand. That shallow part of me wonders if this is what it looks like to be in a relationship, two people holding hands and walking from class. Except we aren't even close to being a couple, and I'm trying really hard to hold myself together, so I won't look like a mess on the outside. I don't need Asher to know how vulnerable I am and use that against me.

I also must look ridiculous in my shirt that's practically lingerie. At least my jeans cover my legs. And Asher, as gorgeous as he is, looks out of place with the dangerous glint in his eye and the tailored suit he wears like a second skin.

Okay, so we look nothing like a normal couple.

I'm saddened by the knowledge that I will never have the opportunity to experience a real relationship. I need to find a way to save myself. There are so many things I want to do with my life, things I've never experienced and won't get the chance to if I die now. I decide it can't hurt to stall.

I turn to Asher and say, "I have another lecture to get to."

I'm stunned when he nods his head. But he doesn't let go of my hand. Instead, he tilts his head, as if asking me to lead the way. I sigh, and we head in the direction of Sproul Hall, where my lecture on the advanced applications of statistics in genetics is being held. This class is smaller, with less than ten people in it, and I wonder what will happen when I enter the class with Asher by my side.

As we walk, I considered my very limited options. I know that Asher won't be letting me out of his sight anytime soon, so whatever I do, I have to do it under his watchful eyes. I don't know anyone well enough to pass any covert I'm-about-to-be-killed-by-the-world's-hottest-man looks.

Plus, if I tell someone, there's a large chance they won't believe me or won't be able to do anything about it. And then I'll be left in the same position, only Asher will have even more reason to hate me. I decide to keep an eye out for any better opportunities to get away.

Part of me doesn't even think I should be trying to get away. Horny Lucy perks up, and I sit her ass right back down. I have enough on my mind without adding Horny Lucy into the mix.

Sane Lucy reasons that there's nothing to do that isn't worse than what's currently happening. If he wants me dead, I would already be dead. I can't hide from him. I don't want to run from him and leave Wilton. Having a degree from here will almost definitely change my life for the better, and there's no way I'll sacrifice that.

I can't go to the police either. I've watched enough movies and read enough Romano fan blogs to know they probably have a lot of police officers on their payroll. I won't know who to trust. It would be a gamble to turn to them. I also don't have anyone in my life besides Aimee, whose advice would be to sleep with Asher.

Inside me, Horny Lucy lifts her head. I mentally duct tape her mouth and force myself to stop thinking of Asher before Horny Lucy takes over my brain and body, and I do something stupid. Like try to jump his bones.

Once we enter the class, I'm flabbergasted when Dr. Lance greets Asher with a warm smile. She's an older woman with white hair, a round body, and keen eyes. But with the way she's looking at Asher like she adores him, I have to question her intelligence.

"Asher! What a pleasant surprise!" she greets. She eyes our joined hands curiously. "Have you come to brush up on your statistics? Unfortunately, this is statistics for science majors not business."

Ah.

I read online that Asher completed a six-year joint Bachelor's and Master's of Science degree program at Wilton's Jefferson School of Business in just three years. I didn't believe it when I read it, but I'm starting to now. Dr. Lance teaches advanced statistics across many disciplines, including business. If Asher has a B.S. and M.S. from Wilton's business school, they have to have crossed paths before.

"May I sit in?" Asher asks. His voice is lacking the hard edge it usually has. He sounds almost... pleasant.

But when I look at him, his face is as impassive as ever.

"Of course, of course. You may sit anywhere you'd like."

I subtly yank my hand out of Asher's grip, knowing he can't grab it back with the attention Dr. Lance is giving us. She's too sharp not to notice something like that. I briefly consider sending her a signal to call the police, but I know they'll never arrive in time.

And Dr. Lance is far too old to take on Asher. Hell, it's unlikely that anyone of any age can. His body is molded into a dangerous weapon that's probably more lethal than a loaded gun. It's definitely scarier, and I would know—I've had experience with both.

With his back turned to Dr. Lance, Asher sends me a warning glare. I try to ignore it, heading towards the seats. These seats aren't stadium style, like the lecture hall's are. These are tiny individual desks, consisting of plastic chairs attached to undersized wooden desks with metal screws.

Everyone is already sitting down, staring at us with varying looks of disbelief. I'm not sure if it's because Asher is one scary dude or because I brought a date to class. I find an empty desk, surrounded on all sides by people. If I sit in this one, Asher won't be able to sit near me. I take a seat at the desk, my face all sorts of smug. I'll get another 50 minutes of peace sitting without him beside me. With the way my day is going, that's more than I can hope for.

My grin drops when Asher glares at the student sitting next to me. He all but jumps out of his seat and scrambles to the empty one on the other side of the classroom. Asher takes a seat at the newly abandoned chair. He reaches over, grips my desk with one hand, and easily drags it closer to him until it's touching his desk. Then, he slings his arm around my shoulders.

I don't react. I'm still too stunned. He just scared off some poor guy and dragged all 125 pounds of me along with this 50 pound desk with one hand. I know that he could have done it even if I weighed 150 pounds more. I am so fucked.

And this, sitting next to him and under his arm, is ridiculous. This is unnecessary. I'm not going anywhere, whether his arm is around me or not. I don't have the guts. We both know that. We also both know that running is an illogical move. He's doing this to spite me, and I know that I won't be paying attention to yet another class.

Not that it matters.

Chances are I'll be dead after this class anyway.

Of course, I don't pay attention to the whole lecture, but I am astonished when Dr. Lance asks questions and Asher answers all of them. *Know it all.* Asher is in the middle of another answer when a rare smile graces Dr. Lance's face, because Asher doesn't just answer the questions.

He explains his answers with a level of depth and thoroughness that is both impressive and inimitable. Not even Dr. Lance, who has long since reached emeritus status at Wilton, can explain the concepts as well as Asher. And the stupid boys in the class are eating it up.

I'm the only girl in the class, which isn't exactly a shocker, because STEM fields are always heavier on the male enrollment.

Couple in the fact that bioinformatics and genomics is such a specialized field, and I'm the only girl at Wilton in the entire major.

It's lonely and it sucks, but what can I do? Go around knocking on doors and asking girls to convert to the sciences, bible salesmen style?

No, thanks.

After a few minutes, the boys in the class stop caring that Asher is intimidating as fuck and affiliated with the Romano family. Hell, I wouldn't be amazed if some of them don't even know, given how focused these guys are on their studies. What they do care about, though, is getting an A. And Asher is someone that can explain convoluted concepts to them better than their professor can.

I can see the worship in their eyes.

It pisses me off.

When class finally ends, the kid Asher scared off actually has the guts to come up to Asher and ask a question about fiduciary inference. And Asher actually answers it. Ronald Fisher, the inventor of fiduciary inference, didn't even fully understand it. But Asher does. I'm stupefied.

Who is this guy?

After fielding a few more questions like a damn celebrity, Asher turns to me and says, "Are you going to talk to me or are we going to waste another hour sitting in a lecture you won't pay attention to?"

I sigh, unsurprised that he caught onto my plan. I don't have another class today anyway. And then I process his words again.

"Talk? You want to *talk*? I thought you were here to '*take care* of me.'" My voice dips at the end, mimicking his deep tone unsuccessfully. I sounded like the prepubescent offspring of the Cookie Monster and Arnold Schwarzenegger.

He finally removes his arm from my shoulders and grabs my hand instead. We're standing up now, and my backpack is somehow already across one of his shoulders.

"I said I *was*," he admits. "But not anymore."

"Not anymore," I parrot, disbelief coloring my words. "And why the Hell not?"

Gosh, I'm stupid. I didn't just say that. It's like looking a gift horse in the face and spitting on it. And stomping on its toes and throwing 'yo mama jokes its way.

Why can't I be mute?

"Let's go somewhere private," he says.

It's then that I notice we have the attention of everyone. Even Dr. Lance. They may not know or care about Asher's mafia connections, but drama is still drama, and these boys look hooked on ours. I'm glad that we were whispering.

I nod to him. Asher would take my hand and drag me away if I say no anyways. I might as well go of my own volition. We leave Sproul, and Asher tugs on my hand, pulling me into another building and hallway I didn't even know exists.

I'm led into an elevator, where there's a sudden and quick flash of light that startles me. He steadies me when I jump back, and I let him because I'm too stunned to stop him. Then, we're headed downward. The elevator opens up into the basement of the building.

It should be scary—I'm in a basement with a killer, a classic setup to just about every horror movie—but I'm way too fascinated to register the threat. The basement is a giant secret lab I've never seen on any Wilton map or directory.

And it's perfection.

I even pass a state of the art centrifuge that's nicer than the expensive ones stocked in the genomics building. This is incredible. It's better than Tumblr porn.

Don't even think about it, Horny Lucy.

I can't help but ask, "How do you know about this place?"

"I don't see how that's any of your business."

His sharp tone snaps me out of my awed reverie. I pause abruptly at the sound of it, then continue looking around, using my wonder as a stalling tactic. I search for exits, pretending that I'm continuing my visual exploration of the lab.

Asher's perceptive eyes narrow at my theatrics, and I suspect he knows what I'm doing. I still pretend that I'm exploring the place anyways. He surprisingly lets me.

There's a door to a stairwell, but it has an ID scanner next to it.

I doubt I have access to it, and my student identification card is in my wallet, which is in the backpack Asher is still holding, anyways. The only other exit is the elevator, which is already on the third floor.

If I want to get in, I'll have to wait for it to come back down to the basement. Plus, the flash in the elevator earlier was probably some crazy security measure, like a biometric scanner or something. I can't know for sure, but I'm not about to take the risk.

Which means I'm trapped.

The look on Asher's face tells me he knows that. That's probably why he took me down here in the first place. How he even knows this place exists, I don't know, but that's a mystery for another time, even though it's killing me not to prod. If I even live past the next few minutes. Now that I think about it, this is the perfect place to kill me —secret, isolated, and full of chemicals.

Done with my perusal, I don't say anything, waiting for Asher to talk.

"You're different than I thought you'd be."

My eyes shoot to his in confused interest. "What'd you think I'd be like?"

"I thought you were a plant. A spy for one of the families. Maybe even a corporate spy, a honey pot to steal secrets. Someone with an agenda at least. But you're not, are you?"

My eyes widen. He thought I was a spy? For one of the five families? The idea is so ridiculous that I have to laugh.

"You thought I was a spy?"

I'm not even going to touch the honey pot comment.

... Because, seriously? *Me? A honey pot?*

If I was a honey pot, he wouldn't have ditched me pre-orgasm...

Must not think about it.

Must not think about it.

Must not think about it.

His voice cuts through my mental mantra. "What was I supposed to think?" His eyes harden with anger. "You called the cops in the middle of an importa—" He stops himself. "You called the cops on an international burner phone paid for in cash over two years ago in a remote city in Mozambique."

When he puts it that way, I actually sound pretty badass.

But he isn't done. "The sim card was in the toilet. It took my tech guys a while to recover it. They didn't even think they could, but when they finally did, there was nothing on it. Not even a single contact."

That's because I knew no one at the time. I have no family, and bouncing around from foster home to foster home makes it hard to make friends. Even now, I only have Aimee and my boss' number. No one I met during my time volunteering has the money for a phone either. It's a luxury most people in America don't even realize is luxurious.

"The phone had severe water damage, and most of its serial number had been scratched off."

I wince. It wasn't scratched off purposely. I'm just horrible at taking care of my electronics. Plus, the phone was a ten dollar flip phone that I didn't really need. It was just a precaution in case of an emergency while abroad. I didn't even consider keeping it unscathed by my carelessness and penchant for ruining electronics.

He continues, "And in every camera footage we had of you, your head was either down or behind that friend of yours. Aimee. I knew how you look like, but we needed an actual photograph to distribute. The sketch artist's wasn't good enough."

I don't even register that he knows Aimee's name. I'm too focused on how lucky I am to have avoided the cameras. I didn't avoid them intentionally. In fact, I didn't even consider the cameras until now.

Aimee is just really tall, especially in heels. It doesn't shock me that her height shielded me from the cameras. As for looking down, I was avoiding looking up because of the dancers hanging above us in the cages.

"That's your dancers' faults!" I cry. "Blame them!"

He frowns. "What are you talking about?"

"I wasn't sure if they were wearing underwear! So, I didn't look up!"

Asher rubs his forehead roughly and glances up at the ceiling in exasperation. It's the universal what-am-I-going-to-do-with-you look. And honestly, I ask myself the same question a lot.

He makes a noise between a sigh and a grunt. "When we saw the video footage, you were the only one that was even near the restrooms at the time the cops were called. That part was easy. Identifying you was the hard part. Your face wasn't on camera, and it looked like you were alone. You didn't dance with Aimee at all, and while you guys were near each other, you didn't look like you guys came together."

I remember. I was lost in my head, imagining Rogue as a strip club. Then, I was focused on Asher when my eyes caught sight of him heading into the VIP area. After that, Aimee danced with some guy, while I danced with strangers.

"Your 9-1-1 call was a dead end. You never identified yourself. Your phone was a dead end. It took forever to trace, and when we finally did, we found out that it was bought in cash." A dry laugh ripples through him. "I thought someone was after me. You were a fucking ghost. Last week, we got our hands on video footage from someone who filmed my encounter with the cops."

Memories of people in the crowd that surrounded the two cops and Asher flashed through my head. I had seen people with their cameras out, but I didn't think to hide my face. I'm so damn stupid.

"Your face wasn't in it. It was shot from behind, but your hands were on your friend's back and that guy she was with. I knew it was you. I recognized the dress. After that, it was easier. We pulled the guy's info from his bar tab. He was just some nobody lawyer you met there. We questioned him, but he knew nothing."

I'm shocked. They questioned him? Guilt fills my stomach, and I hope he didn't get hurt because of me. *Wait*... I remember him exchanging numbers with Aimee. Huh. He didn't rat us out. I'm giving him mad props, but I don't even remember his name.

"But your roommate was even easier to find. She posted dozens of pictures from that night on Instagram." He laughs. "She even geotagged Rogue in them. Imagine my surprise when I saw your face in one of them."

Our resident advisor took a picture of me and Aimee before we left to Rogue, and Aimee immediately posted it to Instagram—#Rogue #Exclusive #Roomies4Lyfe.

He gives me a sardonic laugh. "All we had to do was look at Rogue's Instagram feed. We would've identified you in minutes. Instead, it took a month. I wasted a damn month and almost a million dollars to find someone who isn't even a damn threat."

Hold up. *A million dollars?!* I can't even fathom that amount of money.

"You know, I wasn't even sure whether or not you were a threat when I came here. Your background check came up empty. Not *just* clean but *empty*. As in there's nothing on you past this last month."

That's because my last foster dad, Steve, the one that gave me the shirt I'm currently wearing, is a crazy fuck. He had an unhealthy obsession with me. Maybe he still does. He was starting to act on it, sneaking into my room at night and staring at me.

One time, I woke up to go to the bathroom, and he was there, stroking himself at the foot of my bed. I closed my eyes and pretended to sleep, figuring I was safer asleep than awake. I was relieved when he didn't touch me that night, but I'll always wonder if he had in the past and I just never woke up to it.

The next morning, I packed my bags, ditched school and headed straight to my social worker, who got me the Hell out of there. I spent my last month as a minor in some shitty group home, where Steve kept trying to visit me, even though he was warned by the cops not to.

My social worker even got me an emergency protective order against him, but that didn't stop Steve from trying. It's why I never bothered with a restraining order. I just left once I got the chance.

Once I turned 18, my social worker agreed to seal my file and help me change my name, which used to be Elena Lucy Reeves. Now, it's Lucy Ives. I changed it to my middle name and my biological mother's maiden name. Then, I hightailed it out of the country.

For two years, I was gone. And now, here I am, in danger again and wearing the shirt Steve got me.

The irony isn't lost on me.

Asher laughs again. It's a lifeless sound. "You're a damn ghost, but I don't think you're connected to the mafia. I wasn't sure before, but after meeting you again, I don't think so." His eyes peruse my body, causing me to shiver. His full lips curl up in disgust. "I mean look at you. You're *shaking*, for fuck's sake. It's pathetic." Those chilling blue eyes narrow on me, and he takes a menacing step closer. "Why'd you call the cops?"

I take a step back and occupy myself by eyeing the floor.

It's a really interesting floor.

Looks like a floor.

Feels like a floor.

Floor.

Floor.

Floor.

Floor.

Floo—

Asher interrupts my beautiful ode to the floor. "You're going to have to answer me eventually."

I keep my eyes trained on my dirty friend, the floor. "I-I... I thought that b-big guy was h-hurting that girl."

"He was."

I look up at him, surprised that he would admit it.

He continues, "But that was the point. She knew it. I knew it. He knew it. Everyone that passed them knew it. Everyone but *you*."

He takes a step closer, and I try to take one back, but I'm already pressed against the wall. He's so close now, I can feel his breath on my forehead. I can even smell the mint in it, as cold as the indifference in his eyes.

The look of indifference is replaced by mirth. "Lucy, did you call the cops because you were mad I didn't finish you off?" His hands trail down my body, resting below my hips. "We can fix that easily."

When his fingers brush against my jean-clad ass, I shout, "No!" I'm not sure if it's a reply to his question or a response to his touch.

I can't believe I ever had the courage to touch this man, though that was before I learned that he's in the mob. It's as if the second I found out, my fear extinguished my bravado in its entirety, ensconcing it like a solar eclipse. I can only hope the world will continue to rotate, and one day, the sun will reveal itself—along with my nerve.

The amusement in his face is gone, and he leans down and whispers in my ear, "So, what are we going to do with you?"

Is this where I'm supposed to beg for my life?

I'll do it if it means I'll live. I'm building a future for myself at Wilton, and that's worth begging for. I don't care if that makes me pathetic or weak. I know my strengths and weaknesses enough to know that I will never get away from this man unless he lets me.

"Don't kill me." I look up at him.

Gosh, he's so close right now.

"Please, don't kill me," I beg again, the pleading in my voice so unfamiliar to my own ears.

His smile is patronizing. "I won't kill you. You're an innocent. You stepped wrong, but you're still an innocent."

"What are you going to do to me?" I wince.

That sounded more suggestive than it was supposed to.

The smirk on his face tells me he heard it, too. He leans even closer, dipping his head so we're almost eye level with one another. He lifts his finger under my chin and tilts my face up. I let out a shaky breath, and he breathes it in. It's the most intimate thing I have ever experienced, and I'm not a virgin.

When he speaks, his lips brush lightly against mine. "You'll owe me a favor."

My eyes drop to his lips. "A favor?"

Each time we speak, we're practically kissing, stealing the air from one another but not quite giving it back. I don't fight it. Frozen in fear and lust and stupidity, I can't, and that's frustrating.

What am I doing?

This is a man who has killed before. Hell, a couple hours ago, he was about to *kill me*. Yet, here I am, brushing my lips against his, stealing his breaths like they're mine to take. But other than going along with this, I can't see any other options that don't end with my body floating in the Hudson River.

A part of me sees this for what it is. A fear tactic. A power play. He's letting me know that he controls me, reminding me how afraid I am of him. And he's right. I'm too scared to put up a fight, but I value my education at Wilton too much to run.

He backs away. "A favor. I take it you have a new phone?"

When I nod, still dazed, he holds out his hand. I point to my backpack. He grabs my phone from the front pocket and enters something in. A few seconds later, I hear his phone ringing. He returns my phone to my backpack.

"You have my number. I have yours."

And then he's gone without a goodbye. Though he left the door to the stairwell propped open for me, I stand there for an hour, pressed against the wall. Shocked.

I owe a favor to a *mobster*.

How the Hell did that happen?

CHAPTER SEVEN

He who is not courageous enough to take risks will accomplish nothing in life.
Muhammad Ali

𝓐sher isn't just a mobster. He's a *fixer*, which is "so damn hot." At least, that's what Aimee just told me when she confronted me in our dorm room. She had pounced as soon as I opened the door. I just finished telling her what had happened, starting from the night we went to Rogue and ending with me in a top secret lab on campus. Of course, I left out the part about hooking up with Asher.

"So, let me get this straight." She's currently lounging on my bed in pajamas, because her half of the room is an absolute pigsty like always. She couldn't even find a seat on her bed before she gave up and laid down on mine. "He held your hand as he walked you to class? That is *soooo* cute!"

"*No*, it's not." I cross my arms. "It was to make sure I didn't escape! What's cute about holding someone against their will?!"

I purposely ignore all the romance novels I like to read, where it's more than okay to be kidnapped so long as the kidnapper is rich and handsome. I would be lying if I say I haven't swooned while reading a book where a rich, hot guy stalks a pretty girl and is a major jerk to her, yet they fall in love anyways.

But that's all fiction.

Having it happen in reality is completely different.

And scary.

Very scary.

She shakes her head. "No way was it against your will. I don't believe for a second that you can hold hands with someone that hot and not want to be in that position." Aimee is clearly someone who suffers from Romance Stalker Syndrome.

"He's a *fixer* for the *mafia*," I say again.

That has to have been the tenth time I've said that. I don't expect her to magically abandon her vanity and fantasies, but I can't not bring it up. I'm still having trouble wrapping my brain around my situation.

"That's even hotter!" She claps her hands vigorously, in Elle Woods meets Bruce Banner fashion, the movement dainty yet causing the twin-sized bed to shake. "He's like a real life John Wick, except he's a million times hotter than Keanu Reeves."

I frown. "Except Keanu Reeves is actually a good person. Like, a *really* good person. And did you see him in *The Replacements*?" I fan my face. "Swoon."

She throws her hands up, like *she* is the one that has the right to be frustrated with *me*. "You're digressing! Asher Black is clearly the hotter one."

She's impossible. She's dead-on (Asher is hotter, after all), but she's still ridiculous. He threatened me, for goodness' sake. Doesn't that lower him on the Richter scale of hotness? And Keanu Reeves would never threaten me...

Plus, most of Asher's threats were subliminal, which is even worse. It means he's calculated. Cunning. Asher isn't a schoolyard bully relying on brute strength, though I have no doubt that he possesses it. His greatest strength, however, is in his subtlety, the way he never reveals his hand unless he wants to. I have a feeling that he never does anything without a purpose.

"*You're* digressing." I take a seat on top of my desk and open a new pack of Starbursts. "The point is that I'm in danger. I owe a favor to the fixer for the most dangerous crime family in the country. My life is over. I might as well change my name, surgically alter my face, and move to Tajikistan... where he'll probably *still* be able to track me." I groan. "What am I going to do, Aims? This is the mafia we're talking about."

Aimee's face becomes serious. When she opens her mouth and says, "Here's what you're going to do," I almost expect her to give me actual advice. She doesn't, of course. That would be asking for too much.

Instead, she says, "You're going to dress in your sexiest dress, that LBD I've been eyeing for the past month, and you're going to march up to Rogue and demand to see Asher. Then, you're going to spread your legs for him, he'll fuck you till he's practically living in your V, and you guys will get married out of wedlock. But who cares? No one's judging. Because, and I repeat, he's so fucking hot. You'd get to look at that tight ass all day long."

I throw a Starburst at her forehead. "Yeah, and then, after our wedding, I'll be shot down by a rival family, but not before the poison that Asher has been slipping into my food daily kicks in. And the worst part is that he'll get away with it, because the poison is untraceable." I roll my eyes and huff. "Be serious, Aimee! Gosh, how is this guy not in jail already?"

But I know the answer to that question before I ask it. He's clever, cleverer than any cop, agent, and criminal on his side and against him. That makes him untouchable. I witnessed this firsthand in the way he carries himself, his intelligent eyes always scanning for threats no matter how exposed we were and even when we weren't. He was always on alert, ready. For what, I don't know, and I have a feeling that I don't want to know.

Asher isn't just street smart. He's also a gifted savant with a formal education most people can't even dream of let alone handle. Coupled with his unparalleled looks, he's the full package. It makes him lethal.

"I *am* serious!" Aimee sits up on my bed. A rare frown graces her pretty features. "I'm completely serious, Loosey Goosey." She rolls her eyes at my scowl. She knows I hate that nickname. "You have an in with one of the most eligible bachelors in the country. You'd be a fool not to take advantage of it."

"Eligible bachelor?!" I throw another Starburst at her, and when she catches it in her mouth, I throw the whole tube of them her way. I watch as all of the Starbursts fling out of the rip in the tube and land on her face. "I'm pretty sure being a criminal makes him *in*eligible!"

She gives me a pitiful sigh. "Lucy, Lucy, Lucy. When are you going to get it?" She unwraps the Starburst that landed in her mouth and tosses it back inside, chomping on it with the grace of a gorilla.

It's cherry. My favorite flavor. Fuck her.

"There's nothing to get. He's a criminal, I called the cops on him, and he was going to kill me. End of story."

The End.

Ha! If only.

With her mouth full, Aimee replies, "But he's a hot criminal. It's not like he's a pedophile, domestic abuser, or pimp."

I groan. I'm embarrassed on behalf of my gender. "There's no such thing as 'hot' crime! Crime is crime!" I make a mental note to discover the cure to Romance Stalker Syndrome.

She snorts. "Not if you look like Asher Black. Seriously, Lucy, I'm so jealous of you right now. You should have seen my face when I heard that Asher Black is dating you."

"Jealous?! You're crazy, Aimee. Crazy!" I lay my back on the desk, so I won't have to look at her. "And we're definitely not dating."

"It sure didn't look like it."

"*Look* like it? Seriously? You saw me, and you didn't come save me? Or at least call the police?! As a best friend, you suck."

"I *wish* I was there, so I could get a long peek at his fine ass." She pauses, and I hear some movement from her direction. "See for yourself."

Aimee's giant phone lands on my chest. I flip it over and look at the screen. There's an open text on it from one of the #TeamAimee girls in our hall. The attachment is a picture of me and Asher, walking across the campus quad to Sproul.

With our hands clenched tightly together, we actually do look like a couple. He looks amazing in his suit, and in my fitted black skinny jeans, risqué top, and heeled booties, I look like somebody worthy of his good looks. I would even go as far as saying we look good together.

Even my normally unruly black locks agree with me today, settling neatly below the narrow curve of my waist. My long lashes are coated with black mascara, bringing out the vibrant greens in my eyes. Though I look exhausted, my clear skin is even naturally flushed at the cheeks. It's from fear, but looking at the picture, I can't tell.

We look good together. *Really* good.

Aimee speaks softly, "Look at that, and tell me honestly that you guys wouldn't be good together."

The fight leaves me. I know why Aimee is pressing the issue. After the second week of school, Aimee confronted me, informing me that if I'm a lesbian, she would still want to be friends with me.

When I asked her what she was going on about, she said, "Well, you haven't even looked at a guy since I met you."

Clearly, she equates celibacy to lesbianism. I responded by telling her that men will only distract me from my studies, but that isn't the real reason. Asher is. For the past month, I haven't been able to focus on anything except my fear of retribution. Aimee dropped it then, but she hasn't stopped suggesting guys she would love to set me up with.

This is one of those times, except she doesn't know Asher and doesn't care that he's a suspected criminal. She also doesn't realize that we've already hooked up... and I never got my happy ending.

Okay, so I'm still hung up on that.

He couldn't wait thirty more seconds?

Oh, and err... obviously the threat to my wellbeing is the most dissuasive part about Asher. I can't ignore the fact that he is dangerous and so far out of my league. The hook up feels like a fluke, a lapse in judgement on both his part and mine. His, because he thinks I'm pathetic. And mine, because I can't even be around him without shaking in my boots.

I sigh. "We look good together, sure, but I want more than that." It's my turn to sound crazy. "I want a guy I can talk to comfortably. Someone who makes me feel safe and wanted and beautiful."

It goes unspoken, but we both know that Asher isn't that guy. I don't think he even embodies *one* of those four qualities. Hell, I'm not even sure why Aimee thinks he's a realistic option. It isn't like he wants me. It's unlikely that he'll suddenly express interest after calling me, and I quote, "pathetic."

Plus, I asked for her advice on staying alive not dating, but clearly I went to the wrong person.

Aimee groans. "Ugh, you're depressing me." She sits up and goes to my closet. "Come on. We're going out. Let's find a guy to take your mind off of this. When was the last time you had sex?"

I can't even remember it.

It's not like I'm against sex. I enjoy it, but I've had other priorities —like staying alive in foster care; staying alive despite my psycho ex-foster dad; staying alive while traveling to dangerous countries; and now, well, staying alive despite one very pissed off mobster.

"High school?" I finally answer.

It may have been the end of senior year with Ethan Winters. We hated each other, but it didn't stop us from having explosive hate sex. I grin at the memories. Aimee turns to me, slack jawed. I wait for her to say something. She doesn't, which makes me laugh.

"Seriously?" I say, still laughing. "The only thing that renders you silent is my lack of a sex life? I should bring it up more often."

"Ha. Ha. Laugh away, Virgin Mary." She throws something at me. It lands in my lap. "But you'll be thanking me when you get laid tonight."

I look down at what she tossed into my lap. It's my little black dress. The fabric is tight, reaches mid-thigh, and shows an uncomfortable amount of cleavage. It's sexy, sexier than what I'm used to, but when I spotted it at a thrift shop in Morocco, I knew I had to have it.

I remember when one of my many foster mothers told me that every girl should have a little black dress. Something that makes her feel sexy. Confident. On top of the world. This is that dress for me. I still have yet to find the right moment to wear it, but apparently, Aimee thinks this is it.

So, I give up on bickering over this. I strip and throw it on, because Aimee is impossible to fight with anyway. She likes to argue in circles until the person she disagrees with gets a headache and gives up. I like my head just how it is, thank you very much.

And honestly, I'd much rather fix my nonexistent sex life than the looming threat Asher poses to my well-being. Do I think a night of sex will fix my problems? No, but it'll take my mind away from them. Plus, a few orgasms have never hurt anybody.

Horny Lucy nods her head in agreement and beats her chest from inside the mental cell I stuck her in when Asher and I were brushing lips. Looking back, I realize that I've gone full circle. This all started with Asher pressing me against the wall in the alleyway outside of Rogue, then Bastian pressing that blonde girl against the wall in the restroom hallway. And finally, a few hours ago, I was in the same position again with Asher.

As I get ready, I don't bother with any makeup. I have mascara on, and my face is clear enough that I don't need foundation. We're probably going to a club, where I'll sweat any makeup off anyways. After digging through her bag, Aimee tosses me a tube of Burt's Bees lip balm.

It's mine.

I roll my eyes as I swipe it across my lips. I'm good to go. I toss the lip balm onto my klepto roommate's bed, where it's immediately lost in the mess. Seriously, I don't know how she finds anything on her side of the room. I don't even know how she sleeps at night when her bed is littered with knick knacks.

When I glance up at her, Aimee is already dressed. She's wearing another colorful, sequined mini dress. She loves these. In terms of club wear, they're pretty much all she owns. This particular one is a deep turquoise color that complements her pale skin tone.

Aimee's light blonde hair is coifed into an elegant French twist, and her face is purposefully bare of makeup except for the bold red lipstick she always wears. She once told me that the first thing she wants a man to see when he looks at her is her lips. And after being her roommate for a month, I can vouch that this is exactly what happens whenever a guy looks at her.

Even our R.A. can't help himself.

After putting on another coat of lipstick, Aimee is done. My favorite thing about her is how she can get ready in under ten minutes. She always knows what she wants to wear, and she doesn't waste time putting on a lot of makeup. Neither of us can afford anything other than the essential products anyway.

We both put on heels—nude pumps for me and red stilettos for her—and walk to the street to wait for the Uber she called a few minutes ago. I don't even know where we are headed until we get there and I immediately regret my friendship with Aimee.

CHAPTER EIGHT

*If you could get up the courage to begin,
you have the courage to succeed.*
David Viscott

I **groan as soon** as I see the sign for Rogue above us, a sense of dread filling my empty stomach.

"Aimee, I hate you."

"You're welcome."

"You suck."

"Well, you don't, because you're going to get us into the club with your newfound connections."

And I do.

Or it could be how we look tonight. Either way, the bouncer takes one look at us and ushers Aimee and me inside, much to the chagrin of the hundred-plus people that are waiting in line. When we're personally greeted by a pretty bottle girl and led upstairs to the VIP level, I know this treatment has nothing to do with how we look.

Our first time at Rogue, we waited in line for hours with our stupid heels killing our feet. Now, we're being treated like VIPs, ushered straight from the Uber inside the club and escorted directly to the VIP level. The only thing missing is a damn limo. This has Asher Black written all over it.

The VIP level is stunning. On the sides of the room are glass walls tinted white with bright lights behind them. Through the tinted glass, I can see the outlines of dancing bodies. There are five girls on each side, their shadows forming movements that are clearly the product of formal training. We can make out their shadows, but they can't see us. It's like a one way mirror in that regard.

A long but skinny table lays in front of an expansive booth-style bench. The open booth is made of blood red velvet and is pressed against the center wall. In the middle of the booth sits Asher. He doesn't look surprised to see me. In fact, his handsome face is completely void of emotion, as hard to read as ever.

Aimee grabs my hand and drags me over to him. I nearly topple over my high heels. As we approach, I get a better look at him. He's wearing a suit, of course, but it's a dark navy blue this time. The fabric is tightened around his thighs from sitting, and Horny Lucy admires how muscular they are.

As excessive as Aimee can be, she's right this time.

Horny Lucy needs to get laid.

I sweep a longing glance behind me, wondering if it's too late to head to the dance floor below and find a suitable candidate for what I want. I'm starting to refer to the deviant side of me in the third person.

This is bad.

How long has it been since I've had sex again?

Over two years.

I have to remind myself again and again, because I can hardly believe it. I went from having an almost-daily friend with benefits to quitting cold turkey for years. That has to be some sort of record. And not the kind I'd want advertised.

"Ladies," Asher greets us when we reach him. "What brings you two to these parts?" He looks all too smug for my liking.

I avert my eyes but take a seat anyways.

Aimee speaks for me, "Lucy, here, needs to get laid."

What. The. Fuck.

I'm going to kill her. She must be determined to turn me into a homicidal maniac. Maybe then will her fantasies of Asher and I living happily ever after actually be realistic. I glare at her, hoping that the longer I glare the more likely I am to forget that she just told Asher I need to get laid.

I am so mortified.

Asher laughs. It actually sounds genuine, but a part of me doubts that it is. Everything about this man is too controlled, too purposeful. Like if he doesn't benefit from something, he won't do it. So, what does he gain from having me up here? From laughing at me?

He meets my eyes. "Well, I think I can help you take care of that."

Wait... Is he actually acknowledging our hook up?

His words are said so suggestively, so flirtatiously, that I can't conceal my shock. Aimee even gasps.

My face whips to his so quickly, I'm left dizzy for a brief moment. "What?" I whisper under my breath, but he hears it.

There's mirth in his blue eyes when he continues, "The club is at maximum capacity tonight. There are plenty of suitable candidates below. You're welcome to bring one you like up here for some more *privacy*."

"Oh."

I thought... Never mind what I thought.

My eyes narrow on him. I feel like he's toying with me again, expecting me not to take him up on his offer. To instead sit here and pine for him like I have no other options.

So, I do the opposite of what he thinks I'll do and agree. "Okay. I think I'll do just that."

I get up and leave. When I'm halfway to the stairs, I can't help but turn back to stare at him, a smug grin on my face. But he isn't even looking at me. He has his phone out, his mouth frowning slightly at the screen. Aimee's not looking at me either. She's too busy stealing peaks at his crotch.

The damn traitor.

I sigh and continue toward the staircase. From my vantage point at the top of the stairs, I scan the club for anyone that's my type. Of course, no one looks interesting after seeing Asher here.

I choose a random guy to dance with. He's cute and well-dressed, but he's also significantly shorter than me and a little smelly. To be honest, I'm only dancing with him because he secured a position on the dance floor that has the perfect view of the staircase leading to the VIP level.

I tell myself that I'm only interested because I left Aimee up there with an alleged killer. I have to make sure she's okay. It's the responsible thing to do. Any good friend would do it, right? But when Aimee descends the stairwell and is replaced by the blonde from The Hallway Incident, I don't go anywhere.

Aimee is down here, safe and alive, but I still can't move. I don't understand myself. I watch and wait, even when Smelly Guy wraps his arm around my waist and tugs me closer, invading my personal bubble with his putrid odor.

I endure his scent of pickled cabbages, focusing all of my brain power on the stairs until I can no longer smell it. And when Blondie finally descends with a livid expression plastered all over her pretty face, I can finally breathe again. I regret it instantly.

Two words: *pickled cabbages.*

Gross.

I can't take the scent anymore, so I push away from the guy, mumble a quick thanks and head to the dance floor to find Aimee.

"He kicked me out," she says as soon as she lays eyes on me. "Some chick came up to us, and he kicked me out." She grins, mischievously. "She was glaring at me the whole time, too. I think she was jealous that I had him all to myself."

I think *I* am a little jealous of her myself, but I'm having a hard time admitting my own stupidity

Nope.

I don't have Romance Stalker Syndrome.

No way.

I wait for her to say something more, but she doesn't. We dance instead, losing ourselves in the rhythm of the music. When strong hands slip around my waist from behind and Aimee's eyes widen, I know that they're Asher's.

A part of me is convinced that I knew he was there before he even touched me. I'm definitely crazy. That's for certain.

He molds his hard body into my back, and his lips brush teasingly against my ear. "Relax."

I shudder at the contact but don't reply.

He begins to move his body against mine in a hypnotic rhythm. "Act normally."

I want to scoff. He's *touching* me, and he wants me to act normally? A guy with his looks and his occupation is anything but normal. Plus, I can't even spell the word "normal" let alone be it when I can feel each individual pack of his abdominal muscles pressed against my back. There are eight of them.

Eight!

"Think of this as an audition," he continues. "I'm going to cash in my favor soon, but if you don't pass this audition, I'll have to ask you to do something else for me. And I guarantee you, it won't be as easy as what I am about to ask you." His right arm grips my waist tighter. "Okay?"

I mull over his words. Dancing with him is an audition? My thoughts flash to what this club used to be—a strip club. Does he want to turn me into a stripper? No, that probably isn't it. After all, this isn't a strip club anymore.

Does... does he want me to give him a private strip tease? That's unlikely, too, because let's face it. I was already naked and writhing in front of him once, and he was able to stop himself so easily. Plus, all he has to do is ask and any girl will be willing. He doesn't need me for that.

But a part of me—named Horny Lucy, of course—isn't all that opposed to the idea. In the grand scheme of things, that's fairly tame in comparison to the other nefarious things he can ask of me. I think of Wilton and what I'll be sacrificing if I don't agree.

I make up my mind. He said that whatever he wants now will be easier than what he might come up with later, and I believe him. He may be super scary, but as far as I know, he has yet to lie to me.

I nod and tip my head back, leaning it against his shoulder, so he can hear me when I say, "What do you want me to do?"

"For now? Dance with me like you would any other guy."

Except that's an impossible task, because he isn't just any other guy. He's a guy I want to strip and hump like a dog in heat. He's also a guy I want to cower and run away from. Horny Lucy and Sane Lucy are at war inside of me.

In the end, they compromise. I pretend that Asher is a robot, which makes him less intimidating. The thought even makes me laugh. Aimee, who has finally recovered from seeing Asher again, sends me a concerned look at the sound of my laughter. I ignore her, my mind focused on dehumanizing Asher.

Robot, Sane Lucy says in my head.

Sex bot, Horny Lucy amends.

Fine.

Sex bot.

I can do this.

Asher isn't a human; he's a sex bot, some*thing* for me to use for my own pleasure.

I reach behind me and grab the side of his thigh, pulling his lower body closer to me, until I can feel *him* pressed against my lower back. He's soft right now, but I can tell he's generously endowed, causing the contact to send a shiver through my body.

My other hand wraps around his neck and tugs until we are pressed tightly against one another from his neck down. I grind my ass against him, moving in a sensual pace to the magnetic rhythm of the song, an erotic club mix of Selena Gomez's "Good for You."

Asher wants me to treat him like any other guy, and I am. If he was any run of the mill hot guy and Horny Lucy was in charge, I would discretely take advantage of him in public until I can have my way with him in private. I'm not a prude. I have nothing against casual sex. Hooking up with Asher a month ago is proof of that. My long dry spell has everything to do with a lack of opportunity and nothing to do with a lack of effort.

So, here I am, grinding against the Romano family's fixer and enjoying it. Asher growls, turning me over and positioning me until my breasts are pressed against him. He slips a leg in between my thighs, and I automatically grind myself against it, my dress lifting up a little to reveal more of my skin.

I'm soaking through my underwear, and I hope I'm not leaving a wet spot on Asher's clothes. I barely consider this, though. I'm too lost in the moment, embarrassingly close to coming. I even forget who he is for a second, simply enjoying his company instead of worrying about the inevitable consequences.

Asher lowers his head, burying his face in my neck. I grip his button down at the feel of his tongue running up the length of my jaw. His nose trails along my neck until his lips reach my earlobe, and he nibbles on it.

This is too much. I'm so close. I want to come. I need to. It's been too long. He has to know what he's doing to me. I feel the sudden urge to look into his eyes and see whether or not I'm having the same effect on him.

I sure think I am. After all, he has a massive hard on pressed against me. But my insecurities are there. They haven't forgotten how he left me that night. How I was so close to coming on his fingers, his tongue against my clit, and he was able to walk away.

When I finally gather the courage to look up, I'm rendered frozen. I notice that all eyes around us are on Asher and me. That isn't what unsettles me, though. It's Asher, always Asher. His eyes are tilted upward, focused on a group of people that stand at the balcony of the VIP area. They're looking directly at us.

Understanding floods through me.

This is all a show.

Why? I don't know. All I know is I was so close to coming, and I still need the release. I thought that maybe—just maybe—Asher would be the one providing it to me, but I was wrong.

CHAPTER NINE

*Life shrinks or expands in
proportion to one's courage.*
Anaïs Nin

I take a step back from him, or I try to. He doesn't let me. His eyes return to mine, and he frowns at what he sees. I try to back away again, and thankfully, he allows me to. He grabs my hand, though. I don't mind. It's easier than being pressed against him. I can't think when I'm so close to him, when I can feel his erection cutting deliciously into my stomach.

When he starts to drag me toward the stairwell, I relent, but not before giving Aimee a helpless stare. She looks shocked, yet she still manages to give me a sassy eye roll at my attention.

I can almost hear her saying, "Puh-lease. I am not going to feel bad about you holding hands and dancing with Asher freakin' Black."

At the bottom of the stairs, I dig my heels in the ground, trying to stop our movement. Asher gives me an irritated sigh before turning to meet my stare, but I'm not focused on his face. I'm eyeing the little wet spot on his thigh, a wet spot that *I* made.

He follows my gaze and smirks before wiping it with the index finger on his free hand. I watch with an open mouth as—I kid you not—he dips his finger into his mouth and sucks.

"We'll take care of that later," he promises, before tugging me up the stairs. "When we get up there, play it cool. Just follow my lead."

I just nod, too shocked and turned on to say anything. Unencumbered by a bra, my nipples are straining painful against my dress, the friction pleasant and frustrating all at once. In my defense, the man just *licked* my wetness off of his finger.

At the top of the stairwell, we're greeted by the group of men in suits. The same group Asher was looking at while he danced with me. These are the men he was putting on a show for, so I force myself to pay attention. To look for any clues that might help me. I may be pliant with Asher's demands, but it can't hurt to be more informed.

There are five men here. Each man is accompanied by a beautiful woman. All but one looks like a carbon copy of the blonde girl from the Hallway Incident. Tall and skinny. Small, perky breasts. Heavy make-up. Expensive highlights. Designer dresses.

They're all stunning, of course, which doesn't astonish me. It doesn't intimidate me either, because there's no way I can't feel beautiful after dancing like that with Asher. Plus, I may have been in the middle of nowhere for the last couple of years, but I still know what pretty looks like, and I know that, for most people, I fit the bill.

I stand there warily as a few of the women eye me up and down, not cruelly—for the most part—but judgmentally all the same. The man on the far end looks me up and down as well. The beginnings of an ugly sneer curl against his thin lips.

After a tense amount of time, Asher still hasn't introduced me, so I give a little awkward wave with my free hand and say, "Hi! My name is Lucy. I'm—"

Asher cuts me off, "My fiancée."

His *what?!*

A few of the girls gasp.

I'm amazed I haven't myself.

Is this why one night stands get a bad rep? They up and leave you before you reach an orgasm, track you down a month later, threaten you, then pseudo-propose to you in front of a group of middle aged men and their wives?

"Your fiancée, eh?" a skeptical voice asks. It belongs to the man that has been sneering at us. "That's convenient timing."

Asher waves our joined hands a little, as if it's proof of the legitimacy of our alleged engagement. My hand, which has been sweating since before the news of his fake proposal was announced, almost slips out of his palm. He tightens his grip, which only makes me sweat even more.

Everyone else is still silent.

The sneering man's eyes narrow on my left hand. A smug look crosses his face. He looks all too satisfied. "Where's the ring?"

I can feel Asher's grip tighten around my hand in response. It's almost painful now. I mentally sigh. It's now or never, and I have a feeling that this is the favor he has been leading up to. What I've been auditioning for.

Pretending to be Asher's fiancée is better than carrying out a hit or drowning a puppy or any of the million other damning things I thought he would ask me to do. None of my guesses have even been close to being his fake fiancée, but when I really consider it, this is the best case scenario.

I can live my life normally and just nod my head if anyone asks me if we're engaged. So, I make my decision, resolving to commit to Asher's lie.

I give a fake admonishing gasp and say, "Asher! You were supposed to be keeping our engagement a secret, babe!" I playfully hit his chest with my free hand. Then, I lower my voice conspiratorially, turn towards the sneering man and say, "He wasn't supposed to announce anything until I graduate. I wanted to spend my time at Wilton without any fanfare." I hold up my left hand and wiggle my bare fingers. "Hence the lack of a ring." I mimic a disappointed sigh. "I guess the cat's out of the bag now."

When one of the other men says, "Wow. Wilton? That's very impressive, dear," Asher loosens his grip on my hand and gives it a quick squeeze. I know it's his way of conveying his approval. I turn to look at him, being sure to paste an adoring look across my face.

Damn, I'm a great actress.

My talents are lost on the sciences.

Asher leans in to kiss my temple. The kiss conceals the "thanks" he slips under his breath. I give a slight nod that I know only he will pick up and turn around to lean against him. He wraps his free arm across my body, and one of the girls lets out a long "awwww!" Meanwhile, I'm trying to conceal the way my heart is pounding out of my chest at his gentle touch.

I nod to the man that made the comment about Wilton and say, "Thank you. I'm very thankful to have gotten in. It's truly a wonderful school." And to make our fake engagement more believable, I gush, "You know, Asher actually went there, too." I look up at him with fake googly eyes and say, "He snuck into two of my lectures today and ended up answering all of my stats professor's questions! It was unbelievable."

The sneering man's face is red now. He looks irritated, which gives me the feeling that this charade is for him. And it seems to be working. He's clearly pissed.

"I think we've seen enough," he says. He turns to the rest of his group. "We have a lot to prepare for this upcoming week. I think I'm going to call it a night."

The rest of the group give murmurs of agreements and leave after saying their goodbyes to Asher and me. When they are gone, Asher signals to one of his guards, who nods before pulling a device out of his sleeve.

It's a long, flat stick, like the ones airport security uses to search for any metals. I watch in fascination as the guard waves the stick all around the VIP area, as if searching for something. A bug, probably.

The idea of those men placing a bug in here is disturbing. It makes me tense, and Asher squeezes me in response. It's then that I realize I'm still in his arms. My face flushes. I step away from his body immediately and turn to face him.

He studies me as I study him.

"You know," he begins, "you're a really good liar. If I didn't know better, I might have to reconsider believing you when you say you're not a spy for one of the other families. Or a fed."

He can't afford to. That's unspoken, but we both know it's true. I can tell those men are important, and now they think we're engaged. He needs me. And as long as he needs me, I'm safe in New York and can stay at Wilton. Because of this, I plan to ride the safety of this fake engagement out for as long as I can.

I'm silent for a moment before giving him a shrug. "I grew up in foster care. I learned how to lie when social services came around."

It's grim, but it's my reality. Some of the foster families used to starve me or made it known that they only took me in for the monthly check, but those foster families are better than the ones that beat me.

The ones that physically hurt me, and the families like Steve, are the most dangerous ones. You can always steal food and live with people that don't care about you, but you can't undo death. It's just not possible. So, I trained myself to lie to social workers about my living conditions, and in return, I would be allowed to stay in the "better" homes.

Asher nods. There's no pity in his eyes. Just understanding. "Then I made the right choice. You'll be heading back with me tonight."

"What?" Did I hear that right? "You want me to sleep at your place?"

He sighs, like it's a nuisance to explain his thought process to me. "I doubt they'll have eyes on you yet, but just in case, you will need to stay with me. There cannot be any doubt regarding the validity of this engagement."

No way. I didn't agree to that. I *don't* agree to that. I thought that, at most, I would have to go to a few events, look pretty and smile a lot. But moving in with him? That's asking for too much.

I take another step back, placing even more distance between us. "No. Absolutely not," I say, crossing my arms.

The more time I spend with Asher, the more confident I feel about talking back. I like the newfound fearlessness in me, even if the reason for it is currently giving me a death glare.

He narrows his eyes. "Need I remind you that you owe me a favor of my choosing? You don't get to say no, Lucy." He turns to one of his guards and says, "Let her friend know that Lucy will be coming with me."

I turn to the guard and say, "No. Let my friend know that I will *not* be coming with Mr. Black. Tell her to call the police if I do not come home tonight, for I will undoubtedly have been kidnapped."

Asher growls when the guard doesn't move. "Xavier, ignore her. Do as I say," he barks, before forcibly dragging me into a hidden elevator, located behind one of the tinted glass panels.

I struggle against his hold, but it only brings me closer to him.

He laughs. "Keep doing that, sweetheart. It only makes this more enjoyable."

I stop moving and twist my head to level him with a glare. The scary bastard looks almost... pleased with himself. He presses a button on the panel. The elevator jerks to a downward start, and I stumble on my heels, unprepared for the sudden movement. Asher steadies me, tightening his grip around my waist.

"Let go of me," I demand.

A fleeting smirk graces his face. "Are you going to fall?"

I scowl. "No."

"Are you going to behave?"

"No, but I'll scream if you don't let go."

He laughs. "Go ahead. No one will hear you."

And when the doors open into an empty, private garage, I see that he's right.

I sigh. "Fine. I won't scream. Promise." I hold up four fingers, which I think is Scout's Honor or something like that.

He looks at my hand, rolls his eyes, and pushes one of my fingers down, so I'm only holding three up. Then, he nods and walks away after releasing me. I follow after him, reluctantly, though I'm actually not too concerned about my safety. I know I'll be okay for as long as he needs me, though I would appreciate it if he could turn down the scary factor a bit.

"You know," I begin, eyeing him warily. "If we're going to do this, you're going to have to be less scary."

"Less scary?"

I nod and make a sweeping gesture at him with my hand. "See? Scary."

He has a scowl on his face. His arms are crossed, causing his biceps to bulge formidably. At my gesture, though, he releases his arms, but it doesn't make a big difference. He's still ripped, and it's still intimidating.

"I don't know what you expect me to do, Lucy."

"You could try smiling more."

I watch as his lips turn up into a forced grin. He looks like the offspring of The Lakeshore Strangler and the Joker. The sight is so frightening, I trip over my heels and nearly face plant onto the concrete. Asher steadies me, but I shove his arm off of me and scowl.

"Never do that again." The scowl is still on my face.

"Duly noted," he says dryly.

When we approach a fancy looking car, I see Asher play with his watch before the doors automatically lift like bird wings. As soon as he sees my gaping face, Asher just rolls his eyes and gets in. I slide into the passenger seat and jump when the doors automatically close as soon as my butt hits the buttery leather.

I eye Asher's magical watch in suspicion as he starts the car and drives out of the garage.

He sees my look and says, "It's a smart watch. It won't bite."

I have never seen a smart watch like that before. It doesn't even look like a watch. A camel colored leather strap is attached to the face of it. Though it has an electronic interface, the face is set to mimic the analog appearance of a regular watch. It's so realistic I can't tell the difference. The electronic screen is circular, encased in an expensive black setting that looks more like it belongs to a Rolex or Cartier than an electronic watch.

"That is so ostentatious," I say, thinking of all the suffering I've witnessed abroad.

"In a few years, it will be the norm."

"Yeah," I arch my brow, "for snobby rich guys."

"Smart phones used to be rare, but now they're everywhere. You don't think iPhones are 'ostentatious,' do you?" He eyes the iPhone I'm clutching in one of my hands.

His tone is condescending, which annoys me, but I let it go. I don't know why I'm being so confrontational. It's not like I don't know the top one percent of the one percent exists. Hell, I usually don't even care.

But now, because *he* is a part of this lifestyle, I feel compelled to resent it. I also quickly realize my stupidity. I'm poking a bear that has been generous enough not to kill me. I should be curled into the fetal position. Instead, I'm angering it.

"Sorry," I relent, because I don't want to be bear food.

I'm too cute to be bear food. What do bears eat anyway? Fish? Plants? Bugs? Awkward brunettes with a penchant for running away from their problems? I don't look like any of those. Okay, well, maybe the last one describes me to a T.

He gives me a quick glance before returning his eyes to the road. There's a rare, dumbfounded look in those blue eyes.

I explain myself, "I'll stop being petty if you promise we'll revisit the discussion about my living arrangements after we wake up."

He nods. "Fine. I can agree to that. We'll talk about it in the morning, but it won't matter. You're living with me, and that's final."

My jaw drops. "You're impossible!"

A hint of a smile ghosts his lips. "I'm not the one who called the cops. You put yourself in this situation."

I shut up.

We drive a few more minutes in silence before he speaks again. "You're her replacement."

"Whose?" I ask, but I suspect I already know the answer to my own question.

"The girl you saw getting a pat down—"

"Manhandled," I correct.

He rolls his eyes but lets my interjection slide. "That girl you saw that night was supposed to be my fake fiancée, but you ruined that the minute you brought negative attention to her when you called the cops."

"Oh." And because I can't help myself, I ask, "Why was she getting *manhandled*?"

"She was about to go over the marriage contract with my lawyer. She already signed an NDA, but I didn't trust her not to have a recording device on her. It was supposed to be a quick and simple pat down. She was being difficult, not letting Bastian do his job. He may have gotten a little rough, but that's on her."

I nod. I also suspect that I'll be seeing an NDA soon. I'm astonished that I haven't already been forced to sign one, but the whole club ruse seems like it was spontaneous. Like Asher saw an opportunity with both me and those men there, and he seized it.

"Why didn't you pat me down?"

"I already did, Lucy."

"Wh—"

I stop myself as the realization hits. The dance. I thought he was feeling the curves of my body, but he was really patting me down. It's crazy how someone so book smart can be so stupid. You'd think my life abroad and as a foster child would impart on me more wisdom, but it obviously hasn't.

I redirect my line of questioning, noting gratefully that he's actually being pretty open. "Why do you even need a fake fiancée? You have to know how attractive you are." I don't even blush when I say this. It's simply factual. "You could, I don't know, maybe find yourself a real fiancée? Someone you don't have to force into this."

He's smirking when he says, "I didn't have to force Nicole into this. She wanted to all on her own. You were the one who ruined that. You led me to this."

There's no point in arguing against that, so I say, "A fake fiancée is a pretty drastic solution to anything. You're going to need to explain this to me if you want me to play along with your charade."

His face hardens, reminding me that he's a predator. "You'll play along, because you *have to*." He sighs. "I'm only explaining this because it's pertinent to your role as my fiancée. I've been in the process of leaving the Romano family for a while now."

Shock eclipses my ire. "What? Nobody just leaves the mafia."

"I was never actually in it to begin with. I was an independent contractor, someone that was only called in to fix the messes on an as needed basis. I wasn't involved in the day to day operations."

Parts of my Google search say otherwise.

"But you own some of the mob businesses."

"It's just a small percentage of only some of the companies," he corrects. "I came in as a business consultant. They gave me a scholarship under a shell corporation that allowed me to afford Wilton's tuition. In return, I became their business consultant. But only as an independent contractor."

"And this was all legal?" I ask in disbelief.

"I didn't always fix situations through legal means, but in terms of my business consulting, that was mostly legal. I was paid a consultant's fee and even filled out a W-9 for my work. My income was taxed by the government, too. Fully legal."

I don't believe it. "But some of those businesses are money laundering schemes." I read that on a blog that follows the Romano family.

He looks startled by my knowledge. "Are you sure you're not a spy?" But the lack of heat in his tone tells me that he's only joking. "They make a lot of their money through legal means, but one of the on paper businesses is a money laundering scheme."

"Which one?" I ask.

He glances at me. "Are you sure you want to know? You can't un-know it, and this can be dangerous knowledge."

I think about it. I don't really want to know, but my gut is telling me that I need to learn as much about the situation, about him, as I can. Ignorance is often more harmful than knowledge. Just ask Mary Jane Watson when the Green Goblin dragged her all over the city. She's a damsel in distress, which I refuse to be.

I'll settle on being a scaredy cat with random bouts of courage.

I nod and say, "Un-know isn't a word, and the Asher Black the world knows wouldn't let anyone harm his fiancée."

He barks out a stunned laugh. "No, he wouldn't." He's silent for a moment. "It's the strip club chain."

I roll my eyes. "Figures."

"It's actually one of my more brilliant ideas. Stripping is a cash heavy business. The IRS knows and accepts this. The Romano family has their boys come in with their cash earnings, and they spend all that money on tipping the strippers and waitresses. The girls pool the tips, which go to Frankie Romano."

Frankie Romano is the head of the Romano family.

I finish for him, "Let me guess. The girls are legal employees that get paid in wages, which come from the tips and cover fee, while the boys keep their share of profits and tip the rest. The tip income and club employee wages are even taxed as legal earnings." I laugh. "You probably even have the tip policy in the employee contracts."

Asher looks impressed. "Exactly. The feds can't touch the Romano family. The only ones involved in the illegal dealings are technically just customers of the clubs. They'd have to target those guys individually, and even if they're caught, it doesn't trace back to the Romanos. There's no way to cut the head off the snake. Just a never ending supply of tails that are pointless to go after. Tails always grow back."

I study Asher's profile. This is the most animated I've ever seen him. It flows into his appearance, and he looks both refreshed and invigorated—and far less scary than usual. The effect is enough to make my heart skip a few beats.

I whisper. "You're pretty smart, aren't you?" I shake my head, clearing it of whatever just possessed me to compliment him.

He sighs, and it reminds me of why he's telling me this stuff in the first place. I need to know as much as I can about my new "fiancé."

"Not smart enough." His fingers clench harder against the steering wheel. "I signed a contract for 10% of the earnings of all of the businesses I helped create for the Romanos. It was a lot of money, and I used it to invest in my own businesses. All of my businesses are under one company, Black Enterprises."

He pauses, allowing the information to sink in. "One of the board members is trying to vote me out based on my suspected mafia ties, and he can point out my shares in Romano businesses as evidence. Even if they're technically not illegal, those businesses are tied to the Romano family, which has a notorious reputation for organized crime dealings. They've mostly turned away from the hardcore stuff, but it doesn't paint the most favorable picture of me."

"The one that's trying to vote you out... He's the one that was sneering all night, right?"

Asher gives me a dry laugh. It's amused and irritated all at once. "Yeah, that one. His name is René Toussaint. He thinks that, if the board votes me out, he'll be promoted to CEO. The man's after my bonus and power, and he doesn't care how he gets it. Hell, if he can get his hands on my majority shares of the company, he won't hesitate to take them."

"Is there grounds for your dismissal?"

"There's no proof that I've done anything illegal for the mafia, so he can't attack me from that angle. What he's been doing is painting me as young, inexperienced and unstable in order to prove that I'm a threat to the wellbeing of the company. It's a smear campaign, through and through. I haven't exactly made it hard for him, either. In the business world, I *am* young, which automatically makes me inexperienced to them."

He's only 25. Whereas I see that as something that only makes his achievements even more impressive, I can see how René can depict it negatively.

"As for my instability, all of the board members have wives, kids and homes. That's their view of stability. I'm single, have no family, and am living in a penthouse apartment."

"Which is where I come in," I say, putting the pieces together. I can handle this, being involved in an office dispute rather than a mafia one.

"If I have a fiancée, René can't argue that I don't think about the future, that I'm not putting down roots."

"And as a 'ghost,' they won't be able to pull up any dirt on me." I don't bother telling him that Lucy isn't even my real name. It's not like I'm a criminal.

"Exactly. Couple in the fact that you attend an Ivy League and spent the last two years of your life volunteering, you're practically a saint. You're an even better candidate than Nicole ever was."

I can't help myself. "Why was she a candidate anyways?"

"She made sense, because she was someone I'd been fucking

regularly." He says it so casually, I don't even blink. "We've attended events together a few times, she's pretty, and she has a clean record. It was believable. But you're the jackpot. You won't just not make me look bad. You'll actually make me look good."

I almost don't register the compliment. The way he says it isn't flattery. It just *is*.

I'm silent for a moment. "So, tell me. Why should I go along with this fake engagement?"

"Easy. You have no choice."

And just when I am starting to get comfortable around him, he says something like that. I'm almost thankful for the much needed reminder of the looming threat to my life. I was letting myself relax, which could have been the death of me.

I turn to him and give him a serious look, recognizing that I should nip the threat to my life in the bud if I can. "That's not true. At any moment, at any second, I have the power to give you up. What's stopping me from doing that?"

"I'm a dangerous man."

"That may be true, but I don't think you'll hurt me."

"No?" He's amused. It's written all over his face.

"No."

I remember his words from earlier today.

You're an innocent. You stepped wrong, but you're still an innocent.

After spending more time with him, I believe him now more than ever before. Maybe there actually is a line he draws, a moral code of conduct he possesses. Am I really willing to risk my life on a maybe?

I deliberate my next words carefully. "You won't hurt me. Not when there are better alternatives. You're a business man, so sell this to me. Convince me to willingly agree."

Since I owe him and the deed has already been done, I've mentally committed myself to pretending to be his fiancée, but he doesn't need to know that. I figure if I'm going to be his fake fiancée anyway, I might as well get something out of it. I recognize an opportunity when I see one.

He stops the car at a red light and turns to stare at me, his eyes appraising. I don't understand what I'm seeing in them. Is that... *admiration?*

"Are you trying to renegotiate our terms, Ms. Ives?" There's amusement in his icy blue eyes.

I nod and clear my face, taking a lesson from one of Aimee's textbooks—you don't go into a business meeting with emotions. "As far as I'm concerned, we haven't even begun to negotiate."

The light turns green, and I watch as Asher turns right. We pull into the garage of a building. I catch a glance at the street name before we're driving underground. I am pleasantly surprised to learn that we're only a block from Wilton, perfectly within walking range.

Hell, Asher's place is even closer to the main campus than Vaserley Hall is. I'll be able to wake up later in the morning an—... I catch myself before I finish my sentence. I haven't even agreed to move in, yet I'm already making plans.

I'm silent as Asher drives the bat mobile deeper into the garage. I see another garage door, and when he presses a button, the door lifts. My brows lift, too. He has a private garage within the garage. Of course, he does. He parks beside a line of empty cars and kills the engine. Instead of exiting the vehicle, he leans his seat a little further back and looks at me.

"You're flipping the tables on me," he says, his eyes sparking with interest and something akin to appreciation.

I hold my ground, stomping out the stupid butterflies that jitter at his unspoken praise. "I'm just trying to make this a fair deal."

I study him, waiting for him to speak, to tell me whether I made a wrong move or the right one. As I watch a myriad of emotions flit through his face, I'm shocked to realize they're there. I thought he was cold, a killer, but since I stepped into Rogue today, he hasn't been the ruthless killer the city paints him as.

"Have you actually killed someone?" The words slip out of my lips before I can stop them. I cover my mouth, horrified by my lack of filter. "I-I d-didn't mean t-that."

He stares at me, studying the fear on my face. When he finally speaks, I'm dumbfounded by his words.

"Not in a while."

He reaches out for my trembling hands, causing my heart to still as he removes them from their position over my mouth and returns them to my lap. He lets go immediately after, but his eyes remain on mine.

"Don't do that," he says. "Don't be this meek, little girl. Be the woman that challenges me. That's the one I want to be engaged to. I have no use for the cowering little girl that shakes at the mere sight of me. I need the strong woman I know you are. The one that sees an opportunity and takes it. The one that just flipped the tables on me, demanding a fair trade... The one clever enough to test me when all she wanted was for me to slide my cock deep inside her tight walls."

I suck in a sharp breath, unable to exhale until I absolutely have to.

... Sink my cock deep inside...

His words are on repeat in my head—the honesty, tenderness, and vulgarity all slushing around in there, causing my heart to quicken and my face to flush. This girl he described...

That isn't me, is it?

Nevertheless, I *want* to be her. I'm startled that he wants that, too. It's harder than it looks, though. When he's like this, honest and open, it's impossible to reconcile my experiences with this side of him to the one that pinned me against the wall on campus and stalked me to my classes, toying with my emotions and fear.

That's the Asher Black of legends. The one rumored to have executed a hit on more than a dozen members of a rival family in one night. This Asher, the one demanding me to be stronger, is even stranger to me than the killer alter ego. I don't know which side of him to expect, and it's giving me whiplash to accommodate my dueling perceptions of him.

I don't know whether to be fearful or fearless, so I endeavor to be a woman worthy of my own admiration. Strong. I shake away my nerves and replace them with courage—not because he asked me to, but because I'm sick of being weak when I'm capable of being strong.

I turn and make eye contact with him, ignoring the satisfaction on his face. "Why should I agree to this charade?"

He accepts my change in attitude easily, altering his tone to a sexy, dominating boardroom voice. "I've seen your finances and your scholarship situation. You have enough to pay for tuition, but you can't afford to keep living in the dorms. Your job at the coffee shop is enough to pay for the books and a little bit of rent, but what happens when the rent increases in Vaserley? And it will. It does every year."

"I've been looking at jobs in the city."

"And all the money you'll be making at an entry-level summer job will go to your rent. You'll be burnt out by the start of school. That's a shit plan, and you know it."

"I can move out of the dorms and find a cheap apartment," I protest.

"Nowhere near campus, because there's nothing cheaper than five grand a month in this area. This is prime New York real estate. Are you really willing to work that much just to live in a studio apartment?" He softens his voice until it's a seductive lull. *"Move in with me, Lucy."*

Gosh, the way he says my name is a lullaby. I hate that it's working wonders on my resolve. He really is the perfect predator—danger wrapped in a deceptively beautiful package. Except I'm smart enough to know better. I have to be, for my own sake.

"I've already paid rent for the rest of the semester," I say, weakly.

"Send me your leasing contract, and I can get you a refund. I'm familiar with real estate law."

Of course, he is.

"But what about Aimee?" I ask, pulling out my last trump card.

"She'll get her own room in the dorms. It's a sweet deal."

"Until some stranger she might not get along with moves in."

"After the school year has begun? That almost never happens, and you know it."

"But... I don't even know you. You're connected to the mob."

"I haven't been involved with the Romano family's illegal dealings for a while, and when I was, I never hurt women."

I believe him. My internet research supports his words, and looking at him now, I can't help but believe his sincerity. No one is that great of an actor. Not even Leonardo DiCaprio can lie so convincingly. I'll admit that, and I'm the biggest DiCapriHo you'll ever meet.

I'm grasping at straws now. "You could just give me money in exchange for my services." I wince. I sound like a damn hooker.

Thankfully, he ignores my innuendo. "Any cash or electronic exchanges of money runs the risk of showing up on a financial background check, which René will undoubtedly perform. What I can do is alleviate you of some regular expenditures in a way that won't draw suspicion. If you move in with me, you'll save tens of thousands of dollars on rent without raising any eyebrows. I can also supply you with groceries, which would save you another $12,000 over the course of the year."

I choke on a surprised laugh. $12,000 a year on groceries? For one person? Does he eat gold?

He ignores my mocking laughter. "Once you graduate, you'll need a job. I can write you a letter of recommendation. As the CEO of a multinational company, it'll hold a lot of weight."

I sigh. Even I know that's too good of a deal to not accept. I can focus on my studies instead of working and worrying about rent. And when the time comes to get a job, I'll have a letter of recommendation from one of the most powerful men in the city. I'm silent for a few more minutes, trying to think of more reasons not to agree and failing miserably.

He takes in my face and nods. "Good."

It's decided.

I've officially agreed to move in with Asher Black.

CHAPTER TEN

*Courage is what it takes
to stand up and speak.
Courage is also what it takes
to sit down and listen.*
Winston Churchill

There are a lot of cars in Asher's garage. I can't imagine they're all his, especially since some of them are carbon copies of one another. Asher leads me past the line of cars and into an elevator that's located in his private garage. It takes us straight to the penthouse.

I'm impressed to find that, instead of elevator music, the news is playing in the background. It's a rerun of a *Mad Money* episode from yesterday, in which the host discusses Black Enterprise's rumored acquisition of IlluminaGen, a pharmaceutical company whose work I am actually intimately familiar with through my coursework at Wilton.

I turn to Asher and lift a questioning eyebrow.

He smirks. "I can't say anything about that."

A grin graces my lips as I tease, "Not even to your fiancée?"

The grin slips from my lips.

What the Hell was that?

His face turns serious. "Hey. No second thoughts, okay?"

I nod, but I'm still frowning by the time the elevator doors open. The elevator leads to a hallway with a single door in it, the entrance to his apartment. After we enter, I am in awe as Asher gives me a tour of the main area.

The kitchen is large, with clean and shiny state of the art equipment. The penthouse has an open floor plan, so I can see the kitchen, the living room and dining area at once. It makes the already oversized space even larger. This amount of room is almost unheard of in New York City.

"The whole place is bullet and soundproof. There's a panic button in each room." He points to the one in the kitchen, which is hidden in one of the cabinets. "If you press it, my guards will come in." At my widened eyes, he adds, "Don't worry. It's just a precaution. No one involved with any of the families would dare come after me. It's really just protection against corporate espionage now."

I nod dumbly, even though I'm not even processing half of what he's saying. I'm too overwhelmed by the grandeur of the place and terrifying words like "espionage," "bullet" and "panic." Ignoring a wide hallway on the first floor, Asher leads me up a spiral stairwell and straight to a bedroom. It's large, spanning at least 800 square feet.

No way is this a guest room, but I ask just in case. "Is this the guest room for me?"

Asher shakes his head. "It's my bedroom. The master."

It's surreal standing in his bedroom. There's a sitting room that leads into another room for sleeping, separated only by an archway the width of a school bus. In the main area of the room, there's a bed in the center and a large flat screen television set. The bed is a giant Alaskan king, covered in silky black sheets, a black down comforter and a decorative red throw blanket.

The floor, like the rest of the penthouse, is all dark hardwood. There's an opened door that leads into a sleek walk in closet and another doorless archway that serves as the entrance to a giant master bathroom.

I am amazed by the sheer size and opulence of the place. I can't even imagine what my guest room will look like. "Can you show me to my room?" I ask.

Asher spreads his arms out, as if to gesture that this is it.

I frown. "You're giving me the Master?"

"We're sharing the Master."

I shake my head vigorously. "No. No way."

Asher shrugs. "You could always take the couch."

"I'm the one doing you a favor. I'm not taking the couch. I'll take the bed."

He shrugs again. "Go for it."

I nod, satisfied. I leave him there, entering the closet instead to get ready for bed. It's double the size of my dorm room and can easily be mistaken for a high end men's clothing boutique. I shake my head in disbelief at the lavishness. After grabbing a soft cotton t-shirt, I take it with me to the bathroom, purposefully ignoring Asher, who brushes by me on his way to change out of his suit.

Like the rest of the place, the bathroom looks expensive with its white Carrera marble flooring and black modern cabinetry. There's a toilet in its own little room. The standing shower, encased in grey marble, is separated from the room by a glass door. Inside of it is a bench and multiple waterfall style shower heads. Beside the shower is a white, jetted bathtub fit for five.

I go to the toilet. Afterwards, I wash my hands and pull out a drawer under the sink, finding an unopened toothbrush in it. I brush my teeth with it, rinse my face of mascara and grime, and decide to take a quick shower. After tossing my beloved LBD in the hamper. I stop at my underwear, realizing that I have no clean panties to wear. Mine was soiled by the whole dance floor incident. I remember how drenched they were and make a face.

Gross.

I won't be able to sleep in those. I toss the underwear into the hamper, too. Then, I set my phone on the counter, after remembering to send a text to Aimee, letting her know I'm safe.

> At Asher's place, safe and sound. Be safe tonight! See you soon!

And because I'm a coward, I turn off my phone before she can text me back. I know tomorrow I'll be waking up to a million questions that I don't know if I'm allowed to answer. I'll have to talk to Asher about the parameters of this arrangement later. I still haven't signed a nondisclosure agreement, too.

When I'm done with my shower, I have no other choice but to tug Asher's soft t-shirt on over my bare body. I feel incredibly naked underneath. Wearing another man's shirt is intimate enough, especially given the fact that I'm not wearing a bra nor panties. The knowledge that it's Asher's and he's nearby, somewhere in the same penthouse, makes my cheeks flush.

When I reenter the bedroom after blow drying my hair, I'm frightened to find Asher in bed. He's shirtless, wearing only a pair of black Calvin Klein boxer briefs.

I avert my eyes. "I thought we agreed that I'd get the bed."

When I look back at him, he's shrugging, but his eyes are focused on his shirt on my body.

"No one is stopping you," he says.

"But…"

"Don't be ridiculous. Who knows how long you'll be here for? I'm not sleeping on a couch indefinitely in my own damn house."

"This place is huge! It has to be, like, 10,000 square feet!"

"Twenty."

My jaw drops. "Twenty thousand square feet and you can't even make up a guest room for me?"

"It's only a ten bedroom home," the rich prick says.

He ticks each finger in a visual count.

One finger. "Master."

Two. "Office."

Three. "Library."
Four. "Armory."
Five. "Shooting range."
Six. "Theater room."
Seven. "Security room."

He lifts all ten fingers now. "And the rest have been combined and renovated into a personal gym."

I can't believe this. The dude has a shooting range, armory, gym, theater, library, security room, and office in a New York City apartment? I know he has money, but this is just insane.

He continues, "You're welcome to sleep in any room you want to, but I can guarantee you that this bed and the couch are your best options."

I groan. I am not spending who knows how long sleeping on the couch. I might as well start getting used to sleeping on a bed with Asher. With a long, exaggerated sigh, I make my way to the empty side of the bed. When I pass him, I catch his eyes rolling. He seems to do that a lot around me.

Asher goes to brush his teeth and shower before he returns to the bed. By the time he settles in, I still haven't gotten used to the fact that we're going to be sleeping in the same bed for however long I'm here for.

"Lights," he commands into the empty air, and we're immediately flooded in darkness.

I scoot over until I am on the absolute edge of the bed. Since it's an Alaskan King, there's a generous amount of space between Asher and me, but it doesn't feel like enough. I can't sleep like this.

I am considering falling asleep on the couch when Asher sighs and scoots my way. I can picture him rolling his eyes as he wraps a strong arm around my waist and pulls me toward him. He nestles his body into mine, positioning us so he's Big Spoon and I'm Little Spoon.

Now, with his muscled front pressed against my back and the feel of his breath on my shoulder, I really can't sleep. I'm even more aware that I have nothing on underneath Asher's shirt. We stay like that for a moment before Asher squeezes my body and sits up.

In a surprisingly chivalrous move, he takes a pillow and the extra throw blanket and relocates onto the floor. He's out like a light within seconds, leaving me to wonder...

What the Hell was that?

When I wake up, it's still relatively dark. Though the blackout curtains are drawn, I see bright light peeking out underneath an uncovered edge of the wall to wall window. A glance at the clock on the bedside table tells me it's a little past one in the afternoon. After sleeping late last night, I'm still tired, though this is the best sleep I've gotten since the Hallway Incident.

I lift onto my elbows a little when Asher enters the room. He's in a suit and has a pretty black box in his hand. There's an intricately tied bow wrapped around it.

When he sets it on the nightstand and begins to leave, I ask, "Where are you going?"

He pauses for a moment, halfway to the door. "Work."

I nod and lay back down, not bothering to answer. Because, really? Who works on a Saturday? I'm so tired right now, I can't even fathom working at this moment. I let my slumber take over my body, lulling me into another deep, dreamless sleep.

When I wake up again, the place is empty. There's a note on the nightstand attached to the box Asher dropped off earlier.

> *At work. Dinner at six. Wear this.*

It's not signed, but the note is clearly from Asher. Inside the box is a silky, emerald green evening gown. It's safe to assume that wherever we're going is fancy. A glance at the clock tells me I have an hour to get ready. I'm not surprised I slept in until 5 P.M. I haven't been sleeping well lately, but now that I know Asher needs me too much to harm me, I'm looking forward to catching up on many missed hours.

Asher strolls in by the time I have the dress on and am ready to go. My face is bare of makeup, because I don't have my beauty products with me, but I was able to wrestle my hair into an elegant up do with some hair ties and bobby pins I found lying around in one of the bathroom drawers. I don't even stop to consider who they belong to.

Gross.

Asher hasn't looked up at me since he entered, but I know he's aware of my presence. I shift uncomfortably, unable to tear my eyes away from his bare chest as I watch him undress. When he tugs his pants down his legs, revealing taut, muscular thighs, I zero in on his package, encased in navy blue Calvin Klein boxer briefs.

I haven't stopped lusting after Asher. It's stupid, I know, and I'll do well to remember who he is. But when an attractive man is standing in front of me in nothing but his underwear, I'm going to look. It's impossible not to. I'm not a nun. Hell, I doubt a nun would be able to look away from a shirtless Asher.

I clear my throat. "Where are we eating?"

When he looks up at me, his eyes burn a slow trail up my body, starting from my heeled toes, traveling up the exposed skin under the daring slit of my dress, and eventually leveling onto the abundant swells of my cleavage heaving out of the dress. Once his eyes lock on mine, there's no doubt in my mind that this lust is mutual. He's giving me the same look he gave me the first night I met him.

I take an instinctive step back, trying to distance myself from it.

"L'oscurità."

L'oscurità is a fancy Italian restaurant in TriBeCa with a waiting list over a year long. I know this because Minka once stood in the hallway, going on and on about how exclusive it is after going there for a date with some old hedge fund guy. I'm not sure if I have the table manners for a dinner at such an ornamental place.

At my hesitant look, Asher says, "Don't worry about it. We're just eating dinner with my family. Think of it as a trial run to work out our kinks."

I nod, but now I'm even more horrified on the inside...

I'm going to meet his family?!

That's worse!

"Does your family know this is fake?" I gesture back and forth between us.

He nods. "They know *everything*."

Everything?!

Memories of Asher's fingers in me, his lips sucking on my clit, flood through me. I wince, hoping they don't know about what happened in the alley that night.

CHAPTER ELEVEN

> *Being deeply loved by someone gives*
> *you strength, while loving someone*
> *deeply gives you courage.*
> Lao Zi

The drive to the restaurant is a short one. We go straight from the underground private garage of the penthouse building to the underground garage of the restaurant's building. I never even breathe in the New York air.

Asher opens the door for me, offering me a hand that I proudly refuse. I'm a 21st century woman, damn it. I can get myself out of a damn car. Instead of his hand, I use the door to help me up and accidentally press one of the buttons near the door handle. As soon as it happens, wheels pop out of the bottom of the door.

My eyes widen at the bizarre sight. "Did your car just *grow* wheels?!"

"They're there in case the car is halted during a shootout." He ignores my sharp intake of breath. In my defense, the idea of needing protection from a shootout is so foreign that it's outlandish. "The door can be removed from its hinges, and we can hide behind the bulletproof door while we move somewhere safer. The wheels are there so we don't have to carry the door."

That's... genius.

But also ridiculous.

A shootout?!

Asher presses the button again, and the wheels slide slowly back into the car door. He offers his arm to me, and I place my hand on the crook of his elbow, worried that if I don't accept his help again, something might grow out of him, too. Like maybe horns from his temples or a devil's tail.

We're led into the restaurant by the maître d, who calls Asher "Mr. Black" and me "Ms. Ives" without any introductions needed. How he knows my name, I have no clue. He takes us from the private underground garage into a private room. Asher's guards, who accompanied us in the front seat of the town car, station themselves at the door—one outside and one inside.

I take in the room. It's a large room, but there's only one table in it, a fancy ovular table with four place settings made up. On one wall is glass, stretching across the expanse of the entire wall. On the other side of it is the kitchen, though I assume the glass is one way, because the kitchen staff don't seem to realize that we're on the other side.

I'm shocked to see the guy from my first night at Rogue—Bastian, I think—there, talking to what looks like the head chef.

Asher's eyes follow my line of sight. "He's my manager."

My manager.

Boss.

My mind quickly pieces everything together.

Asher owns L'oscurità. Bastian is the manager. That's how Bastian works for him.

When we're seated beside one another, waiters arrive and pour us wine without taking our orders. Once they leave, Bastian enters the room with an older man, probably in his late forties. They're both dressed in suits, walking into the area with confident body language. Asher said we're meeting up with his family, but I notice that neither Bastian nor the man look anything like Asher does.

Asher stands up and hugs the man tightly. Seriously.

When they pull back from each other, Asher asks, "How are you, Vince?"

"Business is well. I can't complain." Vince turns his eyes to me, and they light up. "You must be Lucy. My name is Vincent, but you may call me Vince or Vinny."

I nod and move to shake his hand, but he pulls me into a hug, too.

Flustered, I return it, albeit weakly. When we're all seated, I look between the three men.

I must look curious, because Vince laughs and says, "It's not a blood relation, dear."

Bastian scoffs. "Yeah, no way am I related to that ugly face."

A genuine smirk crosses Asher's "ugly" face. "I can recall a few of your ex-girlfriends that have said otherwise."

Wait.

Back up.

Did he just make a joke?

Asher just made a joke.

This is weird.

Why are they acting like it's normal?

It's definitely weird, right?

Mafia killers don't joke... They sit around in dark rooms by themselves, brooding and listening to classical music in between their kills.

Vince laughs wholeheartedly, ignoring my bewilderment, and says to me, "That's how this all began. Bastian and Asher were dating the same young lady, a—"

Bastian smirks and says, "She was no *lady*," at the same time Asher snorts and says, "We weren't dating. We were fucking."

Bastian's eyes narrow. "Yeah, yeah. You think you're hot shit, Ash. We know."

Vince ignores the two. "Bastian finds out about Asher, and he goes to confront him."

"And I fucked him up," finishes Asher. "He had a baseball bat, too."

"I have three brothers—Elias, Gio, and Frankie," Vince says.

I still. Frankie is the head of the Romano family, which would mean that Vince is not only a Romano but also a high-ranking member. I'm essentially eating dinner with mafia royalty... and I'm not even scared.

How badass am I right now?

"Bastian is Gio's son, which would make him my nephew. I was head of enforcement, so I was sent to deal with Asher personally, Bastian being my nephew and all. I wasn't expecting what I found. Naturally, Bastian lied and told us he was beaten by someone older, but at the time, Asher was just a 15-year old boy, almost five years younger than Bastian. So, I looked at him and said—"

"Where are your shoes, boy?" Asher finishes.

"And Asher said—"

"I ain't got none."

"And I said—"

"Well, let's go get you some."

There's a look of fondness on Asher's face. It's so vulnerable, it takes me completely by surprise. I've been looking for his weaknesses since the moment I met him, and here it is, and it's so unexpected...

Asher *loves* somebody.

His love for this man is palpable, as tangible as the ground I walk on and the chair I'm sitting on. It's the biggest weakness I've seen of his yet, the most vulnerable side of him he has shown me. I didn't even think he had any vulnerabilities. I almost gave up searching.

I'm ashamed that I immediately wonder how I can use this to my benefit.

As perceptive as ever, Asher narrows his eyes at me and leans in, whispering softly into my ear, "Don't mistake my love for a weakness, Lucy. That love was strong enough to turn an eighteen-year-old boy into a ruthless killer. Heed my warning. There is nothing I won't do for the ones I love."

I back up sharply at his words, quickly scooting my chair over a little in the process.

... strong enough to turn an eighteen year old boy into a ruthless killer.

There's a rumor that, when Asher was eighteen, he was living with a Romano *caporegime* when they were attacked by members of the Andretti family. This was during the territory wars, and the Andretti family sent two dozen people to kill the *capo*, which must have been Vince.

After a fight broke out between Vince's guards and the Andretti soldiers, there were still over a dozen Andretti soldiers left alive. They thought they won, that Vince was theirs. They didn't know that Asher was living there. They weren't ready for him. Maybe they never could be. He killed them all, and then he infiltrated the home of one of the Andretti *capos* and did what they had tried to do to Vince.

Only he succeeded, killing an Andretti *capo* and dozens of his men.

A shiver runs down my spine.

There is nothing I won't do for the ones I love.

I'll remember his warning for as long as I live. I was wrong. His love isn't a weakness. It's his greatest strength.

Vince turns his knowing eyes to me and says, "Asher is like my son. He moved into my home soon after I met him, and he lived there, even when he went to Wilton."

When Bastian's face turns into a snarl and he says, "Yeah, and his piece of shit 'parents' didn't even realize he was gone until he started making money, and they wanted a piece of the cut," I realize that he loves Asher, too.

I didn't know love until that moment. Maybe I thought of love as a weakness because I've never felt it. The only relationships I've seen have been nasty, parasitic and volatile parodies, bastardized by the endless stream of foster parents I've had. Until now, I didn't know what it's like to love and be loved. This... the way these three look at each other, interact, and treat one another...

It's magical.

It's the strongest thing I've ever witnessed.

And I want it for myself.

Badly.

CHAPTER TWELVE

Courage is knowing what not to fear.
Plato

I wake up to the sound of a woman's voice. It's angry and confrontational. I definitely don't want to get involved with that drama, so I keep my eyes closed and breathing even, pretending to still be asleep.

"Why is *she* here?" The voice is shrill and fuming.

Asher sighs. "I'm not explaining this again, Monica. You work for me, not the other way around. I shouldn't have to have this conversation with you."

"But—"

"You're pissing me off. Stop."

She's silent for a moment. "Fine, but I don't like it."

"Noted," Asher says dryly. "Do you have what I asked for?"

I hear a ruffling of a bag, probably a purse, before the woman, Monica, says, "Here."

"Thank you, Monica. You may see yourself out now."

It's a dismissal, and my body relaxes when I hear her leave. Asher's footsteps are eerily silent as he approaches the bed and throws something onto it beside me. It's heavy.

"Here," he says.

I peek an eye open slowly, pretending to just wake up. He rolls his eyes at my theatrics.

"How'd you know I was awake?" I ask.

He doesn't answer me, and I don't bother asking again. I haven't forgotten about his time as a fixer. With his super ninja skills, he's probably able to count my heartbeats from a mile away like Edward Cullen or something equally cool and predator-like.

Instead, I look at the thing he threw at me. It's a black, nondescript binder, unlabeled and about an inch thick.

"What is it?" I ask.

"It's full of paperwork and activities for marriages involving a noncitizen. Green card marriages. They use these activities and questionnaires in preparation for their interviews with immigration officers."

"And you thought we could use these to get to know one another," I finish.

He raises one of his hands, showing me an identical binder. "It's a quick and efficient way, yes."

I moan and nod. "Fine, but let me brush my teeth first."

When I'm done brushing my teeth, I find Asher on the bed, sitting crisscross applesauce. Bare chested and in jogger sweats, he looks mouthwatering and almost... approachable. He has a pen cap in his mouth and has already begun filling out his questionnaire.

He glances up at me as I approach him, perching myself on the other side of the bed. I catch the pen he throws my way, open the binder, set it comfortably on my lap, and start my questionnaire.

We sit in comfortable silence, the only sound coming from the scribbles of our pens. The questions are simple at first, just general background questions... But the problem is that my background is shady at best. My name isn't even my real name.

I answer the questions as best as I can, filling out my legal name and being truthful about my birthplace. I leave my biological parents' names empty, because answering those lines will just lead to more questions about why I have my mother's last name and not my father's. If the rest of the questions are like this, this is going to be a long day.

By the time an hour has passed, I've only answered a handful of questions, skipping about ninety-nine percent of them.

I groan, finally deciding to give up. "This isn't going to work."

Asher studies my face, lingering on the light sheen of sweat on my forehead. (Some of the questions made me nervous. Sue me.)

"Why not?" he asks, his tone even but annoyed, which I find typical.

I settle for a half truth. "Because I'm a foster kid. I don't know a lot of things about my past, and what I do know is complicated. Like the parents section. Am I supposed to list all the foster parents that had a hand in raising me? There's a lot of them."

He reaches out and grabs my binder. A frown graces his face as he scans the pages, presumably annoyed by all the empty blanks. He sighs. "We'll have to do this verbally."

Great.

Now I have to lie convincingly aloud.

I nod reluctantly. "How do you want to do this?"

"We'll go question by question, taking turns to answer them."

"Okay. You go first."

"My name is Asher Aaron Black, and I was born on May 17, 1991."

He snorts when he catches me taking notes on the Quizlet app of my phone. I make sure to set my profile to private first. I don't want people to wonder why I have flashcards on Asher's life, like I'm a stalker or something. I wave for him to continue.

"I was born at Mount Sinai Queens Hospital to a junkie mother and a pimp father. No siblings that I know of."

I wince at how casually he said that, my fingers hesitating on my iPhone screen before completing the flashcards.

Mother's occupation? Junkie.

Father's occupation? Pimp.

Asher stops talking and pulls out a slip of paper from the back of his binder. He places it in front of me. It's a nondisclosure agreement.

I skim through it, as he says, "You need to sign this before I continue."

I nod and sign it after reading the whole thing. It's pretty straight forward. I don't have to give up the blood of my firstborn or anything… but under no circumstances can I disclose anything about my time with Asher in relation to the fake nature of the relationship. I am also not allowed to discuss any sensitive information regarding Asher or his businesses with anyone other than him or any other relevant, involved parties. Basically, I need to use some common sense when talking to people about Asher.

After I hand the signed NDA back to him, I begin my turn:

"My name is Lucy Ives." *Currently true, previously false.*

"I don't have a middle name." *False.*

"I also don't really know much about my biological parents." *False.*

"I don't know where I was born either." *False.*

"Someone dropped me off at a fire station." *Truth.*

"And social services came to pick me up." *Truth.*

"As for my foster parents, there have been way too many to count." *Truth.*

"I've had a lot of foster siblings, too, but I was never close to any of them." *Truth.*

"I never stayed anywhere for more than a few months anyways." *False.*

"Should I name all of my foster dads, moms, sisters and brothers? I really don't want to." *Biggest Truth I've told yet.*

I don't want to open up the Pandora's Box that is Steve and my name and, most embarrassingly, the way I ran away from my problems rather than facing them. It's also disconcerting how much of my life is a lie. Asher may have a dubious background, but so do I. I have no right to be alarmed by him when my history has just as much gray matter as his.

There's a contemplative look on Asher's face before he shakes his head. "If it comes up, I'll just say that you bounced from foster home to foster home, never staying anywhere longer than a few months."

I nod, hiding my relief behind a trite smile. I'm happy to be done with my round of lies. Honestly, I'm wondering why I didn't go into politics. With all the lies I'm used to telling, I think I would be pretty good at it. Politifact would probably give me a pants on fire rating on their Truth-O-Meter™, but that seems to propel careers rather than damage them.

I'm picturing myself in a stuffy pantsuit, speaking at dozens of campaign rallies, when Asher gestures for me to continue. I do, endeavoring to be as truthful as possible from here on out. Because, honestly, who am I kidding? I can't pull off a pantsuit, I'm afraid of public speaking, and I usually fall asleep within the first few minutes of a lecture, let alone hours of congressional hearings. The only political trait I possess is a thoroughly sculpted affinity for telling lies.

"The foster homes were in the High Desert of California, above the Inland Empire. It's a pretty poor area with a high crime rate and ridiculously high temperatures." I wince. "You can probably guess what type of place that was."

Not all of it was bad, but it certainly wasn't safe or fun. It's the meth lab of the nation. From what I remember, there are a lot of trailer homes there that house meth labs. It wasn't unusual for a home to suddenly go up in flames, and when that would happen, everyone knew what type of home that was.

At Asher's silence, I continue, figuring it's safe to mention my social worker, "My social worker's name is Mary Peters. She was my social worker from the time I entered the system to the time I aged out. She's good people. She's probably the closest thing to a parental figure I've ever had, but even then, we're not really close. I haven't talked to her since the day I aged out."

I really should talk to Mary, but I'm too ashamed of myself. I ran, even though she'd advised me not to jeopardize my future like that. She told me we could do something about Steve, but I didn't believe her. I still don't, but I do feel bad about losing touch with her. She went above and beyond for me. There's no denying that.

As we continue, I'm relieved and amazed to see there's no judgment in Asher's face. He just nods and internalizes the information I give him, easily memorizing it with that savant brain of his. Me? I have over a thousand flashcards by the time we're done with the questionnaire. I now know way more than I ever expected to know about Asher.

I have flashcards full of mundane stuff, like:

Name? Asher Aaron Black.

Favorite color? Black.
Childhood pet? A black Pitbull terrier named Dog.
Beverage of choice? Water or black tea. Nothing else.

It's very subtle, but I think Asher really likes the color black.

It's when we delve into the darker aspects of Asher's life that I realize how honest he's being. The courage to speak about painful life experiences is foreign to me, so seeing it in Asher is as impressive as it is alarming.

"Where did you learn to fight?" I ask, remembering how he beat Bastian when he was only fifteen.

We've slowly steered our way from the questions on the worksheets to unexpectedly easy conversation. I'm genuinely curious about him and his past. This is more than learning about things to use against him.

"My parents didn't have a lot of money, so I grew up in a pretty shitty area. There were a lot of gangs. I didn't join one, but I did have to learn to fight and defend myself. I ended up signing up for MMA classes at a local gym." He laughs, unashamed. "I stole the money for the classes from my mom's drug fund. I'd mix her drugs with sugar water, so it'd last her longer. Then, I'd steal the money it saved and use it on classes.

"One night, I was finished sparring, and some chick comes up to me. We end up fucking in the locker room. We get caught, and it turns out she's dating Bastian. A week later, he comes at me with a baseball bat, and I fight back. Beat the shit out of him, too.

"I should have been put down after that, but the *capos* were impressed. So, Vince took me in. He didn't have kids of his own, and for some reason, he wanted me. I moved into his house on the Upper East Side, and he enrolled me into a private prep school nearby. After that, I went to Wilton. Vince could've paid my tuition, but he already did so much for me, so I didn't want to ask. I ended up working out a deal with the family, and well, you know the rest."

As for my part of the getting to know you, I lie about what I have to and tell the truth about what I can. I don't think Asher is suspicious of me. My foster care upbringing makes it easy to divert attention from my lack of a personal life growing up, and I'm able to parrot the same theme over and over—that my childhood sucked but was typical for a foster kid in a poor area.

Blah, blah, blah.

To be fair, that's pretty close to the truth. Because that's my past—a whole lot of *blah*.

But now? Even though this whole situation is really messed up, it's still exciting.

I feel like I'm living for the first time, and I have Asher to thank—and blame—for that.

CHAPTER THIRTEEN

The courage of life is often a less dramatic spectacle than the courage of a final moment; but it is no less a magnificent mixture of triumph and tragedy.
John F. Kennedy

"What do you want to eat?" Asher asks.

We're currently taking a break, because my stomach won't stop growling. The questionnaire took longer than we originally thought it would, so we ended up skipping breakfast. The hunger has been torturous given my love for food. I even listed eating as my biggest hobby. Asher's is MMA.

I smirk. "You tell me, Lucy Expert."

I'm becoming way too comfortable around Asher, but I genuinely trust him not to hurt me. I actually like his company. It's better than what I normally do on a Sunday, which is homework. And if I'm being honest, I can see myself enjoying this whole fake fiancée thing.

This is a nice place to live, I don't have to pay for food and housing, I'm closer to the heart of campus than I was before, and I can sleep through the night without waking up from Aimee's snores or the sound of someone drunkenly stumbling through the hall.

Asher playfully shakes his head at me. He seems less annoyed with me now. "Chicken *Pad Thai*?"

I nod. "If we're doing Thai, you'll get the *Pad See Ew* with Beef and Shrimp."

I bask in his look of approval at my awesome memorizing skills. Truthfully, my skills aren't as good as Asher's, which I suspect is the result of him having an eidetic memory. Me, on the other hand? I'm a pig. I just never forget anything food related.

Asher picks up his phone to call Monica, who I learned is his assistant, for the food order. According to our questionnaire led conversation, she's been having an attitude problem lately, but Asher's reluctant to fire her because she's been working with him since he started the company while at Wilton.

It'll take too fucking long for him to train someone else. His words, not mine. Personally, I don't commend her for working for him for over half a decade without a promotion. What is she thinking? No wonder she's so crabby.

While Asher is talking to Monica, I decided to turn my phone off airplane mode. My phone vibrates for a solid minute with a bunch of incoming texts before stopping. I have 27 unread texts, all from Aimee, and a voicemail from her, too. They're all from around 4 A.M. on the night we went to Rogue, except the most recent one, which is a lone text from last night.

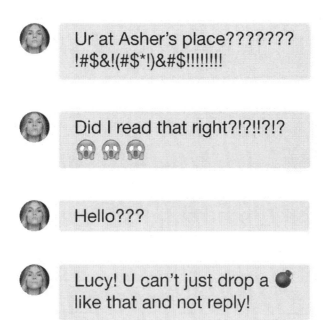

I hate u.

Omw home. Safe and sound no thanks to u. 💀

Eating all ur Starbursts if u don't reply in 3... 2... 1...

All ur Starbursts are in my tummy. Pink next.

Pink gone. Yellow's next.

Seriously? Not gonna reply? Not even for Starburst????

I hate u so much! Don't leave me hanging! ASHER BLACK?! 🖕😈

Seriously? Not gonna reply? Not even for Starburst????

Take a pic of Little Asher. I need to know.

 How big is he????

 I bet he's reaaaaaaaallllllyyy big.

 U guys have to have babies. 👶👧🍼

 And get married. 💍💒👰

 He won't poison u, I promise. I won't let him.

 If u don't fuck him, I will....... 💁‍♀️🧚‍♀️

Lucccccccccyyyyyyy, I need to know.

 Ur the worst roomie ever.

 I ate alllllllllllllllllllllll ur Starbursts. 😾😿😿

 I'm sleeping on ur bed. The only way u can stop me is by replying.

 Grrrrrrr........

 I'm calling the cops if u don't text back...

 Ugh.... U suck....

 I'm givin u 24 hrs to txt back then I'm calling the cops. I mean it, Loosey Goosey! 👊

I roll my eyes. Those texts have pretty decent grammar and spelling given how drunk Aimee probably was when she typed them. I open my call log and tap the voicemail button. I click play, pressing the phone to my ear and plugging my other ear with a finger to hear well.

When I glance up at Asher, he's staring at me, no longer on the phone with Monica. I mouth Aimee's name as the beginnings of the voicemail start to play. Asher takes the phone from my hands.

"Hey!" I say, watching helplessly as he puts the phone on speaker and restarts the voicemail.

I wait in mortified anticipation as Aimee's message commences, her drunken voice crisp and loud on the speakers.

"Loosey Goosey! You better answer your phone. What happened to bros before hos?" She pauses. "Or is it chicks before dicks?" There's some rustling. "I'm eating all of your Starbursts, Lucy. There are only oranges left for me to eat, while you're at Asher's, probably enjoying his yummy cock."

Oh, gosh.

My hands cover my face. I can't even look at Asher.

Aimee isn't done embarrassing me. "I bet he's huge. What is he? 8 inches? 9? Don't tell me he's, like, a one incher. I swear, I'll be so disappointed. I won't be able to look at another dick again."

I leap up, trying to snatch the phone from Asher's hand. But he's unsurprisingly quicker than me, pausing the message before tackling me onto the bed. He has both my wrists bound with one of his hands and my body trapped beneath his. I hold my breath and close my eyes. His whole body is intimately pressed against mine, so I can't think straight.

Then, he presses play on the message again with his free hand.

"Gosh, could you imagine having sex with Asher Black? If anybody deserves it, it's you after that three year dry spell."

Two, I want to correct, but what's the point?

That's still a long time.

I groan and peek an eye open. Asher is grinning, which actually makes him look human. It reminds me of the time I went to Disneyland with my group home on a weekday, and there was no line for Space Mountain. I went on the ride again and again and again that day, wanting to draw out the rare gift until I couldn't anymore. I want to do the same with Asher's smile, because there might not be a next time.

I think about snatching my iPhone out of his hands and taking a picture. But not before deleting the voicemail, of course. This is the largest I've ever seen Asher smile, and it's naturally at my expense.

Aimee is the worst best friend ever.

"Tell me if he makes you orgasm," she continues. "I bet you'll have multiple orgasms." Aimee yawns. "Asher Orgasms. They're probably so good that they deserve their own name. Ashorgasms? Ashgasms? As—" There's a loud snore. Aimee fell asleep over the phone.

We wait for more, Asher's body still pressed against mine, but after thirty more seconds of snores, he ends the voicemail. I note that he doesn't delete it.

"Ashgasms?" he asks.

"Shut up," I say, very aware that he's still on me and my hands are still bound by his.

He dips his head lower, nuzzling his face into my neck before whispering into my ear, "She's not wrong, you know. The things I can do to you will ma—"

Of course, that's when Monica chooses to show up, not even bothering to knock.

"Ashe—" she pauses when she sees us, a harsh look instantly crossing her face.

The things he can do to me will what?! I need to know. I immediately hate Monica for interrupting us. I mentally thank her for it, too. Who knows what would have happened if she didn't?

I take a moment to study her for the first time. She's pretty. *Really* pretty, with pale blonde hair, wide blue eyes, a petite frame and endlessly long legs. Naturally, she's also well-dressed and has on nude pumps painted a famous red at the soles. All in all, she looks like someone more suited to be Asher's fake fiancée than me.

I'm not jealous, though. If I'm going to get through this experience unscathed, I can't like him like that. I can't even *think* like that. Asher still has dangerous mafia connections, and while I know him pretty well after hours of going over green card questionnaires and am confident he won't hurt me, it still isn't enough to form a real relationship bond that only time is capable of. And without that bond, I have no justification for jealousy.

So, yeah... that little clench I feel in my heart?

That's not jealousy.

Nope!

Not even a little!

I eye her ridiculously long legs again.

Is my face turning a little green?

Monica is still staring at me with narrowed eyes when I'm done with my perusal of her. Her eyes focus on my hands, which are bound by his, and I realize that our position looks way too intimate. To be fair, it feels that way, too.

Judging by the pained look on her face as she sees Asher and me in a compromising situation, I realize that she's not stupid for working for the same company—the same man—for more than half a decade without a promotion. She's stupid for doing all that because she loves her boss despite the fact that he clearly doesn't feel the same way.

And he definitely doesn't.

I could tell this when he dismissed her so easily earlier, his tired tone I now know was from exhaustion over her infatuation. I can tell this now, too, in the way that he doesn't give a damn about how close we are, that we're doing this in front of her. He's still looking at me, a stormy expression in his exquisitely blue eyes.

The things I can do to you will...

Gosh, I still want him to finish that sentence.

It is Asher's unnerving attention that makes me sit up quickly, pushing him away. He lets me, though I feel even more self-conscious without him covering me. My legs are in plain view under his t-shirt, which hitched high up my body when he tackled me. I push it down, thankful that it didn't raise high enough to reveal my girly bits. Jumping up, I pretend to be unfazed.

"Let my help you with that," I say, eyeing the takeout bags in her arms.

She has two bags, which look to be holding more than just the *Pad Thai* and *Pad See Ew* Asher and I ordered. That's fine by me. The more food the merrier.

She pushes my hand away and says, "Nonsense. I can do it."

I hold my hands up in mock surrender, hiding my smirk at the annoyed look on Asher's face. She's *his* assistant. If she irritates him, he should show her the door. From what I've seen, she'd just walk back in… without knocking.

We follow Monica downstairs, my stomach grumbling a few times along the way. I shove Asher with my shoulder when it makes him laugh for the millionth time. Monica looks on in contempt.

I almost feel bad for the girl. She clearly has the hots for him, and here I am, a complete stranger in a position she desperately wants to be in. She's been here for five years. I've been here for just over a day, and I've made more progress. That has gotta suck.

I watch as she unloads the bags. I'm right. There are three takeout containers instead of just two. She places the three of them down on the dining table. The one labeled *"Pad Thai"* is placed on the tablemat on the left of the one labeled "Fried Rice." On the place mat to the right of the Fried Rice, she places Asher's *Pad See Ew*. I see what she's doing. She's putting herself between Asher and me, separating us so she can sit next to him.

Asher studies her as she takes a seat. She has a nonchalant expression pasted on her face, but I see how tense her shoulders are. Does she really think she can pull this coy shit on someone as smart as Asher?

Asher doesn't sit. Instead, he grabs both of our food containers and makes his way into the living room. "You're welcome to stay in the penthouse while you eat your food, Monica, but Lucy and I will be eating ours over here."

He's drawing boundaries between them, and I wonder how often he has to do this. From the look on Monica's face, I would say it's not often enough. She looks crestfallen and heartbroken rather than used to it. I briefly wonder if they have a history together. If they do, I need to know about it if I'm going to play his fake fiancée well.

When I take the seat on the floor next to him, I say under my breath, "Is she going to be a problem?"

Asher shakes his head, opening my takeout box for me. It's placed on the coffee table in front of us.

"Nah. She just has a little crush on me." He hands me a fork after I shake my head at the chopsticks he offers me.

"Little?" I snort, my voice still low. I point back and forth between us. "I take it she knows that this is fake?" I remember that she was the one to drop off the green card questionnaires.

"Yeah," Asher sighs. "It can't be helped. She's my assistant, so she has to know everything. She signed an NDA as part of her employee contract, though."

"And you trust her?"

"She hasn't let me down thus far."

I nod, but my mind isn't at ease. Over the past 24 hours, I've come to realize that I have something to lose in this, too, beyond the financial benefits. I'm already a part of this. My fate was sealed as soon as I was introduced to people as Asher's fiancée.

If word gets out that I lied about this, that *we* are lying about this relationship, my professional reputation will be ruined. New York City is a big city, but Asher's celebrity is even bigger. Being branded a liar so publicly will ruin my job opportunities here. My future here.

And all it'll take for everything to come crashing down is Monica opening her mouth about what she knows. She likes Asher. I sympathize with that, but it doesn't mean I like the power her knowledge has over me. She has the motive to hurt me, and I'll be damned if I let that happen.

The thought sends a dark shudder down my back.

CHAPTER FOURTEEN

Courage does not always roar.
Sometimes courage is the quiet voice
at the end of the day saying,
"I will try again tomorrow."
Mary Anne Radmacher

Asher leaves with Monica after we finish eating. He has some commercial properties to look at and clients to meet, and I have packing and homework to do anyways.

The smug look on Monica's face when she walks out of the penthouse with Asher annoys me. I'm not jealous that they're spending time together. I'm irritated that she has the power to ruin my future, and judging by how petty she was earlier and the faces she makes at me when Asher's not looking, she seems like the type to use it.

I am left with strict instructions to return to my dorms with one of Asher's guards and discretely clear my dorm room. I text Aimee, informing her that I am on my way, and forward my ironclad leasing contract to Asher's email address before I leave. He promised that he'll get it nullified when he has the chance, and it will be like I never even signed it.

And my name is Aphrodite, and I invented the orgasm.

I can be delusional, too.

While Xavier, the guard that scanned the VIP level for bugs two nights ago, drives me to Vaserley, I consider what I will tell Aimee. As my best friend (well, my only friend), she needs answers and probably won't stop until she gets them.

I don't think she'll tell anyone that my relationship with Asher is fake, but I don't want to take the chance. As much as I like her, I've only known her for about a month, after all. Plus, I already signed an NDA, so I legally can't tell her anything anyway.

On the other hand, I know that Aimee has a pretty good nose for bullshit. She'll recognize if I'm lying to her, and I have to tell her something. If it can't be a lie, the only alternative is the truth.

Plus, she's aware of the timeline of our relationship. She thinks that Asher and I have only really just met yesterday. She'll call bullshit on a one-day engagement, and so will anyone else if they know that Asher and I only just properly met.

But as far as the rest of the world is concerned, Asher and I have looked as cozy as a couple should each time we've been seen in public together. For instance, when he stalked me around campus, he always either had his arm around my shoulders or held my hand in one of his. When I was at his club two nights ago, the staff gave Aimee and me the VIP treatment, immediately ushering us to Asher on the VIP level.

I also practically dry humped Asher on the dance floor in front of everyone, but I don't want to think about that. It's currently the Voldemort of my life right now, never to be named nor spoken about.

Anyway, the cherry on top is that we left the club together, we went to dinner with his family, and I just left Asher's place after staying with him the whole weekend, although I did so out of his private garage in a black town car with windows tinted pitch black...

Asher's favorite color, of course.

I go over our relationship cover story again: The first night I went to Rogue, we locked eyes and it was love at first sight. He followed me outside, where we talked and had our first kiss. When I left, I forgot my phone in the restroom due to the chaos.

Asher was so taken by me, he tracked me down, using my phone as an excuse when what he really wanted was a date. By the time he found me and gave it back, I already had a new phone, but I was still moved by the gesture. I agreed to the date, and we've been dating in secret ever since. He proposed to me last week outside of Rogue, where we had our first kiss.

It's like a modern day Cinderella story, only I lost a burner phone not a glass slipper.

And it's also a botched version of the truth, which just makes it easier to remember. Of course, we switched the timeline a little, so he supposedly found me three weeks ago, and we fell quickly in love. Even though it would be more realistic, we can't press the timeline back any further, since I only arrived in the country a month ago on the first night I went to Rogue.

We'll just have to work harder to sell how smitten we are.

Joy.

"We're here, Miss Ives," Xavier says, as he pulls the car into one of the visitor's spots.

"Lucy," I correct, automatically.

I sigh, because I still haven't figured out what to do about Aimee. I decide to just ask Asher. I text him on the number he programmed into my phone days ago in the top secret lab.

> What do I tell Aimee?

 Xavier has an NDA for her to sign.

> K...

I frown. It took Asher less than a minute to reply, almost as if he had been waiting for the text. And Xavier is already prepped with an NDA catered to Aimee? This feels like a setup, my first test of loyalty.

I would bet my life that Asher wanted to know whether or not I'll break my NDA to tell Aimee about us. I didn't. I passed this first test, but what about the next? And what would have happened if I hadn't passed?

Xavier follows me into the building. We pass one of the students manning the front desk. Her eyes widen when she sees Xavier. I understand her reaction. He's tall, handsome and well-built, even under the fabric of his suit.

But he isn't as handsome as Asher. Because of Asher, I'm quickly becoming immune to attractive men. My heart doesn't even quicken when I enter my hall and catch sight of Kyle, my hall's program coordinator and Vaserley Hall's very own heartthrob.

Kyle is a senior. Not only is he brainy, but he's also tall and super attractive in the all-American, Abercrombie and Fitch kind of way. Aimee and the other girls in the hall were obsessed with him as soon as they laid eyes on him. Even I thought he was hot when I first met him the day after the whole Rogue incident that left me walking around with my tail tucked between my legs for a month.

I still think he's attractive, and this is post-Asher engagement... but I resent him, nevertheless. He's actually the original source of the Minka vs. Aimee rivalry. Both of the girls think they saw him first, and both of them want him, never mind the fact that R.A.s and P.C.s are not allowed to hook up with their residents.

"Hey, Luce," Kyle greets me. "Whoa." His eyes widen when he sees Xavier.

Vaserley is a co-ed dorm, and bringing people of the opposite gender into our rooms is allowed, but I think Kyle is dazed because I'm one of the few who have yet to do it. Up until now, that is.

It's not that I'm opposed to the idea. It's just that I've been too focused on staying alive after calling the cops at Rogue to even consider meeting boys. Now, I'm fake engaged to one and bringing another into my room. It's crazy how much has changed in just one weekend.

"Kyle, this is Xavier," I say. And because he'll probably find out soon enough, I add, "He's helping me move out."

"You're moving out?" Kyle looks blindsided.

"Yep," I confirm, but I don't add anything else. It's none of his business. That was just a courtesy notice.

I step past him, while Kyle and Xavier do some weird head nod greeting that I always see guys do. When I walk into my room, Aimee is already laying on my bed, patiently waiting for me. She sits up as soon as she sees me.

Before she can talk, I hand her the NDA I got from Xavier in the car and say, "You have to sign this before I can tell you anything."

Aimee's eyes widen as she scans the NDA. "Oh, my Gosh! This is so exciting. It's like you're dating a real life Christian Grey. Is he into BDSM? Does he want you to be his submissive?" She lowers her voice conspiratorially. "Does he have a red room at his place?"

I flush at the idea of Asher using me as his submissive. Then, I rub at my temples, trying to fight the burgeoning headache Aimee's bringing on with her fire round of questions. "Sign first. Then, I'll talk."

She nods and signs, just like that. I don't even think she fully read the NDA. Before I can say anything, Xavier enters the room behind me, bumping the door into my body, which was in its trajectory. I fall to the ground, landing on one of Aimee's spiky heels and scraping my palms against the sharp point. It draws blood, and I glare at Aimee for leaving her shit all over the place, but she's too busy looking at Xavier.

"Fuck. Sorry, Miss Ives," Xavier says. The curse sounds funny juxtaposed beside the formal use of my last name.

"Lucy," I correct.

Again.

After all, Xavier works for Asher not me.

He helps me up, and I'm amazed when Aimee remains silent. She's studying Xavier with the scrutiny of a FBI profiler.

"Aimee, this is Xavier. Xavier, this is my roommate, Aimee."

Xavier nods at Aimee. "Hello."

He holds his hand out for her to shake, but she leaves him hanging. There's another minute of silence before a look of understanding spreads across her face.

She whips her gaze from Xavier to me and says, "You kinky bitch! You had a threesome, didn't you?" She waves the NDA that is still in her hands. "That's what this is about, isn't it?! You didn't even think to invite me?! That hurts! Do you guys need a fourth?" Her eyes rake over Xavier's form as she licks her lips. "I volunteer as tribute!" She stands up and lifts a leg and an arm in a buzz light year pose.

"Aimee," I groan. "That's Buzz Lightyear. You're trying to do Katniss Everdeen."

But she isn't done. She sits back down with a dramatic humph. "Tell me, Loosey Goosey." She rolls her eyes at my cringe. She knows how much I hate the nickname. "I signed the damn thing." She waves the NDA again. It flaps wildly in her hands. "Was it MMF? MFM? You have to at least tell me that."

Before she rips it with all of her waving, I pluck the nondisclosure agreement from her fingers and place it safely in a folder from my desk. I hand it to Xavier, who slips it into the front of his suit.

I turn back to Aimee. "What are you talking about? What do those letters even mean?"

I look to Xavier for help, but he has an amused expression on his face that hasn't left his chiseled features since he met Aimee. He quirks an eyebrow at me.

That's helpful.

"Gosh, Lucy," Aimee says. "You need to read more." Under her breath, she mutters, "And to think I thought *she's* the smart one…"

"I—"

She starts to cut me off. Before she can say anything else, I cover Aimee's mouth with my palm. It's my bloody one.

Oops.

"Ew!" she shrieks.

Xavier passes her a handkerchief, and I swear she swoons. I groan. We're getting nowhere at this rate.

I grab a new tube of Starbursts from my secret stash in my dresser and hold it up. "This is the Holy Stick," I wince at my dirty choice of words, "and whoever is holding it gets to speak. Everyone else has to stay quiet."

I look pointedly at Aimee, because, really, Xavier hasn't even said five words since he entered the room. The stick is to shut Aimee up and no one else. She leaps for the stick, but Xavier cuts in front of me, quicker than lightning, preventing Aimee's body from reaching mine. It's then that I realize that he isn't just here to help me move out. He's *my* bodyguard.

Holy Hell.

I have a personal *bodyguard.*

This is a crazy reminder of the kind of life Asher lives, the kind of life I've gotten myself into.

I clear my throat. And then I clear it again, because I can feel a panic attack coming on. I take a deep breath and answer Aimee's questions one by one. "As far as I can tell, the only similarities between Asher Black and Christian Grey are their wealth, reclusiveness, and attractiveness. Oh, and both of their last names are the names of colors!

"I'm not sure if Asher's into BDSM. I wouldn't know. No, he doesn't want me to be his submissive. I don't think he has a red room. No, we didn't have a threesome. We didn't even have a *two*some," *though we almost did.* "That isn't what this is about.

"We're not going to have a foursome either, and," I take a much needed breath, "if I were to have a foursome, you would *not* be in it, you weirdo!" I pause, wondering if I covered all of her questions. "Oh, and I also don't know what MMM and FM or whatever you said means, so I can't answer that."

Aimee backs away from Xavier and returns to her perch on my bed. "Okay," she drags out the word. "So, if you guys didn't have sex and he didn't ask you to be his submissive, what did he want?"

I steal a glance at Xavier, wondering if he knows that my engagement with Asher is fake. He was there when Asher announced our engagement, but I'm not sure if he heard Asher and me talking afterward or if Asher told him that it's not real. This might be another test. I can ask Xavier if he has an NDA, but even if he says yes, he can easily be lying.

I turn back to Aimee and say, "Hold that thought."

I pull out my phone and text Asher.

> Does Xavier know about our deal?

I wait a few minutes, but he doesn't reply. Aimee is looking antsy, her mouth already opened. I wave the Starburst tube, aka the Holy Stick of permission granting powers. She closes her mouth. Another minute passes, and I lose my patience.

"Be right back," I say and dart into the hall.

I run into the bathroom and slam the door in front of Xavier's face. No way am I letting him follow me into the bathroom. I have boundaries. I dial Asher's number, tapping my toes on the tile as I wait for him to pick up.

"Hello?" It's Monica.

"Hey, Monica. Can you put Asher on the phone?" I ask sweetly, mindful that she knows the truth and can burn me and Asher in a snap.

"Sorry." She doesn't sound sorry at all. "He's in a meeting right now."

I don't believe her. The sound of honking in the background confirms my suspicions.

I roll my eyes, my tolerance for Monica already gone. "No, he's not. Put him on the phone."

"I said he's in a meeting. Are you deaf?"

In the background, I hear Asher say, "Who is that?"

"No one," Monica says at the same time I shout "MEEEEE!!!!!" into the microphone.

I feel like I'm five. Xavier peeks his head into the restroom, eyeing me in confusion. I push his head back out with my free hand and close the door again, locking it this time.

There's a shuffle on the line.

"Lucy?" It's Asher this time.

"Hey," I say. And because I already shouted like a five year old, I decide to go all in and tattle on Monica. "Is this a bad time? Monica said you were in a meeting."

He sucks in his breath. "I wasn't in a meeting. I'll have to talk to Monica about always putting your calls directly through to me." He pauses. "Is everything alright?"

"Yeah..." I lower my voice, "I was just wondering if Xavier knows about our deal. I already asked you through text, but Aimee is really itching for me to tell her everything. And Xavier is there with us, so I can't say anything if he doesn't know anything."

"Oh. Yeah, he knows. Go ahead and say whatever you want in front of him."

"Okay," I say.

"Okay," he says back.

We stay on the line, not saying anything. It's surprisingly not awkward. I like the sound of his breathing.

Wait... what?!

I like the sound of his breathing?!

Who thinks shit like that?

I don't even recognize myself.

Finally, he says, "See you later? Feel free to help yourself to whatever's in the kitchen. I won't be home until late."

I thank him and hang up the phone, but I'm distracted by what he said.

Home.

It still hasn't sunk in that I'm living with Asher, but after hearing him call it that, I'm beginning to realize the gravity of our situation.

I'm about to move in with Asher Black.

And suddenly, I'm glad Aimee signed the NDA and I have someone to talk to... Even though she'll inevitably give me some piss poor advice about having sex with Asher before he changes his mind about this.

When I enter the hall again, Xavier is leaning against the wall beside the bathroom door. Some of the girls are in the hallway chatting with one another, but I can see their eyes darting to Xavier.

These are the neutrals in the hall, neither ascribing to Aimee's side nor Minka's.

Like Switzerland.

I wonder which team Switzerland would be on—#TeamAimee or #TeamMinka? Probably Team Minka, because Aimee's really messy. And aren't Swiss people obsessed with cleanliness? I know they like cheese and chocolate, and they vote a bajillion times a year, and they keep to themselves, and they're used to the cold and mountains, and something about Swiss knives, and I wonder if Asher has a Swiss knife or likes Swiss girls, and…

Okay, I'm mentally rambling. Again.

Being in the hallway makes me nervous. I'm always on alert, worried that Minka might round a corner and pounce on me. I'm also trying really hard not to think about how I like Asher's *breathing*, and I'm moving in with him, and—

Nope.

Not thinking about any of it.

The girls eye me curiously but not unkindly when Xavier straightens up at the sight of me. I ignore them, because even though they haven't added to Team Minka's torment of me, they haven't been helping either. Plus, soon they won't be my neighbors anyway. Hopefully, this is the end of my time dealing with Minka & Co., too.

"Sorry," I say to Xavier. "I had to ask Asher if you know about my deal with him."

"You could have just asked me," he murmurs, keeping his voice appropriately low.

I whisper, too. "No, I couldn't."

He could have lied. We both know it. When I see the look of approval in his eyes, I know I just passed another test. This one may not be from Asher, but it's from one of his guards, and that means something. It's flattering, even.

The first words out of my mouth when I enter the dorm room are, "I'm fake engaged to Asher Black." I grab the Holy Stick from my desk and toss it Aimee's way.

She's so shocked, she lets it drop to the floor. She recovers, picking it up quickly. "No way."

I hold my handout for the stick and catch it when she throws it my way. "Yep."

She takes the stick. "Who? What? When? Where? And Why?"

I take a deep breath and begin, "*Who?* Asher Black in front of Black Enterprise's board of directors.

"*What?* It was a fake proposal to make him look stable in front of the board. One of the douchenozzles," Xavier snorts, "is trying to get Asher voted off the island.

"*When?* Asher announced our engagement to the board a couple nights ago, as soon as we headed upstairs after we danced. It caught me the Hell off guard, but I played along.

"*Where?* It was at the part of the VIP floor that overlooks the rest of the club. That balcony area.

"*Why?* Like I said, he needs to appear stable in front of the board. They all have wives and families, so marriage is how they judge stability." I toss the Holy Stick her way.

She impresses me by catching it midair. "Wow. You're engaged to Asher Black."

"Fake engaged," I butt in.

She tuts at me and waves the Holy Stick in my face. "When are you guys having sex?"

I knew it.

I roll my eyes, expecting nothing less of Aimee. I tug the stick out of her hands. "We aren't. We're *fake* engaged, I repeat. Fake. Fake. Fake."

She takes the stick. "You don't have to be engaged to someone to have sex. You just have to be near them."

Because Aimee is on her best behavior, I snatch the stick and toss it in my desk, so we can talk freely without the tedious back and forth. "Fair point."

"I say you use your access to his home to show up in his bed in tiny lingerie. Seduce the Hell out of him."

I roll my eyes. "That would make the rest of this engagement so awkward."

"Sex is only awkward if the two consenting parties are immature or not ready to have it." She looks me up and down. "What you're experiencing right now isn't a dry spell. Hell, it isn't even a drought. It's a *dust bowl*. Tell me, do you find cobwebs in there every time you get yourself off?"

Xavier snorts beside me.

I glare at him. "I'm not having sex with Asher. Drop it."

"Fine." She sighs like she's thinking it's not fine at all. "So, how is this going to work?"

I hesitate. "That's the thing. I'm moving into his place."

She sits up straighter. "But..." A pout crosses her red lips. "What about the dorms? You're my roommate! You can't leave me!"

"I have to! It won't make any sense if I don't live with him."

"But what about me? What about our friendship?"

"We'll be fine! You'll still be my best friend, and I'll be walking distance from you. Asher's home is right next to campus."

"Your home," she corrects.

"What?"

"It's your home now, too." Her eyes roam over my tense form. "If you're going to move in together, at least call it your place, too."

I sigh and sit beside her on my bed. "This feels unreal."

She wraps an arm around me. "Please, tell me you'll be sharing the same bed."

I cover my face with my hands. "I don't know. I think we actually will be. Hell, we almost did the first night until he got up and slept on the floor. I think he did that for me. We haven't slept together since."

She stands up, rummages through her closet, and then hands me something. "Here. Keep it. He won't know what hit him."

I glance down at what she gave me. It's a slinky negligee, cute and sexy all at once. No way am I wearing this anywhere near Asher.

"Thanks," I say, because I know she'll fight back if I decline her gift.

She narrows her eyes in suspicion, but she doesn't call me out on my bullshit. "I guess you're here to pack up your stuff, huh?"

I nod. "He wants me out of here by the end of the day."

She stands up. "Come on. I'll help you."

I astound us both when I stand up and wrap my arms around her in a hug. One she honestly deserves. She really is a great friend.

We spend the next half hour packing with Xavier's help. It doesn't take long, because as an orphan, I don't have much. It takes Xavier only two trips to carry all of my possessions to the car. While he's making his last trip, I change out of the LBD from two nights ago, which I threw on again before I left Asher's. I didn't want to wear his shirt down the hall while I did my walk of shame. And the evening gown would have drawn way too much attention.

I pull on a romper I put aside while packing earlier and throw my dress into my backpack with the rest of my schoolwork. Then, I'm hugging Aimee goodbye like it's the last time we'll ever see each other. I don't know why this feels so final. I mean, we already agreed to meet at an off-campus restaurant for lunch later next week.

But my gut is telling me that this is the end of *something*.

I just don't know what.

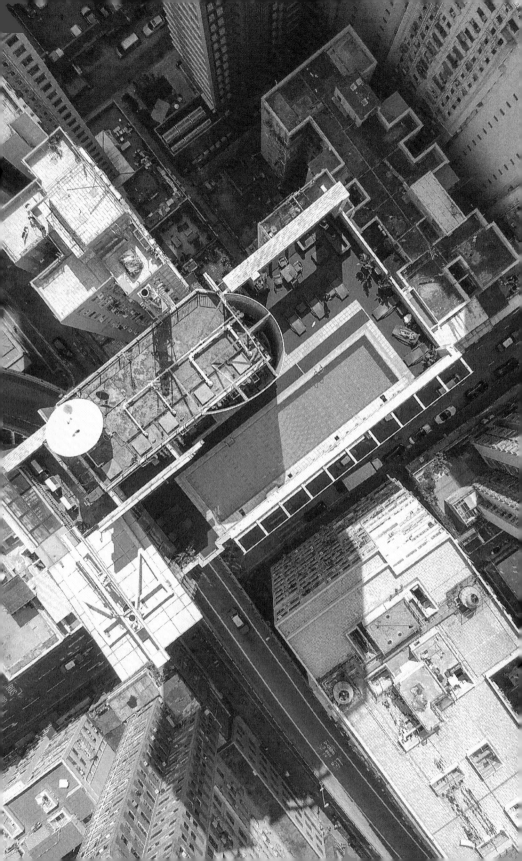

CHAPTER FIFTEEN

Courage is doing what you're afraid to do.
There can be no courage unless you're scared.
Eddie Rickenbacker

*I*t's quiet when Xavier and I get home.
Home.
I tremble at the word.

Xavier helps me carry my things into the master bedroom. We work silently, hanging my clothes in a corner of the closet that I cleared of Asher's clothes. Other than my laptop, chargers and school stuff, I don't have much else. I left my bedding behind for Aimee, because she's always liked my bed better. We both know it's because hers is a mess. In a week's time, my old bed will be the same way.

My stomach grumbles. The sound of it is the only familiar thing about this place. I sigh and go downstairs to make dinner. The kitchen is stocked, which is a nice surprise. Vaserley Hall doesn't have kitchens. All of the residents eat in a communal dining room that serves food buffet style. Having food whenever I want was nice at first, but I eventually got sick of the limited choices. It's nice to be able to prepare food for myself for a change.

I pull out the ingredients for a lasagna, along with a knife, a wooden cutting board and a large pot. I mince some garlic and fennel seeds, dice an onion, and chop some parsley, oregano and rosemary. I sauté the onions in olive oil and add the garlic, fennel seeds and some ground chicken. After adding the rest of the ingredients, some spices and a shit ton of red wine, I turn the stove to a simmer and wash the tomatoes out of my hands.

Xavier follows me upstairs as I grab my textbook. By the time the sauce is done, I have finished most of my homework for the week at the kitchen table. I beat an egg into the ricotta cheese and add some parsley. Then, I grab a large baking dish, shredded mozzarella and some gourmet no boil lasagna noodles I find in the hidden butler's pantry. I layer the lasagna and put it into the preheated oven.

I try to finish my stats homework, the only homework I have left for the week, but fiduciary inference is kicking my ass. I push it aside, giving up, and turn my attention to Xavier. He's sitting next to me at the dining room table, his arms crossed over his chest and his eyes focused on the front door.

Periodically, he has been getting up to scan the room and walk around the house, probably searching for threats. It's a pointless effort, though. This place is like Fort Knox. The Secret Service can probably learn a thing or two from Asher and his security team.

Earlier, I passed by the security room and saw four security guards sitting in there, looking at more than a dozen flat screens filled with live, HD video of the building. There are cameras positioned at the hallways for all floors of the entire building, all around the exterior of the building, in the parking garages, and in all the public areas inside the building. I even saw some camera angles that had to be taken from the buildings across from ours.

Looking at the footage, I learned that there's a communal theater room and gym in the first floor of the building, too, but judging by how crowded the tower's gym is, I don't fault Asher for wanting his own. Plus, for security reasons, the only entrance into the penthouse is from the elevator in Asher's private garage and the emergency stairwell next to it. Both of these can only be accessed from the penthouse and from the garage.

It would be annoying to take the elevator downstairs, walk through the private garage to the residents' garage, take an elevator into the lobby, and then walk to the gym from there every time I want to work out. The walk there is enough of a workout for my lazy ass.

"How are you not bored?" I finally ask Xavier after watching him scan the room with his eyes for the millionth time.

"Bored?" His brows are drawn together. "Why would I be bored?"

"Because you've been sitting there, doing nothing."

"I'm doing my job."

I sigh. "What's up with the security? I understand the heavy security at the club, but here, too?"

"The security guards at the club belong to the Romano family. Mr. Black never fired them when he got full ownership of Rogue. It would take too long to train new guys, and he already trusts the ones working there. Plus, the guys like it. It's much safer than a security detail at one of the other clubs would be.

"Only Mr. Black's personal security team has access to the VIP level of the club, this penthouse, and personal security details anyway. You can tell us apart by our ear pieces. Theirs are coiled and visible, whereas ours are skin-toned to be covert."

"Oh," I say. "Why are there so many of you?"

"There's usually not so many of us. There's about twenty-six of us in total that rotate from shift to shift. You have a night guard for when I'm not here. His name is Wilson, but if you keep regular sleeping hours and nothing bad happens, you'll probably never meet him. The guards stay in the security room at night, only leaving when they do their rounds. They never go into the bedroom, though."

"Rounds," I repeat. "Is that when you press those button things?"

I noticed that when Xavier does his "rounds," he presses little buttons in each room. They're super small and the color of the walls. I wouldn't even know they're there if I didn't see him press them.

"They're another security precaution. I have a ten minute window to press them during each of my scheduled rounds. If I don't press them in time, an alert goes out to the entire team, all twenty-six of us. There are protocols for when that happens, but it never has before. It's not always me doing the rounds either. When I'm not here because I'm off shift or out with you, there's always three people in the security room. One of them does it then."

"Wow," I gasp.

I've never heard of such heavy security for one person, especially one that can take care of himself. Is all of this really necessary? He says he's not in the mob anymore, but how can I believe him when he has more security than the mayor?

I eye Xavier, wondering what detail I pulled him from. "What did you do before you were assigned to me?"

"I got pulled from my old rounds in the security room to work your personal detail, so they're training a newbie right now. That's why there's four guys in the security room instead of only three."

"Only?"

"Mr. Black has a lot of enemies, Ms. Ives."

"Lucy," I correct, absently.

His words chill me to the core. They're yet another reminder of the dangers of knowing Asher. I suspect that whenever I look at Xavier, I'll always be reminded of the danger I'm exposing myself to.

A part of me can't wrap my mind around the idea of a threat large enough to necessitate the existence of such heavy security. I have to assure myself that it's just a precaution for a wealthy man. That it's for his corporate enemies not the criminal ones.

I remind myself that the deal I have with Asher is a good one. I'll gain financial security for as long as this charade lasts, and after I graduate, I'll have my job of choice with Asher's letter of recommendation and connections. My thoughts flash to the rumors of Asher's company acquiring IllumaGen. Working there would be a dream come true.

If I'm being honest, the benefits far outweigh the cons. Asher has no reason to hurt me now that he knows I'm not a threat. In fact, I have a security guard to *protect* me! There's no way Asher's "enemies" can get through this insane security.

Bulletproof glass and walls? Panic buttons? Panic rooms? An armory? Twenty-six guards? Rounds every half hour? This is security suitable for the president. Plus, Asher is no longer involved in the Romano family business.

... *Or is he?*

When the lasagna is finished, I divide it into eight large pieces and plate them. I give one to each of the guards in the security room, much to their amazement, and hand a plate to Xavier. By the time Asher gets home, I've just finished off the last of my lasagna and Xavier has already nabbed one of the extra pieces. He finished that one, too.

"Damn, girl," Xavier says at the same time Asher enters our line of sight. "You can cook."

"What'd you make?" Asher asks.

"Lasagna." I get up and heat the remaining piece for him, because it's technically his food anyway.

When I'm done, I set it on the place mat next to my seat. He loosens his tie and puts it on the kitchen counter before sitting down beside me. He looks exhausted, yet he still manages to appear alert. I avert my eyes as he undoes the top few buttons of his button down. Even the slightest sliver of skin is enough to tease me, so I don't let myself look.

"You never told me you can cook." He moans when he takes a bite.

I force away the dirty images his moan elicits and shrug. "One of my foster dads was a chef, and I loved to eat enough to want to learn how to make food. He ended up teaching me a lot."

I also learned how to make a lot of different cuisines from all the families I've lived with, from Peruvian to Irish food. My Vietnamese dishes are ridiculously good, too. My *Bo Luc Lac* is melt-in-your-mouth delicious.

Jumping from foster home to foster home is like traveling the world in so many ways. You're exposed to such a diverse group of people and get to learn from the experiences they give you. I'm not sure if I would have traded it all for a stable childhood and family, though I could certainly have done without some of the creeps.

Asher nods and takes another bite. The sensual way he closes his eyes and bites down sends dirty thoughts through my mind.

He swallows and turns to Xavier, who takes my dish and his to the dishwasher. "You can go for the day."

Xavier nods, says his goodbyes to us and the rest of the security team and leaves. When he's gone, it's just Asher and I in the room. After the questionnaires from this morning, I'm more comfortable around him, but he still has me on edge. So, I distract myself with my stats homework, opening up my overpriced textbook and getting to work.

I've bitten off a chunk of my No. 2 pencil by the time Asher asks, "What's wrong?"

I exhale deeply, reluctant to admit my failure. "I don't understand this."

He leans over, skims my work, and shrugs. "Don't beat yourself up over it. Fiduciary inference is outdated anyways. You probably won't ever use it."

"That may be, but it doesn't change the fact that I'll still be tested on it."

Asher stands up and places his dish in the dishwasher along with all the other dishes Xavier brought back from the security room before he left. I try not to watch as Asher loads the dishwasher with all the kitchen utensils and dishes I used to make the lasagna. He puts soap in the machine and turns it on. It's weird watching him perform domestic acts. It's like watching a wild lion play fetch.

After he returns to the seat next to me, I'm shocked when he starts to explain the math to me. I listen, and half an hour later, I'm a proud pro at fiduciary inference. I almost wish that it's used more often.

"You should've been a teacher," I say, as I pack up my work into my backpack. I follow him up the stairs.

He pauses to think about it before shaking his head. "It never would have worked out. I don't like people, and teachers deal with a lot of them."

"So do you as a business man."

"That's different. I'm the boss at work. I have control. Teachers don't. They answer to parents and administrators and students and the government. It makes what they do infinitely harder than what I do." He hesitates. "At least for someone like me."

I nod in understanding. I make a horrible teacher. Teaching requires skill sets that I don't possess, like patience and compassion. I have immense respect for those who can do it, mostly because I tried my hand at teaching at one of the orphanages I volunteered at in Africa. I failed miserably.

I find myself telling Asher, "I tried to teach once. I was at an orphanage in Djibouti. The head of the place thought it would be a good idea for me to teach English to the kids, since all of the other volunteers either spoke French or Arabic." I chuckle. "It was a disaster. I made half of the kids cry by the end of a one hour class period. They ended up moving me to the kitchens, where my only interactions with a living being were with an elderly woman who never talked to me.

"After a while, I finally had enough of her silence and demanded that she speak to me." I wince. "When she signed something back with her hands, I felt like the biggest bitch in the world. There I was, hating her for not talking to me, and she was mute the whole time. What's worse was I couldn't even understand what she was signing. It was in Somali Sign Language."

Asher and I are in *our* room now. He's taking off his clothes, getting ready to shower, but he pauses to give me a sympathetic look. "What'd you end up doing?"

I avert my eyes as he takes off his boxers and heads into the bathroom. I don't see his package, just a very, very firm backside, but I'm still breathing heavy after.

How can he be so comfortable naked?

I like my body, but I don't have the kind of body confidence he possesses. I wish I did, but I doubt most people do anyway. The world will probably be overrun by nudist colonies if that ever happens.

I clear my throat and raise my voice, so he can hear me in the bathroom. "I left."

I was ashamed of myself then, and I'm ashamed of myself now. Like I said, when things get tough, I usually run away.

"What'd you say?" Asher shouts from the shower.

I sigh. He turned the shower head on and probably can't hear me over the noise. But what does he expect me to do? Go into the bathroom so he can hear? I don't even want to repeat myself, and I don't know what will come out of my mouth if I see him naked, full frontal.

"I said, 'I ran.'" I repeat, louder this time.

"Huh?"

"I ran!" I'm yelling now.

"Come again?"

"Ugh!" I curse under my breath, get up and enter the bathroom, his nudity be damned. When I see him, I don't even bother catching a glimpse of his private parts. I stare him dead in the eye and say, "I. RAN. Is that what you want to hear?! That I'm a runner? That I run from everything?"

What I see in his face staggers me. A look of understanding passes between us, but Asher also seems unperturbed by my outburst.

I briefly consider that he pretended not to hear me, so he could see me admit my cowardice face to face. The thought makes me angry.

I'm shaking in fury when he looks me in the eyes and says, "But you didn't run from me."

I reel back from him as if I've been slapped. He's right. I didn't run from him. Is it because I have more to lose now? A degree? A future to think about? A better option? I don't know. All I know is that I'm sick of running. I ran from foster home to foster home. I ran from Steve. I ran from one country to the next. I ran from Rogue.

But I didn't run from him.

I'm not running now. I'm dealing with my problems, acknowledging them and finding solutions. I'm trying to be a better person, and like it or not, he's been a part of that process. Even if he is both the cause of my problems and the solution.

He gives me a knowing look that would have sent me running for the hills had we not just discussed my embarrassing running habits.

"What do you expect me to say to that?" My voice is a whisper, but I'm not surprised that he hears me over the sound of the shower head.

His blue eyes pierce my soul. "Why aren't you running now?"

"I don't know."

CHAPTER SIXTEEN

Sometimes even to live is an act of courage.
Seneca the Younger

"No," Asher says for the fifteenth time.

"Are you serious?!" I demand. "You can't just trap me here, Asher. I'm getting stir crazy. My voice doesn't even sound like my voice anymore. I never agreed to stay cooped up in your tower like I'm freakin' Rapunzel or something." I laugh sardonically. "Do I need a prince to come rescue me? I'll be sure to ask *René* once he dethrones you."

Usually, I wouldn't talk to Asher like this, but between the stir craziness and the fact that he has actually been letting me get away with talking back, I don't pull my verbal punches.

Asher sends a scowl my way. It's ugly and beautiful all at once. "You can leave once Tommy comes."

Tommy is my new stylist. Asher hired him the day after I moved into his place. I woke up that morning to a gorgeous, well-groomed Asian man pressing measuring tape around my breasts.

The first words out of his mouth were, "Girl, I wish I had tits as big as yours."

Then, he pulled me out of the bed and proceeded to measure my body in places I didn't know needed measuring. Two days later, he came back with a bunch of fabric for fittings, but I haven't seen him since. And I also didn't realize my freedom depends on him.

"Tommy?!" I say, though it's more like a yell. "Oh, my goodness! You are such a jerk! This is about my clothes?! You didn't seem to have a problem with how I dress when YOU TOLD YOUR

COLLEAGUES THAT WE'RE ENGAGED!" I wince, embarrassed by how shrill my shouting got towards the tail end of that sentence. Because I can't help myself, I add, "Unbelievable!" and stomp my way to the gym.

I was floored when I found out that Asher's gym isn't just a gym, though it also has all the standard equipment and more. It's a UFC gym, too, with fighting equipment, a sparring ring, and enough punching bags for me to punch and kick away my anger. That's been useful lately, since I'm angry a lot now.

Because after I realized that I didn't run from Asher, I also realized that I'm not as afraid of him as I initially thought I was. It's like the fear that was there only existed because I let it, but once I recognized that it was just a construct, it evaporated. It also helps that, lately, he has been pissing me off to the point where even fear can't stop me from standing up for myself.

Hell hath no fury like a woman trapped, or whatever the saying is.

I'm not afraid of Asher, which is good for me and bad for him. It's good for me, because I'm able to stand up for myself now. It's bad for him, because he's giving me a lot to stand up to. First, he hired Tommy without asking, which is awesome and akin to having my own fairy godmother, but that's not the point. He didn't *ask* me if I wanted new clothes. He just decided I did.

Then, when I tried to go to class on Monday, he told me that I can't. No reason was given, just a "no." I tried to leave anyway with Xavier hot on my heels, but apparently there's a biometric scanner to access the elevator.

And guess who doesn't have access?

Me.

When my glare cut to Xavier, he held up his hands and said, "Can't do it. Gotta pay the bills."

I growled and stomped my way back to Asher, where I demanded he let me out. When he gave me an infuriating "no" again, I lost it, kicking and punching whatever part of him I could. I didn't even scratch him, which only pissed me off even more. Instead, he stepped around me, easily lifted me up by the waist, dropped me into the gym, and told me to "have at it."

Two Sundays have passed since then, and that has been our routine every day since. I wake up and ask if I can leave. He says, "No." I scream and yell until my throat hurts, then I try to escape. I inevitably fail and stomp back to him.

Because my voice is usually gone from my morning scream sessions, I resort to kicking and punching. He drops me off in the gym, where I kick and punch every bag in sight. Eventually, Xavier gets tired of my poor form and teaches me to fight properly. I've even gotten better.

Yesterday, when one of my punches landed on Asher's stomach, I swear he smiled for a second before it was gone. Today, I'm not even bothering to escape. I head straight to my very own pink punching bag, which Asher surprised me with yesterday. I may have printed out a picture of his face on the office printer last night and taped it to the bag for target practice. I'm actually excited to test it out.

If Asher really wants to make it up to me, he'll either let me out of here or have a punching bag that looks like him custom made for me. Because as fun as punching a picture of him is, it's certainly not the same.

When I'm done with my fighting, I head to the office and log onto Asher's desktop, which is way faster than my laptop. It's a Black Enterprises product, after all. I open up the picture of Asher on Photoshop, a close up of his face I found on the internet, and edit some bruises onto his face. I digitally give him a busted lip and a black eye, because I can. When I print it out, I smile and proudly show it to Xavier, who rolls his eyes.

It's ridiculous. I know. A few weeks ago, I was attending labs at a prestigious Ivy League research university and turning in insightful essays on the practical applications of MITE research in the Human Genome Project. Today, I'm photoshopping bruises onto my warden/fake fiancé's face, because I can't do it in real life. I'm also proudly showing it to my bodyguard, who doubles as my prison guard, like I expect it to be framed on the fridge or something.

Wait...

I reboot the printer, print out another copy and write a giant "A+" at the top right corner in red Sharpie. I hear Xavier groan when he sees what I'm doing, but I ignore him. I take the tape with me, because Asher doesn't strike me as the type to have refrigerator magnets laying around. I'm taping my masterpiece onto the shiny, stainless steel surface of the gigantic hunk of metal that's our fridge when Asher descends from the stairwell with Monica trailing closely behind like the little brown noser she is.

Obviously, my relationship with Monica is the one thing that hasn't changed. Well, if possible, we hate each other more now. She scowls at me every morning when she goes into the bedroom to wake Asher up at 5 A.M. like an annoying human rooster.

She doesn't like that I sleep on the bed while he sleeps on the floor, but I guarantee she would like it even less if we both sleep on the bed... because I absolutely refuse to sleep on the floor. Hell, I think Asher *deserves* to sleep on the floor for holding me prisoner here. I certainly don't feel bad about our sleeping arrangement.

"What are you doing?" Asher asks, approaching Xavier and I.

I take a couple steps back and admire my master piece, mentally patting myself on the back for a job well done. I tilt my head to the side, like I'm admiring priceless artwork at the Louvre, and say in a heavy, fake French accent, "Ze black eye is wonderfulzee done, is zeet not?"

I slide a glance at Asher's face. He's looking at the picture, his lips twitching. He's trying to hide his amusement, but it's there. I know it. I can see it in his blue eyes, which are lighter than usual. Making Asher smile is another way I try to win this fight we've got going. As you can see, I've really lost it when I think I can win a fight with this man by making him smile.

I need to get out of here.

I have no idea why I'm being held hostage, too. I'm being fed well, and he's actually treating me better than I expected. Apparently, my teachers know that I haven't been attending class and have been emailing me my homework assignments and sending me lecture slides and notes, which is odd and definitely not in accordance to university policy, which states that a student must withdrawal from a class after two unexcused absences.

After missing several weeks of class, I have definitely been absent more than two times. I should be kicked out of these classes, but instead I'm getting the VIP treatment. My teachers are even sending me emails with phrases like, "I'm looking forward to seeing you soon!" in them.

Not soon enough.

"Tastefully done," Asher says.

That's another surprise I've learned.

Asher has a sense of humor.

It's subtle, but it's there.

I drop the French accent. "I think I can easily get a six-figure bid for it."

I cross my arms and walk from one side of the fridge to the other, pretending to look at it from multiple angles. I hear Monica humph in annoyance, which almost makes me lose it, but I'm able to reel my laughter in.

I step back next to Asher. "I'd say it's worth a quarter of a million dollars. At least."

Asher taps his chin with his pointer finger, his face mimicking a thoughtful expression. "It's missing something," he says. Then, he pulls out a paper from the binder in Monica's hand and sticks it onto the fridge, covering his photoshopped face in the process.

In Asher's picture is a rooster, wearing nude Louboutin stilettos. Its feathers are even the exact shade of Monica's hair. There's an alarm clock hanging around its neck, set to 5 AM. The background of the picture is pitch black, clearly still night time.

That's it.

I lose it.

I'm nearly in tears on the floor, laughing my ass off, not even caring that I just lost this stupid game I think I'm playing. When I look back up, Asher's replacement picture is still there. I laugh again.

Asher and Xavier are smiling, but Monica has a constipated expression on her face.

I don't think she gets that she's the rooster, waltzing into Asher's room at five every morning, uninvited and unannounced. She doesn't get why this is funny, but that's okay. I think hearing her laughter would break my already delirious brain anyway.

I lift the picture away from the fridge, moving it so it's beside my master piece. "They should be sold as a set."

"Ugh, do you have to act like such a child?" Monica says, her voice extra snarky today.

If I'm being honest, I *am* acting like a child. To be fair, I haven't left the penthouse in almost a month. I've had to skip out on all of my lunch dates with Aimee, who must hate me by now. I haven't felt the sun on my skin in ages.

I even found myself trying to sunbathe by leaning against the window in a bikini. It wasn't a good idea. I learned that I'm afraid of heights. Xavier, of course, thought it was hilarious and always asks me when I'm going to do it again.

Because she already thinks I'm being juvenile and it's actually true, I decide that until I'm allowed to return to civilization, I don't care.

So, I mimic her pose and voice and mock her words, "Ugh, do you have to be here right now?"

It's not even a half decent burn, but Monica doesn't care. I can read *Harry Potter* to her, and she'll still be angry. That's when you know someone's hatred is irrational. How does one possess a beating heart and not enjoy *Harry Potter*?! Seriously, there's a special place in Hell for those *Harry Potter* one-star reviewers on Amazon and Goodreads.

"Maybe you should go," Asher tells Monica while I'm busy making up a 10th circle of Hell for *Harry Potter* haters.

Her eyes widen and irritation flashes through them, but she doesn't say anything. She walks out the door, slamming it on her way out. I try to chase after her, hoping I can escape with her, but a strong arm slides around my waist and pulls me back. I'm flush against Asher's powerful chest.

"Seriously?! She's hooked into that biometric thingy and I'm not?!" I abandon the little pride I have left and whine. "I have to get out of here, Asher. It's been so long. Please, please, please, please, please. I don't even know what it smells like outside anymore."

"Pollution," Xavier says, helpfully.

That lands him an attempted uppercut.

I miss, of course.

I'm not even usually a violent person. I swear. I just can't stand being trapped in one place for this long. I've always been on the move, either from foster home to foster home or country to country. I don't think I can handle this for much longer.

Hell, I don't think I'm *handling* it right now.

Asher's place is huge, but it's not freedom. I want my freedom. I'm going crazy without it. I have a newfound respect for prisoners. How do they do it? How do they handle it? I'm stuck in a twenty-thousand square foot luxury apartment, and it's driving me crazy.

Last week, the highlight of my week was when I hid under Asher's desk for 13 hours, waiting for him to come in so I could scare him. I was asleep by the time he got there and pretty much wasted my entire day for nothing. Asher ended up carrying my sleeping self to the bed.

Sighing, Asher hands me a box. "It's a prototype for our newest set of virtual reality glasses. It'll help with the craziness for a little bit. I've already programmed a bunch of games and scenic activities in it. Here are the controls for it."

I take the pair of gloves he hands me. They have little metal circles all over them, which I assume works like a controller.

"They're ugly," I tell him, though I'm flattered he's trusting me with them. That he thought to do this for me... Even though he's the one trapping me here.

"It's a *prototype*, Lucy." There's a darkness in his eyes as he says, "Plus, beauty is overrated."

The words are weird coming from his mouth, considering he's the most physically beautiful person I've ever met. Unsure of what to say to that, I instead look through the list of apps he programmed into the VR console. There are dozens of them, all catered towards my interests, but a few catch my eyes quickest:

Lucy's Lab
From sodium monofluoroacetate to batrachotoxin and everything in between, experiment with dangerous chemicals you wouldn't normally be able to in real life.

Adventures for Lucy
From the bright and frosty peaks of Machu Picchu to the mysterious and dark depths of the Mariana Trench, the world is your oyster, Lucy Ives.

Lucy's Kitchen
Any tool, any appliance, any ingredient—it's all yours. Make your dream cake or favorite lasagna without the mess.

Dozens of apps—Lucy's Lab, Adventures for Lucy, Lucy's Kitchen, and so many more—are all named after me and catered towards my interests, mostly things about me I've only mentioned briefly since I've known him. I can't believe he remembers all these things about me.

There's an app of a virtually sold out Madison Square Garden arena meant for getting rid of stage fright. I mentioned my stage fright to him *once* in passing. Another app is intended to teach me to play the triangle. I barely even remember telling him that I can't play any instruments—"Not even the triangle," I said, at the time. It has never been brought up again.

Just like the subjects of most of the apps. It's alarming and flattering that he's been paying so much attention to me, to the things I tell him and the things I don't.

My God.

He did all this *for me*.

But he also trapped me here.

How should I feel about this?

I'm not sure, but I do know my heart is racing a marathon a minute, and when I glance up to thank him, he's already gone.

Like the enigmatic ghost he is.

CHAPTER SEVENTEEN

It is curious that physical courage should be so common in the world and moral courage so rare.
Mark Twain

An hour later, I'm skiing down some slopes in Athens at full speed with Xavier trailing closely behind me. I can't actually see him, since I have the glasses on, but I can definitely hear him, shuffling furniture around so I don't blindly hit anything.

He even has thick, cushy pillows in each of his hands for when I'm about to walk into a wall. He sticks them in front of my face, and I'm met with a face full of pillow plushness instead of a face full of wall.

I'm midway through my Olympic-worthy jump off a ski lift when I hear, "No way, girlfriend. What in the world are you wearing? I don't ever want to see those gloves and those hideous glasses again."

"Tommy!" I shout, whipping off the glasses and throwing them at Xavier's face.

He catches them.

Barely.

"*Expensive* prototype," he says.

I shrug. I'm not in the mood to be gentle with Asher's things when he trapped me here. I'm in the mood to get the Hell out of this building, and my ticket out has just arrived... yet, I find myself gently taking off the gloves and setting them down carefully on the coffee table.

Xavier lifts a questioning brow at my change of pace, but I ignore it. I don't know what to tell him. So, maybe I am grateful for Asher's gift and don't want to ruin it. So what? I turn quickly away from Xavier's inquisitive eyes and envelope Tommy in a hug, squishing his pudginess into my eager arms, which are far more toned than they used to be, thanks to Xavier's training sessions.

I hope the newfound definition in my body doesn't require Tommy to spend another month altering clothes. Speaking of taking forever, I want to ask him why it took him so long to make a few outfits, but I don't want to be rude and upset my ticket out of here. So, I keep my mouth shut and wait.

He doesn't make me wait long. "Try these on," he says, shoving a garment bag into my dumbstruck hands. "I'll go grab the rest of the clothes from the hall."

I decide to change in the living room, so Tommy doesn't have to carry his creations up the stairs. Plus, I don't want this to take longer than it needs to take. Now that I have the clothes, I can get out of here.

A part of me sours at the thought, unable to believe that Asher kept me trapped in his home because I wasn't clothed appropriately. I even asked him if I could just head to some designer store on 5th Avenue to buy something to wear. I would have even let him choose the outfit.

He gave me a resounding "no."

The clothes have to be from Tommy.

As I open the bag, I can see why. There's a gorgeous burgundy colored dress inside, consisting of a mesh and lace corset top bodice and a fitted skirt. The corset top is hand sewn with beautiful rubies and what I hope isn't real diamonds. I've never seen anything like it. I'm excited to get this dress on.

Xavier averts his eyes as I change, struggling to hook the back up until Tommy comes bustling in and does it for me. He heads to a switch by a flip panel in the wall, pressing a few buttons until the floor to ceiling glass window that separates Asher's penthouse from the rest of New York shifts. It turns into a mirror, causing my mouth to gape.

"What just happened?" I ask.

"It's a version of electrochromic glass made from nanotech. Black Enterprises manufactures it," Xavier says.

Our eyes meet in the mirror, and I see his widen as he takes me in. I turn to my reflection, remembering the dress and eager to see how it looks.

"Wow," I breathe out.

The dress fits like a glove, hugging every curve of my body. The corset is all mesh and lace, which looks like lingerie yet somehow still appears elegant. There's a nude slip stitched into the lining underneath, so I'm not actually naked under there. The skirt of the dress clings tightly to my body, ending just at the knee. I can see myself wearing this to an elegant dinner or cocktail party, though I've never actually been to one.

"I know. I'm awesome," Tommy says smugly.

When Xavier turns to take me in properly, he doesn't say anything. He simply stares, and it's all I need to know. I look damn good in this dress.

"Tommy, if the rest of the clothes look like this, I'm kidnapping you," I tell him, unable to stop staring at the dress.

"Speaking of," he replies. "The rest of the clothes should fit you, so you don't have to try on everything. But there are a few things that might need altering, so you'll just have to try on those items only."

I nod, overwhelmed as I turn to see what he brought me. There are hangers upon hangers of clothes, hanging off of wheeled metal racks. This is more clothes than even Asher owns. I have no idea where we're going to store them or how we're even going to bring everything upstairs. Now I understand why it took Tommy this long to make all of this. He built me an entire boutique's worth of clothes.

"I would have finished everything sooner, but Asher said you've been working out. He sent me an updated picture, and I fixed everything for you." Tommy's eyeing my new figure.

I decide to ignore the part about Asher having a recent picture of me. "You refitted all this off of a picture?!"

"I'm very good at my job."

"Yeah. No kidding," I agree, ogling the collection in disbelief.

There are at least a dozen evening gowns in the mix, all stunning of course. I have no idea when I'll wear them, seeing as I've never been invited to a fancy event and Asher hasn't taken me out since our engagement. But I'm excited to try every single one of them on.

I feel like I'm Cinderella without the part where she's chased around the kingdom by a stranger she danced with over a damn shoe. Can you imagine going to a club, dancing with some random guy and having him chase you all over the country afterwards?

That's called stalking.

And it's not sexy.

By the time I'm done trying on clothes, I'm exhausted. A few items turned into me trying on most of the collection, only for Tommy to take merely two dresses for more altering. The security guards come out of the security room to help Xavier carry the clothing racks upstairs. Tommy and I follow with at least a thousand new velvet hangers.

We have to switch out the thick wooden hangers from Asher's clothes with the new, ultrathin ones Tommy brought in order for my clothes to fit in our shared closet. Even then, our clothes are packed so tightly together, it's difficult to pull an item out. And this is a giant closet. I'm amazed that Tommy got all of this done in such a short amount of time.

It's not until Tommy and I are stepping back to admire our work that I realize all my old clothes are in a bag on the floor. Tommy picks the bag up and heads towards the door.

"What are you doing?" The accusation in my voice is clear.

"I'm taking these to Goodwill for donating."

"You're what?!"

I know I have all these wonderful new clothes, and Asher said he'll let me keep them after this is over, but I can't help but feel attached to my old clothes. They're mine. I worked my butt off during high school to afford a lot of what Tommy is so ready to give away. I didn't have a family to buy these things for me. I worked for them, and because of that, I'm attached. At the very least, I want to keep my little black dress.

Tommy shrugs. "Asher's orders." He eyes the clothes, packed like sardines beside one another. "You don't seem to have any more room, too."

He's right. I should be grateful for these new clothes. No way should I want to get rid of some of them to make room for the old, but I can't help myself.

"But I—"

His eyes dart towards Xavier, who's sitting on a chair in the center of the closet, purposely minding his own business. "I have strict orders to give these away. Sorry." And then he runs off quickly.

I let him, because I don't have another choice. I can't chase him down the elevators when the stupid biometric lock won't allow me access.

"This is your fault," I tell Xavier.

He finished his rounds a few minutes ago and has been sitting in the closet since.

"How?!"

"If I had access to the elevator, I could have chased him down."

"I can give you access now."

And he does.

For the first time in a month, I'm free.

CHAPTER EIGHTEEN

*Courage is to never let your actions
be influenced by your fears.*
Arthur Koestler

The freedom almost eases the burn of losing all of my clothes, but the pain of the loss isn't quite gone. I can feel a heaviness settling in my chest, overpowering the excitement of liberty. Am I overreacting? Probably. I can't help it, though. Those tatty clothes are the only damn things I've kept from my past.

I send Aimee a text, asking her to meet me for an early dinner at Carmen's Cantina, a Mexican bar and grill near campus. Courtesy of Tommy, I'm dressed in fitted dark blue jeans, a skintight black long sleeved turtleneck shirt, and velvet black thigh high stiletto boots that make my frame tower four inches off the ground.

I look good.

It's almost weird.

Last time I saw Aimee, I was wearing my own raggedy clothes. Now, I'm wearing handmade, one of a kind creations. Is this what Julia Roberts' character feels like in *Pretty Woman*? Two parts princess, one part whore?

Xavier and I take one of the many town cars parked in the private garage. Apparently, all the identical cars do belong to Asher, but they're assigned to an employee during their tenure working for Asher. The employees leave the cars parked in the garage for security and practicality purposes.

The town car we're in is black, roomy and filled with cream colored leather seats. I'm not focused on the softness of the seats though. My nose is pressed against the window as we exit into the streets. I'm wide eyed, body humming in anticipation, as I catch sight of New York from ground level for the first time in almost a month.

I feel like a prisoner being released. The experience of freedom is almost too overwhelming. When I move to roll down the window, Xavier rolls it back up and locks it, saying something about a potential security risk.

I don't mind, because Carmen's is only a block away. We could have walked, really. It's far more practical than finding parking in New York City, especially near campus.

Turns out, we don't have to worry about parking, since Xavier parks in a no parking zone without a care in the world.

"We're not going to have a car to come back to when we leave." Frowning, I point at the sign that reads, "Tow Zone."

Xavier nods towards the front license plate. "They won't tow this car or ticket it."

I look at it. My eyes bulge when I realize they're diplomatic plates. Seriously? How does one acquire diplomatic plates without actually being a diplomat? The amount of clout Asher has is astounding. I may have to steal a car from him when this is all done. I can get used to parking wherever I want in New York City.

Carmen's is a family owned bar, whose main customers are students. I see a lot of them as I walk in. Most of them are congregated at the bar area, watching some sports game. The guys are watching the game, but the girls are watching the guys. It's a sight so familiar it's comforting.

I pass the bar area entirely and seat myself at one of the booths in the far back corner. Xavier, thankfully, sits himself at a different table while I wait for Aimee. He's far enough that I'll have privacy but close enough that he can get to me quickly if something goes wrong.

"I hate you. You missed—I don't know—about four of our scheduled weekly lunches and dinners, you bitch." Aimee sits down across from me, her arms crossed, clearly expecting me to grovel.

"You can blame Asher for that. I was being held hostage." I turn the tables. "You didn't think to come save me?" A fleeting smile crosses my lips as I mock, "You bitch."

Aimee rolls her eyes and holds up her phone. "I didn't even get an SOS text. Not a single one."

She's right. I didn't want her to call in the cavalry. A few days into the engagement, I signed a formal contract, outlining the details of my arrangement with Asher. I'm getting a *lot* out of this deal. In addition to the free housing, food, job recommendation and clothes, he's prepared to give me a condo in the area and a $2.5 million divorce settlement upon our separation.

We'll be getting married quietly in a courthouse sometime within the next year and divorcing a year after that. All in all, I'll be committing two years to this ruse, but I'll be financially secure for the rest of my life. It's a generous offer, one Asher certainly didn't have to offer me.

But I'm starting to see why he did.

It's the bait, and I've taken it—hook, line and sinker.

No way am I going to ruin this for myself, even if I do have to hide in his penthouse while I wait for some damn clothes to be made. *God forbid I make a fashion faux paus and embarrass Asher.*

I sigh and give her the apology she deserves. "I'm sorry. I really have missed you."

And I have. When she was my roommate, I often found myself needing space from her. But now that she isn't, I find myself missing her. I've heard the saying "you don't know what you've got 'til it's gone" before, but I never knew it applies to friendships, too.

Like all lessons in life, I learned the hard way.

Her eyes are glistening as she says, "I didn't realize how important you are to me until you vanished off the face of the planet."

I'm glad it's not just me. My heart swells at her words, though I try to steer our conversation away from the heavy stuff. I've never been too good at talking about feelings.

"I didn't vanish! You could've come visit me."

"I tried."

"What?!" I'm angry now. "And they didn't let you up?"

"No." A faint blush spreads across her face.

I've never seen her blush before, and it causes me to sit up straight.

She admits, "I couldn't bring myself to go up. I was outside the building, too. I just saw all of these guards, and it was pretty intimidating."

Shocked doesn't even begin to describe what I'm feeling right now. Aimee is the fearless one between the two of us, yet here I am, living in a building she's afraid to enter. When did the tables turn in our friendship? How did we get here?

"It's not as scary as you're picturing. It's actually a really nice place."

Her eyes dart cautiously to Xavier's table. Her tone is gentle but serious when she asks in a whisper, "Are you in danger, Lucy? You would tell me if you are, right? I promise I'll take it seriously."

My heart warms, unfamiliar with being cared for but liking it nevertheless. "I'm safe, Aimee. I wouldn't be doing this if I didn't feel right. There are contracts and agreements in place to protect me if anything goes wrong. The only way I see this going wrong is if I breach the contract, which I have no reason to. I'm being treated well, and I'll gain so much from this when it's over. This is a smart decision for me."

"If you say so. I trust you." And then my best friend is back, smirk and all. "Have you fucked him yet?"

I scowl. "No, you perv! Can we not focus on my nonexistent sex life and talk about something else?"

"You've been living with Asher Black for a month, and you still haven't gotten laid?! Now, I know you're a lesbian."

"I am not a lesbian," I say just as a waiter approaches us. I recognize him from one of my genome labs.

"What's wrong with lesbians?" he asks, a charming grin on his face, probably from catching two pretty girls talking about lesbianism.

"Nothing is wrong with being a lesbian." I try to keep a blush off my face. "I'm just not one." I hold up my left hand as proof.

We all eye the ring on my ring finger. It's a beautiful 5-karat, princess cut diamond valued in the six figures. Monica was actually the one to give it to me. Asher was at a meeting in Los Angeles when she barged into the bedroom and threw the velvet ring box onto the bed. She gave me a vicious sneer and left without saying anything. The whole thing made me pity her.

Aimee's eyes widen. "Wow, that's some rock."

"So, the rumors are true?" the waiter says. "When I didn't see you in lab, I kind of assumed the worst."

"And what would the worst be?" Aimee asks saucily. Her arms are crossed, and she has a defensive look on her face.

I love her for it.

He mumbles, "Ya know… That maybe she flunked out or switched class sections or… waskilledbyAsherBlack."

"What was that last part?" Aimee asks for me.

He eyes Xavier warily, turning his body to put more distance between himself and Xavier's table. It doesn't really work, and it only makes Xavier more suspicious. I see him leaning forward, but I cut him off with a small shake of my head. He nods and relaxes in his seat.

The waiter says, a little slower this time, "I thought maybe she was killed by Asher Black."

"And why would you think that?" I ask.

"Because he's in the mob." His voice is defensive with a dash of hysteria.

"Allegedly," Aimee butts in, like the best friend she truly is.

"I'll take some carne asada fries," Xavier says loudly from the next table over. He's looking at the waiter, who fumbles and drops his pen.

"Oooh! Me, too!" I raise my hand like a child, eager to chase away the tension with some great food.

"Ditto." Aimee leans back in her seat. Her arms are no longer crossed, and her facial expression is back to normal.

The guy nods his head and runs away, his face pointed downward and shoulders slumped. I almost feel bad for him. I make a mental note to tip him well.

"So, speaking of missing classes, how have you not been dismissed from Wilton? When I missed one of my business law sessions last week, I got a sternly worded email from the Dean of Jefferson." She's referring to the name of Wilton's business school, the Jefferson School of Business. "Seriously, it made me feel like I was being spanked via email." A canary grin stretches across her signature red lips. "Have you seen Jefferson's dean? I'd let him spank me any day."

When I don't even groan at her one track mind, I realize how much I've missed her. "I bet your head is just a never ending stream of Tumblr porn."

"Basically, and every guy featured is hung like a horse. And in this magical world of mental Tumblr porn, I have your 32 triple Ds."

I cross my arms over my chest, self-consciously. "They're only triple Ds at Victoria's Secret. I swear, their cup sizes are one size too small. A C-cup at Victoria's Secret is really a B-cup everywhere else."

She nods her head in agreement. "Very true. It's why I shop there." She snaps the strap of her bra. "Gotta turn these Bs into Cs however I can." She gives me a knowing look. "Stop changing the subject."

She's impossible.

"You're the one that brought up your dean an—"

"*My* dean? I like the sound of that."

"—and spanking," I finish, ignoring her comment. "But to answer your question, my professors have been emailing me with coursework. I turn in my assignments through email. In lieu of my labs, I've been turning in essays based on the practical applications of the skills learned in the given week's lab. When I have a test, a proctor gets sent over to the penthouse with the exam and hovers over me while I finish."

I smirk at the last part. When one of the proctors got too close to me during a stats exam, Xavier had her pinned against the wall in seconds. She was married, but that didn't stop her from enjoying his touch. I could see it in the way her pupils dilated and she pressed her body harder into Xavier's. She sent flirtatious smiles

Xavier's way for the rest of the testing period. They went unreturned.

Aimee is silent for a moment. "It's Asher's connections that are giving you this hookup, right?"

I nod. "Probably. It kind of just happened. The professors just started to email me lecture slides, notes and assignments out of nowhere, and I never asked how they knew I'd be gone. I kind of just assumed it was Asher's doing."

There's a foreign wariness in her eyes. "It doesn't scare you that he has this kind of clout at Wilton?"

I understand her worries. I do. Wilton is notorious for valuing intellect over wealth and power. They don't do favorites at Wilton, yet here I am, being given preferential treatment because of my connection to Asher. I doubt anyone will say a word about it when I get back either. Not even the students, though they have every right to complain about my special treatment.

I'm starting to notice that, when Asher does something, no one has the guts to question him. The only thing that makes me uneasy about it is the dooming inevitability of something going wrong. You can't be untouchable forever.

"No," I tell her. "Honestly, he doesn't scare me."

Her eyes narrow. "Bullshit. I've seen you around him. Even though you're lusting for him, there's fear there."

I remember my conversation with him about running. "Of course, there was some fear at first. I would have been stupid not to fear him. But now, I'm comfortable around him. He has no reason to hurt me. In fact, it's the opposite. I have a full protection detail. It's not just Xavier in it."

We both glance at Xavier, who somehow got his carne asada fries first. He's already halfway done with his plate.

I continue, thinking about my app full of Asher flashcards, detailing his rough childhood. "I know him better now. I understand why he is the way he is. I'm not afraid of him."

And a part of me never was, I realize. At any moment since I met him, I could have fled. I could have run from this country, but I didn't.

I wonder if there's more to that decision than my unwillingness to sacrifice my degree. As frightening as it is to admit, my fight or flight responses have never kicked in around Asher. Maybe my subconscious has never seen him as a threat.

Aimee's eyes study me carefully. "Do you like him?"

"No!" I'm quick to deny it, but I have to admit, "I am more attracted to him than I was a month ago."

Her eyes widen. "You were *really* attracted to him a month ago."

"Yeah."

"A month ago, you were dry humping him on the dance floor at Rogue."

"Yeah."

"And now you're even more attracted to him?"

"Yeah."

She leans back. "Whoa. Are you sure you guys haven't had sex yet?"

I groan and am thankful when a server drops the food off, cutting off any further conversation. Because if I'm being honest, I won't be able to say "no" if Asher asks. Sex will just make this arrangement far more complicated than it needs to be, so I almost hope he doesn't ask.

But, then again, I can't keep Horny Lucy away forever. Two more years without sex will be the death of me. I know this with absolute certainty. It's even worse that I'm living with the hottest man alive.

Seriously.

Asher was named *People Magazine's* Hottest Man of the Year both years I was out of the country. He's probably a shoo in for this year, too.

The waiter comes by with an empty plate for Aimee. She puts all the carne asada from the top of the fries onto it and slides the plate over to me. Xavier leans over and steals the plate, reminding me that he's not only paying attention to everyone else in the bar but also us, too.

I stare at her "carne asada" fries, which is just cheese, beans, salsa, and guacamole now. "Why don't you just order the fries without the meat?"

She lifts a fry into her mouth. "Because they charge the same price even without the meat."

"So you order the meat even though you won't eat it?"

She shrugs. "Someone else always does."

We both look at Xavier, who's already done eating the steak. He's scanning the bar for "potential threats." I swear, those are his two favorite words. I wonder what will happen if he ever sees a potential threat.

I spot a glimpse of distinctly red hair from behind Xavier and groan, because she's most definitely a potential threat. "Wicked Witch up ahead."

A glower crosses Aimee's face when she sees Minka with her crew, Nella and some other girl I don't know the name of. They haven't caught sight of us yet, but I have no doubt they eventually will.

Minka is a supernatural force of nature. She probably has a Team Aimee radar jammed somewhere in that size double zero sundress of hers.

"I don't know why she's even here. It's not like she eats." Aimee pushes her food away from her and stands up. "I think I just lost my appetite. I have to pee." She moves to go but stops when she sees me stealing her guacamole. Her eyes narrow. "I didn't actually lose my appetite. It's just something people say when they see something disgusting."

"I know." I smile and dip a fry in the guac. "You snooze you lose."

I watch as she makes her way to the bathroom. Once she's in the door and out of sight, the loud murmuring in the restaurant swiftly dies down.

I find the source of the silence immediately.

Asher's here.

CHAPTER NINETEEN

Courage is contagious. When a brave man takes a stand, the spines of others are stiffened.
Billy Graham

Asher is making his way toward me, dressed in a tailored three piece suit. Tommy's work, no doubt. It's all dark grey, along with the button down and tie. Whereas the button down is a silky Egyptian cotton, the suit is a lightweight wool, single breasted with slim lapels running down the front.

Wow.

He looks like he stepped off the cover of *GQ*. He returns the heat in my eyes with a searing glance of his own. The turtleneck I'm wearing shows no skin, yet I feel sexy in it. It's tight, and I can see Asher's approval as he runs his eyes down my torso, stopping for a second longer on my breasts, like he has done in the past.

He takes in the seating arrangement, eyeing Aimee's food with a frown. After nodding to Xavier, he unbuttons both buttons on his suit jacket and takes a seat beside me. I see a flash of a holstered gun before the flap of his suit swings shut again.

As he slides in, I'm pushed further into the booth until I'm against the wall. It's a little too small for the two of us, especially given how huge Asher is, so I'm entirely aware of the way the sides of our bodies are pressed tightly together.

When he leans over and kisses my temple, I forget to breathe.

"What are you doing here?" I eye the restroom door, hoping Aimee will hurry up and come back.

"Meeting my fiancée and her best friend for an early dinner. I wouldn't want anyone thinking there's trouble in paradise." He says the last sentence sarcastically before pulling out his phone and typing something into it. Once he's done, he hands the device to me.

On the screen is an article that literally reads, "Trouble in Paradise." Below the headline is a picture of me walking into Carmen's. I'm suddenly glad I'm wearing Tommy's clothes, because I actually look good.

Really good.

I didn't even consider that the paparazzi would take an interest in me, but now I'm glad I'm not in my typical hand me downs and thrift store clothes, most of which have been owned by at least three people before they even got to me.

I read the article:

TROUBLE IN PARADISE?
by Justin Sider

Hi, ladies (and gents—we see you, too)! Asher Black's new fiancée, Lucy Ives, 20, was *finally* spotted—at Carmen's Cantina sans fiancé. This is the first time she's been pictured since rumors spread of her engagement to self-made billionaire Asher Black, 25. Hmm... Could it be that there's *already* trouble in paradise for the two lovebirds? What do you guys think? We'd love to hear your thoughts on this! But let's be real, we know you all have your fingers crossed, hoping they don't make it down the aisle.

I scroll down further and read a few of the most liked comments:

> **Alyssa (Downey, CA):** Finally he's come to his senses! Took him long enough. We all knew that he's too good for her.

> **Hannah Marie (Richmond, VA):** Like if you'd have Asher Black's babies!

David (Devils Lake, ND) : I'd bone. Don't even care if she's his sloppy seconds, too.

Aaron (El Paso, TX) : Bet she has a mouth like a vacuum to match those porn star tits. Am I right or am I right?

Disgusted, I hand Asher his phone back.

Looking around, I notice Monica isn't here, even though she's usually with him this time of day. It's only him and one of his main bodyguards, who's sitting at the same table as Xavier. With matching goliath frames and serious, brooding expressions, the two of them are the picture of intimidation.

I turn back to Asher. "Where's Monica?"

"I sent her home for the day." At my confounded look, he adds, "Her attitude has been getting worse. She's been getting on my last nerves. I'll have to do something about her."

"But you won't."

It would be done already if he really wants to. He's not the type to wait around.

He sends an appraising look my way. It sends goosebumps up and down my arms. I shiver a little, causing a ghost of a smile to appear on his lips.

"I won't," he agrees. "It's not a good idea to fire my long-time assistant before the vote. It won't exactly say, 'stable.'"

"And after?"

"As soon as it's done, she's gone."

I nod, relieved. She can't stand me, and I can't stand her. I have a contract that requires me to be here for two more years. She doesn't. If one of us is going, it's her.

I think she knows it, too, and it's causing her to be even crueler to me. She's another Minka, only she has the power to hurt me. Speaking of Minka, I see her heading our way just as Aimee plops herself down at the table.

"Something wicked this way comes," I say, quoting the title of the Ray Bradbury novel.

Aimee tears her stunned eyes away from Asher just as Minka settles herself in front of our table. There's a screeching of chairs as Xavier and Asher's guard stand up behind her. Asher gives a shake of his head at the two, and they both sit back down. Asher's guard keeps his eyes on our table, while Xavier continues to scan the crowd.

"Minka." Aimee's voice is curt, but it delivers a greeting more pleasant than the situation merits.

Minka has her vulture claws out, but she isn't focused on me or Aimee. She has her sights set on Asher, who choses that moment to wrap his arm around my shoulders. I maintain eye contact with her as I shift in my seat, snuggling closer to him until my head is resting comfortably on his shoulder.

We're clearly putting on a good show for her, because Minka's hands clench tightly into little balled fists. Her eyes twitch, and she just stares at us. Behind Minka, Nella's eyes bulge. The other girl clutches tightly onto Nella's arm, her expression one of stupefaction.

Minka changes her face into an angelic countenance. "Hey, Aimee and Lucy." She sends a sweet smile our way. "We just wanted to say hi. We miss you in the dorms, Lucy."

Her lies are convincing. Hell, I'd believe them if I didn't know any better.

She eyes my shirt, her disdain clear to me as a cloudless day. "I love your new clothes. They look very expensive." She smirks, so I prepare myself for a verbal hit. "Did you get a new *job*? Find a *boss* that pays well?"

I wince at the obvious innuendo. She just accused me of being a whore. The allegation hits a little too close to home, because while Asher isn't paying me to fuck him, he *is* paying me to marry him.

If I'm being honest, having sex with Asher would just be a perk. He wouldn't even have to pay me for that. If he asked, I'd spread my legs for him in a heartbeat.

How did I get here?

How did I get from being coerced into a false engagement to wanting to have sex with my fake fiancé?

Maybe it's Stockholm Syndrome or the fact that I've overcome my fear of him, but when you get rid of the fear, Asher is funny and thoughtful. It's just sheer absurdity that he's handsome on top of that.

He's the type of man a girl can fall in love with at first sight, and nobody would fault her.

Have I become one of those girls? Someone blinded by looks? I feel like I'm in the passenger seat of my hormones, while Horny Lucy has her foot on the gas and Sane Lucy is floundering at the wheel.

I spare a glance at Aimee. Her face is too shocked for her mouth to say anything. I can't blame her. I can't believe Minka is saying all this in front of Asher either. Speaking of Asher, his body has gone completely rigid beside me. My heart squeezes sharply in my chest, remembering that his mom has actually done what Minka is accusing me of.

I shift one of my hands so it's touching his thigh under the table and give him a comforting squeeze. I'm speechless when Asher's hand finds mine under the table, and we link our fingers together, hidden from view by the white table cloth.

Minka shifts her gaze onto Asher, her true purpose for being here. "It's a pleasure to meet you." She grins flirtatiously, holding onto one of her forearms with the opposite hand, so her breasts push together. "Asher, right? I'm a good friend of Lucy's. I'd *love* to get to know you better." She winks at him, and the hidden message is abundantly clear.

I tense as Asher looks at her, his gaze slowly moving from her toes to her head. She fidgets a little under his attention, her confidence wavering slightly.

When he's done checking her out, I almost expect him to take her up on her offer, but he shocks me by saying, "If you're going to be two-faced, at least make one of them pretty."

She takes an immediate step back, bumping into Nella and the other girl. They reach out to steady her, but their hands are shaking.

Asher isn't finished. "Do you make a habit of being a bitch to the woman I love?"

Everyone looks at me, causing me to flush under the sudden attention.

Asher leans forward, shifting his body so he's staring her dead in the eyes as he says, "I know your type. You're not at Wilton for a degree. You're there to find someone to marry. Some rich sucker you can leech off of for the rest of your parasitic life." Minka sucks in a sharp breath, but he continues ruthlessly, "Come near Lucy again, and I'll blackball you so fast, no man in the city will dare touch you with a ten foot pole. You clearly know who I am. You know I'll do it."

There's a shocked silence before Aimee breaks it with her raucous laughter. Minka huffs and holds her head high as she walks away, but I can see the tremor in her legs. Her two lackeys follow closely after her without half of her grace.

I'm still silent, though. No one has ever stood up for me like that. Logically, I know Asher probably did that for himself. It would have made him look bad if he didn't defend me... but even if he didn't do this for me, I can't help but be grateful.

And emotional.

I've been alive for over twenty years, and this is the first time anyone has ever defended me like that. I'm shocked when a few tears leak out of the corner of my eyes, trailing silently down my cheeks. I'm helpless to stop them.

Asher turns to me, a frown marring his perfect face. "Are you okay?"

Aimee looks uneasily between the two of us and says, "I think it's time for me to leave." She leans across the table and squeezes my hand. "Love you, Luce."

And then it's just Asher and me.

And my embarrassing tears.

I lean back a little, putting some much needed distance between us. "I don't know why I'm crying." I take a deep, raggedy breath and force myself to calm down.

When Asher shifts his body, shielding me from everyone else in the bar, I'm grateful. I would be mortified if Minka were to see me crying.

"It's not about what she said, is it?"

It never ceases to amaze me how perceptive he is.

I shake my head. It wasn't Minka at all. I'm used to her saying things like that to me. Hell, she's usually more overt with her offensive remarks. She probably toned them down because Asher's here.

I'm emotional because he defended me. I can't tell him this, though. It makes me too vulnerable. So, I stay silent, waiting for him to talk.

It takes a few minutes, but he finally speaks. "I cried the first time Vince bought shoes for me."

"What?" My eyes are clear now, and I'm fully turned to face him. I'm flummoxed by what he's telling me, that he's confiding in me to make me feel better.

He lets out a derisive laugh. It's empty and gut wrenching. "It was the first pair of shoes anyone ever bought me. Before that, I used to steal them from neighbors or trash bins. I fucking *cried* when Vince took me in and bought me shoes."

My heart weeps at the thought of a young Asher, crying at the first kind thing to happen to him. "Why are you telling me this?"

His eyes look earnest and void of judgment when he says, "It's okay to cry at kindness. This is the first time someone has stood up for you, but it won't be the last. I'll always look after you, okay?"

"How did you kno—" I cut myself off.

Of course, he figured it out.

This is Asher Black.

I laugh a little as I repeat the words he said to me the second time we met, "You're different than I thought you'd be."

Back then, I thought he was cruel, calculated, and perceptive.

A lethal weapon.

I was right.

But I was also wrong.

He's so much *more* than that.

He's witty, protective and also kind. This depiction of Asher is at odds with so many of my previous misconceptions of him, and I find myself promising to let my bias go. To judge Asher by the way he treats me, not what other people claim he is.

I've been prejudiced from the start. I know that now.

Asher is so much more than foregone conclusions, and what I'm learning about him, I really, really like.

CHAPTER TWENTY

One man with courage makes a majority.
Andrew Jackson

The next week, I'm happy to find an invitation to Wilton's senior networking cocktail party sitting in my email inbox. The school hosted event is an opportunity for graduating seniors majoring in the sciences to meet the who's who of the medical field.

It's exclusive to the seniors graduating magna or suma cum laude. As a junior, I shouldn't even be getting an invitation. Asher is probably behind it, and I find the gesture surprisingly sweet.

It's custom to take a date, so when I ask him if he'll go with me, I'm glad Asher agrees. I'm tempted to ask him how he got me an invitation, but if something illegal is involved, I'd rather not know. Because this, an invitation to the hottest networking event on campus, is too big to turn down.

On the day of the party, I dress in the jeweled burgundy dress Tommy made me, the first dress I tried on when he came over last week. I'm feeling confident when I step out of the bathroom, done with my light makeup.

Asher is exiting the closet with his head down, but he looks up when he hears me. I stand still as he takes me in, his eyes traveling from my heeled feet to my hair, which is pulled up into an elegant French twist.

"You look stunning," he says, the compliment sounding foreign on his lips but still genuine.

At his approval, I force myself not to make a fool of myself. I still manage to blush, which causes him to shake his head and smile. He walks back into the closet, and when he comes out, he's wearing a tie the same color as my dress. It goes well with his all black suit and white button down.

I'm surprised when he hands me his cuff links and lifts a questioning brow, the blackness of lust still lurking within the depths of his eyes. I've seen Asher put on cuff links himself at least a dozen times. He doesn't need my help.

I know this, but I help him anyway. When I take the cuff links from his palms and slip one into the cuff of his sleeve, my fingers brush lightly against his skin, and I immediately know why he asked for my help.

He was giving me an excuse to touch him.

When we get to the event, I'm surprised to see Minka there on the arm of a much older man. She scowls at me, but she wisely keeps her distance. I see her sending a worried glance Asher's way and wonder if Minka's date is one of the poor saps she's trying to gold dig from.

After we check in, Asher and I mingle around. He introduces me to a lot of people, and I'm stunned to see how well he knows all these powerful players in my field. These are influential people, all of whom seem to respect Asher. Despite his youth, he stands more self-assured than anyone else here.

I'm proud to be on his arm.

I'm also grateful for the way he's careful to keep me engaged in these conversations, not as an accessory but rather a partner. He treats me like his equal, and in response, everyone we've talked to gives me the same respect.

I'm ecstatic from all of the connections I've made by the time I head to the bar for a water with Xavier following a few feet behind me. I frown when I see Minka's date there. He's leaning against the bar when his eyes scan his surroundings.

There are two drinks in front of him. He pops something—a pill, maybe?—into one of the drinks and stirs it with his finger. I stumble a little when I see where he's headed, both drinks in hand. My eyes follow his path as he takes the drinks to a table a few feet away, where he hands the spiked drink to Minka.

I hate Minka. She treats me poorly, has a superiority complex, and has been hell bent on making my life miserable since I met her. But she also doesn't deserve to be drugged and who knows what else. There isn't even a doubt in my mind that I have to do something about this. And quickly.

I turn towards Xavier and tell him what I saw. He leads me back to Asher before he takes off with an event security guard in tow. They're headed in Minka's direction, so I turn away. She's in capable hands. I know she'll be safe now. I don't owe her anything else.

"Can we leave now?" I ask Asher, unsure of how Minka will react.

If there's a scene and she's humiliated, I know she'll blame me. I hope it doesn't happen, but I don't want to be here in the off chance that it does. That's just asking for trouble, which I definitely don't need in front of people that can potentially be my future bosses.

Asher nods. We say our goodbyes to a few people before we head out, his guard following closely behind. Xavier stays behind at the event to deal with Minka's date, so only the three of us head out the front door of the building.

It's a short walk back to the penthouse, so I ask Asher if we can walk before he calls his driver to pick us up. We make our way down the sidewalk adjacent to Sproul Hall, where my statistics class is held. Asher and I are holding hands, probably to keep up appearances, but

I don't mind it. I also don't mind that Asher's guard is trailing behind us from a comfortable distance.

The sidewalk is on a busy street, close to a crowded intersection. I mindlessly look at the hectic street, watching the congestion of cars slowly passing by in traffic. There are bicyclists and motorcyclists swerving in and out of the traffic, bypassing the gridlocked cars.

I smile when I see a funny duo on a matte black Ducati. There are two men on the bike, but they're so ripped they can barely fit together on the seat. I'm trying not to laugh, but a little chuckle slips through.

Asher hears it and follows my line of sight. I frown, reacting to his narrowed eyes. I look back at the duo, trying to see what he's seeing in those calculated eyes of his, when I spot it, danger and death wrapped in a sleek package.

A gun.

The one in the back locks his eyes on me and reaches for the weapon. Asher and I react at the same time, and all Hell breaks loose. He tries to pull me behind him, but I'm already moving at the same time. When the bullet pierces through the air, I accidentally push him into its trajectory.

It hits him square in the chest.

Meanwhile, I'm safely crouched on the ground, shielded by his falling body. The world moves in slow motion as I watch him fall. *No way he survived that*, I think, but I'm proven wrong when he reaches behind his back with both hands.

He pulls out a gun in each hand and shoots. Two shots ring out simultaneously, moving in the direction of the motorcyclists that are zipping away. A bullet hits each of their moving forms at the same time Asher finally falls and lands.

On me.

I push him off of me gently, careful not to touch the guns nor his chest. My eyes are wide as I search his torso with my eyes and fingers for a bullet hole. I see a circular gap in the middle of his button down, but there's no blood seeping into the shirt.

I press down on the area anyway, because it's the only thing I know to do—put pressure on the wound.

"Fuck, Lucy!" Asher cringes away from the firm pressure of my hands. "Stop! Babe, *stop*."

My mind doesn't even register that he called me "babe."

I gape at him as he gently pries my fingers away and rubs at his chest. Asher tears the ruined fabric of his button down a little and sticks his finger in, pulling out the bullet. My eyes widen when I see that his undershirt doesn't even have a mark on it.

But I'm so relieved he's alive, I don't think as I crawl into his lap and hug him. There may be tears streaming down my face, but I'm too prideful to admit it. I pull back, look at the place on Asher's chest where he was shot, and hug him again.

And then I lean back and slap him.

He catches my wrist when I move to do it again. "Hey! What was that for?" He's frowning at me, a look of sheer bewilderment in his blue eyes.

"Are you wearing a bulletproof vest?!" I gesture to my cocktail dress. "What about me? What if that bullet had hit me?"

I move to slap him again with my free hand, but he takes both of my wrists and uses them to pull me back against him. I'm still straddling his waist, pressed into his body, so I can't see his face. He's shaking, which causes me to frown.

Wary, I wrap my arms tightly around him. I don't want him to cry. Is he thinking about what would happen if I was the one that got hit? It's unexpected but not unwelcome to learn I mean so much to him.

Then, I realize he's not crying.

He's *laughing*.

It's a deep rumble, and in between breaths, he says, "What you're wearing *is* bulletproof." His laughter subsides, but he's still holding onto me. "It's sewed into the corset and skirt of your dress. It's the same fabric the lining of my suit and button down are made of." And then he laughs again. "And you wouldn't have gotten shot either way. I was moving to shield you when you went all Inspector Clouseau on me and knocked me over."

I feel a shadow over us and turn to find Xavier, who's now

hovering above us. He has a quizzical eyebrow cocked at our position. I'm still on Asher's lap, and we're still hugging each other.

I try to move, but he tightens his hold on me. I can't help but let him, allowing his presence to calm me. To make me feel safe again, because at this point, no one else but him can.

It all makes sense now.

Asher has been protecting me from the start. He didn't let me out of the penthouse until Tommy was done with my clothes. My *bulletproof* clothes. It wasn't because I wasn't dressed nicely. It was because I wasn't dressed *safely*.

I swoon a little.

He wants me safe.

He jumped in front of a bullet for me.

How can I not be affected by that?

I'm only human.

I know it's intimate, but I'm interested to know. It's a burning curiosity and the remaining adrenaline rush that gives me the nerve to run my hands down Asher's chest. I examine his suit thoroughly, feeling the smooth fabric beneath my fingers. I think it's identical to the fabric of the slip lining my dress.

"How is this possible?" I ask.

"We manufacture bulletproof fabric at one of our R & D labs. I give some swatches to Tommy to make our clothes."

"Wow. I didn't know that bulletproof clothes exist."

"It's been out for at least a decade now. President Obama wore a bulletproof suit to his first inauguration in 2009."

I don't reply. I'm still in his arms, hugging him. I'm trying to remain as invisible as possible, because I'm not ready for him to let go. Getting shot at is surreal, and I'm still unsettled. Asher rubs my arms, fighting away the goosebumps caused by fear and replacing them with goosebumps caused by our proximity.

"What do you have?" Asher asks Xavier.

Meanwhile, I'm still clinging to him like a koala bear.

"The two perps have been tied up."

I look past Asher and see the two guys on the ground, tied

together. There's a bit of blood on the sidewalk beside them, and one of them is slouched dangerously low. Asher's personal bodyguard is hovering above them, leaning against their bike, which has been pulled onto the sidewalk opposite of ours.

"What do you know about them?" Asher's arms are still around my waist.

I inch even closer, resting my chin on his shoulder, and he tightens his grip. I don't know if he knows he's doing this, because this position, sitting on his lap, feels so natural. Too natural.

"They have no IDs on them. I don't think they're mafia." Xavier's voice sounds concerned. "Maybe corporate?"

I want to scoff, because really? What corporation hires a hit on someone?

"Do you know which one of us they were after?"

I pull back at that. "You think they might be after *me*?"

Who would want to hurt *me*?

I'm a nobody.

"We can't rule anything out." Asher's voice is firm but gentle, yet I still tense at his words. "I won't let anything happen to you."

I'm taken aback when he kisses my forehead. There are sirens in the distance, coming closer and closer, but I remain seated in his lap. Tense. Because if they consider me as a target, they may look into my past.

Into Steve.

CHAPTER TWENTY-ONE

*History shows that courage can be contagious
and hope can have a life of its own.*
Michelle Obama

I'm not surprised the cops were called. Since we left the cocktail party before dinner was served, it's still pretty light outside. This happened in broad daylight, and there are a lot of witnesses. Someone was bound to call the cops.

What does surprise me is that Asher doesn't seem to care.

Xavier gives me a knowing look. "Asher shot them in self-defense. We did nothing illegal, so we can call the cops. It's okay if they come."

"It actually helps prove my legitimacy." Asher's voice caresses my ears. "If I was still in the mob, I'd call a cleaner and we'd handle this internally. Calling the cops means I'm out. I have nothing to hide."

"Oh," I say, as I see the first police car round the corner and park on the curb.

Two uniformed officers step out, and their weapons are drawn as they walk towards Asher's guard, who holds his hands up in surrender. Another unmarked vehicle pulls up, and the man and woman that step out and head in our direction are wearing street clothes. They must be detectives. Behind them, the shooters are being loaded into an ambulance that has just arrived.

"Mr. Black," the older of the two detectives greets us.

I scramble off Asher's lap as gracefully as possible, allowing Xavier to help me up. When Asher stands, the female detective eyes the hole in his shirt warily. At her look, he hands her the smashed up bullet for evidence. She takes a latex glove out of her pocket and uses it to place the bullet into a little Ziploc bag. I watch as she scribbles something onto the bag with a black Sharpie.

"Can you two give us your statements?" the male detective asks. "Separately?"

I go with the female detective, Xavier trailing closely behind. He stays back a safe enough distance, but he still remains close. The cop sends him a suspicious look, and he gives us a few more yards of distance.

The detective begins grilling me, her tone an odd mixture of firm and gentle, but I'm able to answer all of her questions easily. Except one.

Who were they after?

I'm feeling guilty when I approach Asher after we're both done being questioned. A crowd has gathered around us, and paparazzi are stationed behind the police barricade, obnoxiously shouting questions our way. No way will this turn out to be good press for him.

"Sorry," I say when I reach him.

"What for? It's not your fault we got shot at."

I shrug. "It's my fault we're here. Still, it was sweet of you to get me into the event tonight. I really appreciate the invitation."

Asher stiffens, and his face hardens. "I didn't get you into this event. What are you talking about?"

I falter. "I-I got an invitation through my email. It's a senior networking event, and I'm a junior. I thought you had something to do with the invitation, that maybe you pulled some strings for me." I pause, taking in his frown. "If you didn't, then who did?"

Asher sweeps his gaze over me, taking in my disheveled appearance. His eyes are a frosty navy blue as he says, "I don't know. That's what we need to find out."

It doesn't shock me to learn that I have trouble sleeping that night. It's not images of the shooting that are plaguing my mind, though. As soon as I close my eyes, I dream of Steve at the edge of my bed.

I've had this dream before. It's been awhile, but as soon as I'm immersed in the familiar bedroom, I know what will happen. This dream is a replica of what happened in real life, except in my dreams, there are two Steves.

I'm always unable to move as one remains at the foot of the bed, stroking himself, and the other approaches me, his hand reaching out to touch my body. This is the part where I usually wake up and stay super still with my eyes closed, convinced that if I open them, I'll see both of the Steves there. And they'll tell me which one of them is real—the one who doesn't touch me or the one who does. I always hope it's the former, but I'm too scared to ask. Not knowing has become a torment of its own, no doubt a byproduct of my cowardice.

This time, when I wake up, I keep my eyes closed tightly like I always do. But when I feel the bed dip, they fling open in alarm, relaxing instantly when they lock onto Asher's concerned face. He hovers nearby before I close the distance, snuggling into the safety of his arms, remember how sheltered I felt when he hugged me after the shooting.

"Nightmare?" he asks.

I nod, but I don't say anything, letting him assume that it's from what happened earlier today. I'm not about to tell him about the unanswered questions I have for Steve Who Likes to Watch and Steve Who Likes to Touch.

"If I let you sleep on the bed, can we not talk about it tomorrow? Or ever?"

There's a rumbling of laughter in his chest before I feel him pull me tighter against him. "Yeah, Lucy. I just want you to sleep well."

I miss half of my lab the next morning. Sleeping in Asher's arms was so comfortable, we both slept in later than we normally would. It helps that Monica didn't come in at 5 A.M. to wake Asher up like she usually does.

Maybe she decided to let him rest after the whole getting shot in the chest thing.

Or maybe she lost her keys.

Or maybe—fingers crossed—she's finally rethinking her job here.

Who knows what goes through that woman's mind?

By the time I make it to lab, about an hour has passed, and there's only two more hours left in the class period. I'm already feeling awkward after missing so many classes without a reprimand, so when I show up, I take my punishment like a champ, not even bothering to ask for a makeup lab. A normal student wouldn't get one, so it's only fair if I don't either.

There are eyes on me as I start extracting DNA from a tomato for PCR. It'll take almost two hours in the machine before the thermal cycling is complete, and by that time, the class period will be over. I do it anyway, so I can at least get partial participation points.

The write up for this lab, which I can't do without the data from a completed lab, is worth fifteen percent of my overall grade in the class. At most, I'll get half credit for it, which means the highest grade I can get in the class is now a 92.5%. And that's assuming I get a perfect score on everything else I turn in for the rest of the semester.

A 93% is an A-. I need a 3.7 GPA, which is an A- average, to maintain my scholarship. I've been gunning for straight As, because getting an A- is a little too close to my GPA cut off for my taste. I already have enough excitement with Asher in my life.

Which basically means that this sucks, and the guaranteed plummet of my GPA is enough to sink my spirits. Between the shooting, the nightmare, and the grade, I'm in a really shitty mood.

It's almost enough to make me rethink this whole charade.

Once I enter Rogue, I leave Xavier to talk to some of his guard friends about whatever super buff security guards like to talk about. Probably about how many people they've killed and how they've gotten away with it. Xavier looks like he's got at least a dozen under his belt.

There's only one guard in front of the stairwell leading to the VIP floor when I approach the bottom of it. It's the middle of the day, so it's not operating hours. The music isn't on, and the dancers aren't in their cage-stages, but the security is certainly there in spades. There are even more guards than there usually is, which isn't surprising given the shooting that happened a few days ago.

When I reach the guard, one of the Romano guys, he smirks and says, "Let me guess. Model? Actress?"

"Fiancée."

I shove past him, ignoring his widened eyes. I feel him following behind me, so I quicken my pace until I'm practically running up the stairs.

When he sees me, Asher's eyes widen. "Lucy? Whoa! What happened? Was there another shooti—"

"What the fuck is wrong with you?" I demand.

His eyes grow wary, and they cut to the guard that followed me up there. I wait impatiently, my right foot tapping a rude rhythm against the floor, as he shakes his head at the guy, who soundlessly retreats back down the stairwell.

When Asher's eyes come back to me, he says cautiously, "Me? What did I do?"

"My lab, Asher." I cross my arms and try to plaster a fierce look onto my face.

I hope it's scary, because the pastel pink blouse I have on doesn't exactly scream: *FEAR ME*. Though he should be scared, because I am pissed the fuck off right now. I can practically feel my cells humming in sheer anger.

I try not to yell, but I do anyway. "*My* fucking lab!"

"Oh." His face relaxes. "You're welcome."

"You're welcome? Are you fucking kidding me? That's what you say to me after interfering with my grades?"

"Wha—" Asher's jaw drops a little. "You're mad about that?"

"Of course, I'm mad," though my anger is quickly dissipating. I'm just tired now, and with that comes a newfound vulnerability. "Wilton is the only valuable thing I have in my life that's completely mine, and it's *already* tainted.

"People stare at me when I walk into class now, and I know they're angry about all the special treatment I'm getting. They won't say anything, because you're you, but I know they're thinking it. I don't even blame them. I *can't* blame them. The special treatment I'm getting is unfair for them. That's a fact.

"The worst part is that I can't even decline your help, because without it, I'm just a random girl that missed dozens of classes and deserves to be placed on academic suspension not to mention have her scholarship revoked.

"But this? This lab? I didn't ask you to help me with that. I could have taken the hit to my GPA. I *deserve* to take the hit."

Asher's eyes soften. "I'm sorry. I just thought... It was my fault you overslept and failed the lab, so I fixed it."

He still thinks I was up all night with nightmares about the shooting—not the two Steves.

I don't correct him.

"This is my life, Asher! *Mine*. There's nothing to be 'fixed,' especially not by you." I sigh, forcing myself to release my residual anger, since his heart was in the right place. "Look, I know you thought you were doing the right thing, but I would appreciate it if, from now on, you don't interfere with my life any more than necessary."

"And the aspects that I need to interfere with?"

"There's nothing that you 'need' to interfere with."

"We're engaged, Lucy. There are aspects of our life that are intertwined."

"Consult with me first."

He looks at me, his eyes taking in my face and then my body. I struggle to control my body's reaction to his perusal.

Asher nods stiffly. "Fine."

"Fine."

"Fine."

I roll my eyes. "I'm not doing this with you, Asher."

A boyish smirk etches itself onto his face. "Fine."

I don't bother answering. I turn and leave.

But my heart is pounding, because even though I don't want his help, he went out of his way to do something nice for me.

And damn if that doesn't make me like him a little more.

CHAPTER TWENTY-TWO

*Success is not final, failure is not fatal:
it is the courage to continue that counts.*
— Winston Churchill

My jaw drops at the sight of the pair in front of us. Asher and I are in his penthouse, surrounded by his security team. All twenty-six of them. In front of us are a man and a woman that look just like Asher and I. Sure, there are some noticeable differences, but from afar, no one will be able to tell us apart.

I study my female doppelgänger. She looks like me, but not quite. Whereas my chest is fuller and I'm a little taller, she's far paler than I am. She's also missing a lot of hair and has eyes that are dim and sunken in.

Asher's double is the same height as him, but the double's eyes are brown, his hair is blonde, and his ears aren't quite right either. He's also wearing thick reading glasses and is bouncing around the room like he's tweaked out of his mind. Yet, when I caught sight of his pupils, they looked fairly normal.

When the two are ushered to a team of stylists, I pull Asher aside. "Do they know what you're asking of them?"

I try not to blush as Asher studies my face. We almost died together, and he used his body to shield mine. I don't care that he was wearing a bulletproof suit. It was still incredibly brave, an act of bravery I never in a million years would have imagined someone doing for me.

The few lingering concerns I had about Asher evaporated after that. In its place is respect. I respect Asher for the kind of man he is to me. Respecting a man I find attractive is dangerous territory.

If I'm not careful, I might begin to blur the lines in this relationship. I'm already far more aware of his body than I've ever been, struggling to come up with valid reasons for not pursuing a man that would risk his life for mine. It doesn't help that I know what it feels like to be kissed by him.

Asher sighs. "They know the risks. Damien is an adrenaline junkie. He gets off on this shit. Caroline has cancer. She's dying. She can't do anything about it, but the two million dollars I'm paying her will go a long way in helping the family she's leaving behind."

My eyes widen.

Two million dollars?!

Is that how much a life is worth?

Is it how much *his* life is worth or *mine*?

Or is the figure somewhere in between?

I nod to Asher. I can't judge him for this. Like always, he's right. Caroline and Damien know what they're doing. He's not tricking them or anything like that. Still, a part of me can't grasp the fact that they're about to risk their lives for us.

"Hey. Come with me," Asher says gently.

He leads me upstairs into our room. Once the door is closed, he backs me up into the wall, his hands pressed on either side of my face. I let him, because I need the comfort right now. I need to know that what we're doing isn't wrong and immoral.

His blue eyes stare into mine, searching for something, though I'm not sure what. "Don't feel bad about this. It's their decision to make. We're not forcing them to do anything, okay?"

It's hard to process what he's saying when we're in such an intimate position, but I know this is important. This needs to be said.

"I just... I can't help but feel like I should be doing this. Not Caroline."

"Don't." The harshness in his voice is shocking. "Don't even think about it, Lucy. Between your life and hers, yours is the one that matters. Every. Single. Time."

"Because she's dying?"

"Because you're mine."

My eyes widen, and I instinctively take a step back from him, but I'm already trapped against the wall. I study him, trying to decipher what he means by that. His eyes are guarded, and I can't read them, so I'm left drawing my own conclusions.

And my emotions are at war with logic.

If I'm his, is he mine?
Stop what you're thinking.
I can't help it.
He doesn't mean it like that.
But what if he does?
You're not actually his.
He just told me I am.
This isn't real.
It feels so damn real to me.

I release a shaky breath. "You can't just say stuff like that."

"I can't?" There's amusement in his eyes.

"It's confusing."

Like when you go out of your way to help me with school.
And slip into bed with me because I'm having a nightmare.
And step in front of a bullet for me.
And defend me against Minka.
And whisper in my ear that you'll do anything for the ones you love.

His eyes drop to my lips, and he opens his mouth to say something, but something in my face makes him stop. Instead, he nods and takes a step back from me. Asher leads me downstairs, where his security team is waiting.

They're going over the plan again, so I leave them alone, entering the kitchen for a bottle of water. I don't need a recap. My part of the plan is pretty simple anyways. I just have to stay here with Asher, Xavier and a few other guards while Caroline and Damien go out in public, pretending to be us.

I remember my conversation with Asher earlier.

"It's a Cold Charlie. You put your helmet on the end of your sniper rifle.

Someone takes a shot, and you flush them out. Then, you take the shot. It's a Cold Charlie."

"American Sniper? *That's just a movie, Asher."*

"And a book, but that doesn't make it any less true."

We're trying to draw out any more shooters, so we know which one of us they're targeting. If Caroline and Damien stay realistically close but far enough apart that a shot will hit the intended target, we'll know who they're after.

Asher has a private detective tracking down who hired the shooter. So, until he figures that out, the best we can do is figure out which one of us is the intended target. And apparently, the quickest way to do that is to lure the shooters out.

Asher's team has already made a route for our doppelgängers to take. Most of Asher's guards will be following them discreetly, hoping to capture the new shooters. Meanwhile, three guards will stay in the security room with me along with Xavier and Asher's personal guard. We'll monitor the situation from there, using live high definition footage from the miniature body cameras attached on all the guards, Damien and Caroline.

When I approach Asher, he reaches behind him and sticks a finger in my belt loop, tugging until I'm beside him. It's an intimate gesture, but it's not an unexpected one. Since the shooting a few days ago, we've been more aware of each other.

Even though I have Xavier, Asher has barely left my side. He even went to lecture with me a few times this week. Whenever we went, Asher always dressed in black jogger sweats and a black hoodie to keep a low profile. We would sit in the dark back corners of the class, hidden from view, while I'd try and fail to pay attention to the professors.

To be fair, Asher in a suit is sexy as sin, but Asher in sweats and a hoodie? I'm more likely to go to Heaven than find a man hotter than him.

"We're still waiting on hair and makeup," Asher tells me.

I eye the group, noting that there's a ~~rooster~~ person missing. "Where's Monica?"

"This is need to know. Only security personnel and my family know."

And me.

I have to ask, "Are you sure this isn't mob related?"

"I'm not in the mob anymore, Lucy."

Yet he asked Vincent *Romano* for these doubles, and Vince delivered them in record time. How does one even find a look-a-like so quickly?

"Mmhmm," I say, shrugging, but it's clear I don't believe Asher.

His finger unhooks from my jeans, and he takes a step to the side, putting more distance between the two of us.

I already miss his touch.

"This is surreal," I say, looking at the screen in awe. Asher's outside the room, while I'm in the security room with Xavier, Asher's personal guard and the newbie guard, who I suppose isn't a newbie anymore. We're looking at the screen, where Caroline and Damien are walking into a boutique on 5th Avenue. They have their hands linked together and look like a happy couple.

They're dressed in our bulletproof clothes, though the two don't know they're bulletproof. That's apparently only divulged on a need-to-know basis "for security reasons." I swear, if I hear "for security reasons" one more time, I'll give them a reason for security.

Instead of telling them about the bulletproof fabric, Asher gave Damien and Caroline super thin bulletproof vests to go under their clothes, even though they don't need the extra layer of protection. Dare Devil Damien didn't seem to care, but Caroline was shaking like a leaf before she left, and the vest is doing wonders to ease her nerves.

I watch as Caroline picks up a dress and holds it against her body, pretending to see whether or not it looks nice on her. The fabric covers her body camera. We still have about eleven cameras on her and twelve on Damien, thanks to the guards trailing both of them.

I still can't believe the resemblances between me and Caroline and Asher and Damien. Though it took almost two hours, the hair and makeup team did wonders with the prosthetic nose and chin they attached onto Caroline's face. They also gave her a handmade wig that's identical to my hair and looks unbelievably real. With a push up bra and sunglasses on, she looks just like me.

Damien looks pretty darn close to Asher, too. The prosthetics helped fix the differences in their ears. He was given contacts, a haircut, and some hair dye. He also has some makeup on to even his tan. In Asher's suit, he bears an uncanny resemblance to him.

Vince did a great job in picking these two out. I wonder how he did it. Is there an underground search engine for this type of scenario? Like Google for the damned and deranged? I picture his internet search history in my head.

Browser History

www.StraightTalkWithSatan.com/
search=how+to+dump+a+body/

www.BeelzebubKnowsBest.com/
search=how+to+conjure+a+doppelganger/

www.LifeLessonsFromLucifer.com/
search=how+to+talk+in+a+bad+ass+voice+like+Batman/

www.TheDailyDevil.com/

search=so+is+he+into+me+or+not/

www.AskElDiablo.com/
search=Oh+shit+I+think+I+like+him+
what+do+I+do+fuck+fuck+fuck/

*O*kay, the last couple searches might be what my search history looks like.

And assuming that Vince gets his internet advice from the Devil isn't fair.

Vince, Bastian, and Asher—the only mobsters I actually know—have been really nice to me. I'm just suffering from second hand bitchiness, courtesy of Monica, who called Asher a few minutes ago and demanded to know where he is and why it's not on her schedule. He's still outside the security room, talking to her when he should be in here.

On the screen, Caroline grabs a random scarf from the rack and purchases it. After it's bagged, they head outside again. This is the part that makes me tensest. Caroline and Damien are exposed, and anything can happen to them out in the open.

This is probably the fifteenth store they've been into, and they're running out of hands to carry bags. If something is going to happen, it has to happen now. Caroline and Damien can't keep shopping forever. They have to stop eventually, and it's almost that time.

I lean against Asher as soon as I sense him settling beside me. The contact eases my tension, and I revel in the feel of his thumb brushing against my arm. We watch together as Caroline and Damien leave the sidewalk and cross the street.

When they reach the middle of the crosswalk, we lose sight of them on the monitors briefly, the crowded New York street covering their exit. I'm waiting patiently for the streets to clear when a single shot goes off. Asher and I lean forward at the same time, our eyes scanning all the monitors, trying to find one with a clear view of Caroline and Damien, but there isn't one.

There's only chaos everywhere, as the pedestrians scramble, running in every direction.

I can't tell whose audio it's coming from, but I hear someone shout, "Terrorist attack!"

It only makes the chaos worse.

But then I see it, a little gap in the crowd. There's a body on the ground, and I'm stunned to realize that it's Caroline's. She's lying there on the ground, her arms clutching her stomach over her bullet-proof dress.

The evidence is there, right before my eyes, yet I can hardly believe it.

I'm the target.

CHAPTER TWENTY-THREE

> *Mistakes are always forgivable,
> if one has the courage to admit them.*
> Bruce Lee

It turns out living with Asher is easier than I previously thought it would be. After we learned that I'm the target, we both agreed that a lockdown is the safest route.

Unfortunately, there have also been whisperings of the vote being moved up, so Asher had to act. He ended up starting a new line of hotels at Black Enterprises. Because he's the resident expert in real estate law and has the most connections, this is the best move. It's making him invaluable to the company, so they had to push the vote back until the beginning of the next business quarter.

But scouting locations for new hotels also means he has been traveling a lot lately, so he's rarely home. But when he is here, he's easier to be around than I initially expected. We have a nice roommate thing going on here, where we leave each other alone until bedtime comes.

Since I let him sleep on the bed after my nightmare, he hasn't moved back to the floor. And I'm not about to ask him to. After doing it a lot, sleeping with him isn't awkward anymore. I actually like it. I don't dwell on it, but I enjoy his touch at night and even miss it when he's gone.

Sometimes, I'll cook when he's in town, and we'll eat together. But he mostly works when he's in New York, so our contact is at a minimal, typically limited to nights in the bedroom, where he'll cuddle me to stop my fidgeting. At times, I toss and turn just so he'll touch me. I'm playing a dangerous game, but I crave his touch, and with all the time we spend apart, I'll take what I can get.

In fact, I'm starting to wonder how our lack of time spent together is looking to the public and the people we're supposed to be selling this relationship to. We've only been photographed together three times, and we weren't even technically in one of the photographs.

The first time was when we left Carmen's Cantina together. It's the only normal picture of us. We're holding hands, and I'm smiling up at him with a goofy smile on my face. Last week, I caught a glimpse of Asher's phone and saw it as the wallpaper for the home and lock screen.

He must hate me. I swear. That's the only reason he'd set a picture of me looking like a stupid sap as his background. I have to give him credit, though. He's really selling this whole fiancé thing.

The second time we were photographed together was a totally *un*-embarrassing picture of me sitting in Asher's lap after the first shooting. In it, there are ugly tears streaming down my face, and Asher looks like he's about to commit first, second, third, fourth and *fifth* degree murder.

Fifth degree murder is when you make eye contact with Asher while he has an angry glare on his face, and you're stunned to death by his hotness. It's like getting petrified when making eye contact with the Basilisk in Harry Potter and the Chamber of Secrets, only Asher is gorgeous and came from a vagina rather than a chicken egg hatched under a toad. (Yes, we all know what you did, Herpo the Foul.)

The third picture is of Caroline aka Fake Lucy on the ground, a hand over her stomach, while Damien aka Fake Asher holds her hand while they wait for an ambulance to come. Someone is stepping on Fake Me's hair, and Fake Asher looks like he's having a blast. It's an odd picture, and I hope no one ever asks us to explain it.

But as far as the media and everyone else is concerned, Caroline/I survived because she/I was wearing a bulletproof vest under my dress —not bulletproof clothes. I still don't know why Asher is so hush hush about the bulletproof clothes.

The craziest part is that picture has been spread all over social media, and people still think it's us. When I found out that we'd gone viral, I just about had a heart attack, wondering if Steve has seen it. But that old goat would have to learn how to use the internet first, and that'll never happen...

Right?

I'm in the living room with Eduardo, my so called tutor of all things WASP related, when Asher descends the staircase with a suitcase in one hand and a book in the other. I tilt my head a little to read the title.

Sleeping Beauty in the 21st Century: A Modern Retelling.

I snort, causing him to narrow his eyes at me. I back up slowly when he approaches me. The books I'm balancing on my head wobble dangerously.

Eduardo is teaching me to walk properly in heels, which apparently involves using my cranium as his personal bookshelf. Two of the books are thesauruses, which is ironic, considering the only words Eduardo seems to know these days are "Damn it, Lucy!" and "Straighten your spine!"

"Damn it, Lucy!" Eduardo chastises me. "Straighten your spine!"

See what I mean?

I huff out an irritated breath, my wary eyes still focused on Asher as he stalks my way with a rare mischievous look on his face. Over the course of our many months living together, I've come to learn that Asher can be impishly playful when it's just us.

So, I'm justifiably wary when he advances on me, even though I know he won't do anything too ridiculous with Eduardo watching.

"Yeah, Lucy. *Straighten your spine,*" Asher mocks.

And then the fucker puts his heavy hardcover book on my head and heads toward the door.

I teeter in odd little circles, trying to prevent the books from toppling over. This is my longest record thus far, and Asher is about to ruin it.

Because I can't help myself, I shout, "Asher!" I'm satisfied when he pauses at the door, his back still to me. "Are you sure you don't want your book back?" I smirk devilishly. "Don't you want to find out if 21st Century Sleeping Beauty wakes up?"

And of course, that's when the books have to topple over, finishing my comeback in classic Lucy fashion. I swear I hear him laughing when he exits into the hallway.

And because I'm a doomed sap, the melodious sound soars straight to my heart and sends a secret smile to my face.

*A*n hour before noon, Eduardo heads home, leaving me with a massive headache, neck ache and foot ache. I hate days when I have to balance books on my head with sky high heels on, but even I have to admit that I'm a pro in heels now, able to walk in them better than most runway models.

Eduardo was appalled when we first met a month or so ago, not even hesitating to inform me that most of his five year old clients are more talented in walking and table etiquette than I am. After thrice weekly lessons in rich people expectations, I like to think I'm now his star pupil. He'll never admit it, but I know he likes me… so long as my spine is straight.

Monica walks in just as I'm about to head upstairs for a much needed, soothing bath. Unfortunately, she hasn't quit. And she still has a nasty habit of walking in here without knocking like she owns the place. I have no idea how Asher can tolerate it, but other than our conversation a long time ago about how it's not a good idea to fire her yet, I still haven't heard him comment on it.

"Get ready. You'll be leaving with Asher in an hour for a charity event," she says before heading to the door without a goodbye.

I frown. Asher left with a suitcase a few hours ago. He's supposed to be on a plane to Dubai. Over the past month, Asher has traveled to Los Angeles, Hong Kong, London, the Bahamas and, now, Dubai. Well, I guess not, since we're headed to a charity event.

"Wait!" I shout as Monica's hand connects with the doorknob.

She pauses, but she doesn't turn around, causing me to wonder if she picked that up from Asher.

I frown at her back. "What's the charity event?"

"A polo match," she says tritely.

Then, she's gone, much to my delight. I still don't like her, mostly because she's always so rude to me. I'd like to say that I usually go the high road around her, but I'm usually rude right back to her. I can't help it.

It's like watching *Here Comes Honey Boo Boo*. I know it's ridiculous, but I can't help but pay attention when it's on, just like I can't help but give Monica a taste of her own medicine when she's around. I'm playing with fire with someone who has the ability to light a match on my cushy new life, but I lack the willpower to stop myself.

And this new life of mine definitely *is* cushy.

I absolutely love it here.

I learned quickly that Asher has to be very hands on with the real estate division of his company, which is why he's always traveling and meeting with foreign dignitaries and real estate moguls. His interest in real estate makes sense, since he followed through on his word and magically got me out of my ironclad leasing contract.

I even got a full refund, which miraculously included money back for the month that I actually *had* lived in Vaserley Hall. I didn't think he could do it, because my housing was paid by my financial aid package and my lease had a nonrefundable clause, but he did the impossible. I have twenty-three thousand dollars in financial aid money sitting pretty in my bank account to attest to that.

That money means I don't have to work at the coffee shop, where Minka and her friends always hang out, ever again, so I quit permanently. Before the check, I was just on unpaid leave, but now I'm never going back. And I'm one thousand percent okay with that. The life of unemployment means I have a lot more time to enjoy my youth, time even my coursework, which I still do at home, doesn't fill up.

It turns out I don't have to worry about being bored, because Aimee, Tommy and Eduardo come over all the time. Xavier has even become a friend of mine. Now, I have four whole friends! That's more than I've had in a long time.

So, I'm pretty proud of myself.

As I stand in the closet, I consider consulting Tommy for clothing help, but I don't want to bother him on a weekend. If I ask Aimee, she'll just tell me to wear the tightest, shortest dress I can find.

Aimee and I still meet up a few times a week, mostly at the penthouse, and whenever she sees me, she'll squeal over my outfit and ask me why I'm not dressing to seduce Asher. I usually ignore her, because while Asher is insanely attractive and I often wonder what it would be like to go all the way with him, I don't want to ruin the tentative friendship we have going on—yes, we're actually friends.

I think.

Sort of.

So, maybe that means I have four and a half friends?

I shower, blow dry my hair, and put on makeup, keeping it light.

Thanks to Eduardo's lessons, I know that polo is mostly played in an indoor arena during the New York winters, even during the tail end of winter.

So, I pick out a white fitted dress and a fashionable light grey coat to wear over it. I add a pink statement necklace and nude Louboutins to the outfit. Stepping back, I look at my reflection in the mirror. Tommy and Eduardo would be proud.

And then I wait, realizing I still have another fifteen minutes before I have to leave. I pull out the binder with the questionnaires from months ago, anxious about what I might have to know about Asher for tonight. I have all my flashcards memorized by now, but I'm still nervous.

After all, this will be the first time in a long time that we've gone out together. On top of that, it's the first time we'll be in front of his coworkers after we announced our engagement... which is starting to be less and less believable with each passing day.

I skim through the binder, everything looking familiar until I encounter a bump in one of the binder's pockets. I didn't notice it before, but now, there are lines indented into the binder material from being stretched by the folded piece of paper for a long duration of time.

I take it out and read through it. It's an activity worksheet for getting fake couples used to intimacy in public. My best guess is Monica folded the paper up and hid it here before she gave us the binders. She clearly doesn't want us touching, let alone kissing like this activity suggests.

I'm still staring at the paper when Asher comes in.

"What's that?" he asks.

I study him. He's already dressed for the match in fitted white dress pants, a white dress shirt and a tailored, navy blue sports blazer. There's a white pocket square sticking out of the coat pocket. The casual polo outfit is at odds with the tenseness of his face.

I put the paper down on the bed and cautiously approach him. "What's wrong?"

He hesitates, as if debating whether or not he wants to tell me, before he says, "I'm pissed."

I can't help but smile. "I can see that. What are you pissed off about?"

"I was on the jet headed to Dubai when I got a call from Monica, informing me that Black Enterprises bought a tent at the charity match today."

"Okay…" I say, not seeing what is wrong with that.

Charity's a good thing, right?

Asher's company is pretty well-known for donating to a lot of causes. Before I met him, I thought it was just PR to distract from his reputation as a mobster, but now I know that he does it because of the way he was raised. He told me one night that Vincent's generosity helped him escape a grim life, and he hopes he can do the same for someone else. I have never been more attracted to him than I was that night.

"I had to reroute the flight, wasting my time, the pilot's time, the flight crew's time and a lot of fuel. We had to drop the fuel into the ocean." At my sharp look, he says, "It's standard operating procedure. The fuel evaporates before it hits the ocean. No sea life is harmed in the process, Steve-O. Don't go climbing any cranes now."

I roll my eyes at his reference to Steve-O's SeaWorld protest. "So you're this mad about wasting time and fuel?"

I know him well enough to know there's more to it. It takes a lot for him to show his anger.

He exhales. "No, I'm mad because I depend on my staff, on Monica, to keep an eye on things that I don't have the time to do myself. That includes knowing well in advance when René goes behind my back, buys a tent at a charity event, and invites everyone on the board except me."

Oh.

He's mad that René might have gotten an opportunity to further his anti-Asher agenda, and Monica almost missed it. But that doesn't seem like it's all of it either. He already expects René to do something like this…

But Monica?

He wouldn't hire her if she isn't good at her job. Her slip up must have taken him by surprise. It's no wonder she was so angry earlier when she informed me about the event.

I study him, looking for a reaction. "That's not all, is it?"

He looks startled by my keen observation.

I blaze forward, "You're not mad about René. You're mad about Monica. You're mad that she let you down, but you're also mad that you have to depend on someone else."

His face hardens.

Bingo.

I hit the jackpot... and won his ire.

But I don't want him mad at me.

As much as it pains me to admit, Asher actually turned out to be a decent person, maybe even a *good* person. Definitely a better person than I am. And I maybe sorta don't hate his guts and like him more than I should... as a friend, of course.

I don't want Asher to be unhappy, let alone mad at me.

So, I step closer to him and soften my voice, "450 people."

He gives me a confused look. "450 people?"

"That's how many people it takes to maintain the White House." I push him gently until he's sitting down on the bed.

We're eye level now, and he lets me step between his legs. This is the closest I've been to him in a while. At least with the lights on.

I take a moment to relish in the proximity before I continue, "It takes 450 people to run one household. You're only one person. As much as it sucks, you can't expect yourself to know everything that goes on in a company that does business in over seventy countries. Let yourself depend on others, even when someone disappoints you." I pause for a second, scrunch my nose, and add, "Except Monica. You can fire her. You're right. She sucks."

That's my honest opinion.

My heart fills up when he throws his head back and laughs.

He startles me when his hands go to the back of my bare thighs, lifting the hem of my dress a little with the tips of his long fingers. "I never said she sucks." He chuckles again. "There's no love lost between the two of you, is there?"

I shake my head. I have to bite my tongue to stop myself from petulantly saying, "She started it!" It's true, but it's also something expected of a five year old child not a twenty year old woman.

His eyes turn serious again. "Thank you."

The way he thanks me is so honest, so gentle and so genuine. I forget myself for a moment, leaning into him a little further. I want to kiss him, to feel his thanks whispered against my lips. But he backs away and eyes the paper I left on the bed.

"What's that?" he asks, nodding towards it.

There's no point in lying. If we're going to have our first real public appearance together, not including the school event, I need to be prepared for the inevitability of a kiss on the lips. From what I remember, it's something that'll dazzle me, no matter how often he does it. I have to be ready for it to happen, so I don't make a fool of us both and do something like orgasm in public from a kiss.

I reach over and hand the paper to him. Giving him a pointed look that I hope portrays my suspicions about Monica, I say, "I found it folded up and hidden in our questionnaire binders." I deadpan, "I wonder how that happened..."

He takes the activity sheet from me. "Hmm..." he says, ignoring my last comment as he reads it. "I think we should do it before we leave."

I nod. I expected as much. We'll probably have to kiss at least once at the match, and if we have our second kiss in public, my reaction will definitely give this charade away.

I take the paper from him and read aloud, "Step one. Hold hands until the both of you are comfortable enough to move on."

Asher sends me a mischievous grin as he grabs my hand and yanks me into a hug, which is step two.

"Step three," he reads before tearing up the paper and leaning forward to kiss me.

His lips are light against mine, a teasing touch that drives me crazy. It feels unreal, almost virginal, to be kissed again after so long, especially by him. A part of me considers that I'm imagining the whole thing.

But then he presses another closed mouthed kiss onto my lips, harder this time, and I open my mouth in response. He groans into it, causing my cheeks to flush, and slides his tongue into my mouth, brushing it against mine. I grab two fistfuls of his shirt, pushing myself closer to him until there is no more space between us.

With both of his hands, he grips my ass, triggering a moan that escapes my mouth and hurdles into his. When he scoots further back on the bed, I follow him, placing both legs on either side of his thighs until I'm straddling him. One of his hands tugs my hair as he deepens the kiss. I respond enthusiastically, grinding my lower half against his stiff erection and savoring the taste of his tongue against mine.

I distantly hear footsteps approaching, but I don't care. It's not until someone clears their throat that I stop. I don't have to look to know it's Monica. That woman has a cock blocking radar.

I groan softly and hide my face in Asher's chest. I feel his chest vibrate against me as he gives me a light chuckle. Both of his hands are still on my ass, and my entire body is still pressed against his, making it difficult to concentrate.

"You'll have to leave now if you want to make it before the match starts," Monica says, her voice tight and full of thinly veiled disapproval.

"Thanks, Monica. That'll be all." Asher pauses, and I hear the sound of her heels retreating. "And Monica? Knock next time, please."

"Of course, Mr. Black." She doesn't sound sincere.

The door slams shut, louder than necessary. My face is still buried in Asher's chest when he tips my chin back to examine me. There's laughter in his eyes.

"I think we aced this assignment."

I roll my eyes at his words and push off of him. When I spare a glance at the mirror, I see how disheveled I look. I try to fix myself up, but it's a hopeless cause. So much for making Eduardo and Tommy proud.

I'm finger combing my hair when Asher grabs my hands and says, "Stop." His eyes meet mine in the mirror, while his free hand trails down the side of my body, ending at my waist. "You look beautiful."

Given the way he's looking at me, I believe him. This isn't the first time since dancing with him that I've had to remind myself that we aren't actually together. This time, I'm reminding myself that the kiss was just an exercise.

CHAPTER TWENTY-FOUR

*Courage is not simply one of the virtues,
but the form of every virtue at the testing point.*
C.S. Lewis

When we get to the arena and Asher helps me out of the car, I realize that we've been holding hands since we left his bedroom.

"Are you okay?" he asks.

I nod. "It's just... overwhelming."

There are photographers at the entrance, shouting our names. Since our engagement was announced, I've been featured on a few New York blogs—walking to lab (the only class I go to) and eating with Aimee when I'm desperate to get out.

This is my first time being bombarded by a horde of photographers, though. I almost prefer the ones that like to stalk me from afar.

Asher shakes me up by pressing a kiss to my temple, which sends the paparazzi into a frenzy of loud clicks. "You'll be fine. Breathe."

I take a deep breath and plaster a smile on my face. Asher and I are standing side by side, his arm around my waist. For the next few minutes, I endure the paparazzi's shouts and actually follow their helpful pose suggestions...

Until someone shouts, "Are you pregnant? Is that why you guys are already engaged?"

I suck in a sharp breath as Asher's body tenses. I swear I hear an animalistic growl coming from him. Everything happens quickly after that. Xavier steps behind us and Maybe Dominic steps in front of us as we plow our way through the paparazzi, the time for pictures clearly over.

When we enter the arena, we are greeted by a smug looking René.

"Congratulations on the baby," René says.

I understand now why Asher has waited so long to take us out into public. We've been too new. Hell, the paparazzo's comment is proof that we are *still* too new. Barely more than four months have passed since we announced our engagement in October, and only five total months have passed since we supposedly started dating—even though it feels like it has been a lifetime since the first time I went to Rogue.

"There is no baby," I say tightly, though I don't have to. I was skinny when René met me, and many months later, I am still skinny.

He's just being an asshole.

Asher squeezes my hand, and I reel my anger back in.

The familiar blonde beside René steps forward. "Asher, darling, don't be rude. Aren't you going to introduce me to your *bride to be*?"

She says it so sarcastically, I admire Asher for not snapping, though I shouldn't be surprised. Asher's emotions are locked up in a fortress. If he doesn't want you to, it's impossible to tell what he's thinking. I'm shocked by the sudden realization that Asher *confided* in me earlier, something I suspect he has never done with anyone else.

This isn't real.

This isn't real.

This isn't real.

"Forgive me," Asher says, his voice dripping with condescension and bringing me out of my astonishment. "Viola, this is Lucy. Babe, this is Viola, René's wife."

We shake hands, the feel of her grip uncomfortable in mine. I remember her standing beside her husband at Rogue the night of my engagement announcement. Viola Toussaint is a gorgeous woman, whose beauty seems ageless. She has an elegant air about her, from the way she dresses to the way her hair is pulled back into an effortless chignon. The only telltale sign of her age is her hands, which are slightly wrinkled.

"Lovely to meet you, Viola," I lie.

The four of us, plus Xavier and Asher's guard, walk further into the arena. After we journey further into the place, I can barely tell that we are indoors. The floors are all artificial turf, and there is even natural light shining brightly through the glass ceilings.

The only sign that we are indoors is the temperate weather. While it's a chilly fifty or so degrees outside in the March weather, it's a comfortable seventy degrees in here. I'm able to take off my coat and leave it at the coat check.

Asher and I follow René to a tent that is labeled, "Black Enterprises." As one of the primary donors, Black Enterprises has an entire tent for its executive board and their guests. I'm relieved when I see that Monica isn't there. She's probably still licking her wounds.

Asher pulls me to a corner of the tent and says, "See that man René is shaking hands with?"

"Yeah."

"That's Martin Weisman. He's in René's corner." He continues, pointing discreetly at several other men. "That's the rest of the board. Elliot O'Malley, Owen Carter, and Tim Burks. Will you remember that?"

I nod, and because I can't help myself, I say in disgust, "You don't have a single woman on your board?"

He gives me an exaggerated groan. "You're such a pain in the ass," he says, but he's grinning.

I wonder if it's an act for the crowd.

This isn't real.

This isn't real.

This isn't real.

He continues, "Martin will vote for René, and Elliot and Tim will vote for me. They're loyal. The only one that's up from grabs is Owen. He'll be the tie breaker. He's the one we have to impress."

I study Owen again. He's the one that was impressed by my education when it was brought up at Rogue. He has an easy going grin on his face, and he doesn't come off as evil or creepy, like René does.

He looks nice enough, so I roll my shoulders back and nod. "I can do that."

Asher intertwines our fingers and leads me to the center of the tent, formally introducing me to the men. While he isn't as kind as Elliot or Tim are, Martin is at least cordial, treating me with much more respect than René does.

Owen is harder to read. His stoic face reminds me of Asher's, though I'm starting to grasp that I'm privy to a different, private side of Asher. I don't know how I feel about that. It's overwhelming and all-consuming to think about, so I shake the thought out of my head.

This isn't real.
This isn't real.
This isn't real.

The match begins, so we settle at the front of the Black Enterprises tent, which is prime seating in the center of the field. Even though I understand the game, thanks to Eduardo's lessons, I can't pay attention to it.

I can feel Viola's eyes on me. She's sitting to the far right of us with all the other wives. They haven't extended me an invitation to join them, which is fine by me. I feel more comfortable at Asher's side anyway.

I let Viola's creepy staring go. But after ten minutes pass by, I can't help but frown. I've caught Viola's eyes on me for the tenth time in as many minutes.

I whisper under my breath, "Viola keeps staring at us."

Asher gives me an imperceptible nod and squeezes my hand,

which is quickly becoming our way of communicating silently with one another. Then, he surprises me when he lifts our joined hands and places an open mouthed kiss on my wrist.

His tongue swirls around the sensitive skin, even sucking gently for a brief moment, sending a shocking jolt to my aching clit. It's over as quickly as it began. He presses another swift kiss on my wrist and one more on my cheek before he returns his attention to the game as if what just happened is normal.

I'm glad I slipped on my sunglasses a few minutes ago. My face is undoubtedly flushed, and my widened eyes would have portrayed my surprise. I know that was just a show for René's wife, but *holy cow*.

Man, am I affected.

If Asher keeps this up, I'm screwed.

When the match is finished, everyone stays in the tent to socialize. Thanks to Eduardo, I'm well-prepared for this. Asher and I separate. While I go to butter up Owen's wife, Madeline, he goes to charm Owen.

Madeline was the only brunette in the VIP lounge that night at the club. Turns out she is also pretty nice. She's chubbier than I recall her being, but she carries the weight beautifully and gracefully. She's one of the prettiest women I have ever seen, and when I tell her this, she gives me a sweet smile and compliments my eyes.

"Are you two planning on having children anytime soon?"

I groan. "Not you, too?" At her confused look, I say, "The reporters were hounding us on why we're getting married so soon. They think it's out of wedlock." I roll my eyes and pat my flat stomach pointedly.

With my luck, some photographer probably just snapped a picture as my hand connected with my belly. I can imagine what the headlines would read—Asher Black's Fiancée Rubs Pregnant Belly at Charity Polo Match.

"Ah," she says, her amusement sincere. "No, I was just genuinely curious." She points to her belly and grins. "If they ask you that again, you should point them in my direction. This is what a pregnant belly looks like. I'm due in seven months."

Oh.

Now her weight, which is centered on the little pouch of her belly, makes more sense. In my defense, it's been awhile since I've seen a pregnant woman. Plus, what's growing in her belly isn't even as old as my supposed relationship with Asher, which is not very old at all. That's a sobering thought. I clench my fist tightly, fighting the urge to glance at Asher.

Forcing myself to focus on Madeline, I ask, "Boy or girl?"

A melancholy expression flits across her face before she smooths it over. "Owen wants to know, but I refuse to find out. We didn't wait to learn the genders of our last two kids, so I want to be surprised for this one." She pauses, her voice tentative. "It's actually been something we've been fighting about lately. It sounds so stupid when I say it aloud. Maybe I should just give him what he wants again, or maybe he should be giving me what I want because the last two went his way. I don't know. Either way, we're fighting about it, and it sucks."

"One of my foster moms got pregnant," I begin, startling myself.

I hate talking about my foster families, but here I am, about to do it. Is it because I sincerely like her? Or do I want her to like me for Asher's sake? Maybe a little bit of both.

I continue, "She was one of the better ones. I really liked her and her husband. They were kind to one another, and while I don't think they were in love, they were good friends." I sigh. "Their relationship was built on that friendship, too. At the time, that was the closest thing I ever saw to love—between spouses and even between parents and their children. I never witnessed love. But them? They were friends and genuinely enjoyed each other's company. But they changed after they got pregnant. Their fights were tearing their marriage apartment." I eye Madeline's belly. "Want to guess what they fought about?"

Madeline's eyes widen. "Learning the sex of their baby?"

I nod my head. "Yep. Every day."

"But that's so stupid," she says indignantly.

"*Exactly.*"

"Oh." She pauses. "Did you just call my fights with my husband stupid?"

I smile a little. "If I recall correctly, you did."

We laugh together when she grins. "I did, didn't I?"

I shrug. "If it helps, I was thinking it, too."

She barks out a surprised laugh. It fills the room, causing Asher and Owen to look over. Madeline sends Owen a loving grin and a wink. He looks surprised, which makes me think that they really have been fighting a lot.

"You know," she begins. "You're not as bad as I thought you'd be."

"You've known me for all of two minutes. Just wait. My horns are retractable. You just caught me at a good time."

She giggles. "No, really!" Her face turns serious. "I normally hate the girls Asher brings around."

"Are they anything like them?" I glance towards Viola, who's laughing with Martin's wife. When I passed by them earlier, they were rating people's outfits. No one received more than a two.

"They're worse. Asher's girls are vapid airheads. At least Viola and Marla have two brain cells to rub together."

I nod. I can respect intellect. I just think nicer people deserve it more, though how nice can Madeline and I really be if we're talking about other people behind their backs?

"That bad?" I'm referring to Asher's girls.

"Whatever you're picturing, it's worse."

I think of Nicole. "I've sort of met one. I've never actually talked to her, but I've seen her from afar."

"What's her name?"

"Nicole."

"Oh." She grimaces. "That one stuck around longer than welcome."

I laugh, because Asher was planning on having her be his fake fiancée, but he has me instead. And now that's looking like it's turned out to be a positive thing. To be fair, I actually like Madeline. I'm not even trying to butter her up now. At first, sure, but now I'm just enjoying talking to a woman that I respect.

Madeline gives me a hesitant look.

"Just say whatever you want to say." I playfully roll my eyes and nudge her with my shoulder. "I don't scare easy."

Just ask Asher. He used to be a mafia fixer, and I'm living with him.

"Just curious, and you don't have to answer if you don't want to because it's a really invasive question, but why are you guys getting married so soon?"

I groan internally. I've been dreading this question. I spare a glance at Asher. He's talking to Tim, but when I catch his eyes, he sends me a sweet smile. It feels so... *real*.

This isn't real.

This isn't real.

This isn't real.

But I really want it to be.

Maybe it's because I've never had the privilege of being in a genuine relationship, or maybe it's because I like the person I'm discovering he is. But when I get past his previous mafia ties, everything about him is perfect. Don't get me wrong. I know he has flaws, and he's not the perfect guy, but he's perfect for me.

I remember what I said to Aimee a long time ago.

I want a guy I can talk to comfortably. Someone who makes me feel safe and wanted and beautiful.

The funny thing is I said those words thinking Asher was anything but that. I know better now. There's no one in my life I'm more comfortable talking to than Asher, and after our conversation earlier, I'm starting to think he feels the same way. And while I have Xavier and the other guards, I feel safest whenever Asher is with me. Even when he sends Xavier and my night guard home and it's just us, I feel safe. Earlier, when he told me I look beautiful, I genuinely felt it.

But does he want me?

I'm not sure.

He's too hard to read.

Three out of four isn't so bad, though.

Isn't it?

"Ah," Madeline says, giving me a knowing look when I finally turn back to her.

I've been staring at Asher for a little too long, but what's even more surprising is that he's been staring back, a heated look in his eyes. A look that makes me think he hits four out of four of my criteria.

"Ah?" I ask, trying to recover but still distracted.

"You love him."

My eyes widen, and I almost drop the champagne flute I'm holding. I quickly force myself to recover, hoping my reaction doesn't come off as weird. "Yes, I do. I really, really do," I lie.

And honestly, it's too soon to love him.

I'm *just now* realizing I not only consider him to be a friend but also someone I like romantically, and now she's accusing me of *loving* Asher?

I know for a fact that it isn't true.

But... it can be in the future.

If I open my heart to him.

Madeline grins at me and says, "Come on. Let's go over there and cut the man some slack. Your fiancé has been staring at you since you started talking to me."

My eyes widen. I can't help but ask, "He has?"

Madeline laughs. "Don't act like you're surprised. The two of you are the real deal. You two can't even keep your eyes off of each other.

I'm so jealous of you guys right now. It's been so long since Owen and I have been like that."

Or we're just gifted actors, I think, as Asher gives me a convincingly sweet kiss on the lips when we reach him. I lean my head against his shoulder as I focus on what the people around us are saying.

René, Owen and Martin are speaking French. I glance at Asher. I didn't know that he speaks French, but when I realize what they're saying, I know for certain that he doesn't.

Because if he knew what they've been saying about him, he would be pissed.

René and Martin are shit talking Asher in front of his face, and while Owen looks uneasy, he isn't defending or denying anything they're saying.

I'm pissed the fuck off when I interrupt, "*Chacun voit midi à sa porte.*"

It's a French proverb that literally translates to, "Everyone sees noon at his doorstep." What it means is everyone feels like their opinions are the objective truth, but really, they're clouded by their own personal interests.

I'm essentially saying that René's words are spoken out of self-interest.

I just stabbed a metaphorical knife in René's protruding gut, and I'm about to twist it. "*Je me demande ce que vous voulez gagner en parlant mal de l'amour de ma vie.*"

I wonder what you wish to gain by speaking ill of the love of my life.

There's silence for a moment before René reacts. He takes an aggressive step forward, his fists clenched in fury, but Martin grabs a hold of his arm, and René stops. The look of rage remains, though. Madeline glances uneasily between René, Martin and me before settling her eyes on her husband. Both of Owen's brows are raised.

I can feel the tension radiating off of Asher. I squeeze his hand reassuringly and press an apologetic kiss to it. He wants to know what I said, but I can't tell him in front of everyone. Doing so would just bring more attention to his inability to speak French, something René can continue to use to Asher's disadvantage.

A few more seconds of tense silence pass before Owen barks out a loud laugh. A delighted smile crosses his face. "She speaks French!" he says like it's the most wonderful thing in the world.

And it's starting to feel like it is.

They've been trash talking Asher in front of his face, making him look foolish in the process. They've probably done it before, too. And now, they'll have to think twice before doing it again.

René's eyes narrow in suspicion. He's visibly calmer now. "Yeah... Where did you learn to speak French?"

"I spent the last two years volunteering abroad, mostly in predominantly French speaking countries in Africa. I picked up a thing or two."

"A thing or two," he parrots drily.

I like to think it makes him sound like an idiot.

And because I can never help myself, I say, "Now, if you guys don't mind, Asher and I must leave. He may be too polite to say anything, but I'm uncomfortable being around people who would trash talk my fiancé, let alone do it so brazenly and *distastefully*." I turn to Madeline and hug her. "It was a pleasure to meet you." I genuinely mean it, too. Then, I turn to Owen and say, "Anticipation can be more valuable than knowledge." I gaze pointedly at Madeline's belly. "But neither anticipation nor knowledge are more valuable than love." My words are clear enough to get my message across but cryptic enough that all the other prying ears won't understand what I'm saying.

Owen looks stunned. I probably overstepped my boundaries, but I don't dwell on it as I grab Asher's hand and lead him to the coat check with Xavier and Maybe Dominic trailing closely behind us. Asher is tense as we wait in the long line for our coats.

I turn to face him, slipping both hands under his coat to massage his back. I can feel how coiled his muscles are. When I stand on the tips of my toes and kiss under his jaw, I feel a muscle in it clench.

I don't know what I'm doing.

Standing here with my arms in Asher's coat jacket and my lips brushing against his jaw is intimate. But I've already overstepped my boundaries with Madeline and Owen, so I might as well overstep the ones between me and Asher. I'll relish this moment without caring for the consequences that will inevitably follow it.

I press another kiss to the other side of his jawline, darting the tip of my tongue out to trace it. He isn't pushing me away, but he also isn't returning the attention I'm giving him. I sigh, stepping into his body until we're entirely pressed against one another.

He finally wraps his arms around my waist and pulls me closer. I enjoy being in his arms for a moment before the line moves forward. Instead of turning around to walk normally, I take a step backward, remaining in Asher's hold. He follows, and when he tightens his grip on me, I feel like his lifeline.

This isn't real.
This isn't real.
This isn't real.

I glance up at him. He still won't look at me, and it's bothering me. Ignoring how inappropriate it is to do this in public, at a charity event no less, I stand on my tiptoes again and capture Asher's lower lip in my mouth, tugging on it gently and caressing it with my tongue.

A low growl escapes his mouth before he presses his lips completely against mine in a hard, demanding kiss. We kiss until the tension housed in his shoulders leaves him—holding each other, even when the line moves forward and people end up walking around us and Maybe Dominic has to grab my coat for me.

We only stop when Madeline runs up to us and says my name. I turn to her, knowing that my face must look wild.

"Thank you," she says.

I immediately know what she's referring to. "I didn't overstep?"

"You did what I wish I'd done a long time ago." A dark laugh erupts from her lips, sounding out of place against the sunny backdrop of her chartreuse sundress. "Years ago when I had my first kid. It's senseless, isn't it? All of this over the gender of a kid, something we'll figure out eventually."

I give her a pointed look. We've already been through this. I don't have to repeat myself.

She rolls her eyes at me. "Has anyone ever told you that you're so sassy?"

"No."

Never, I realize.

I've always been a runner. Runners aren't sassy. They're never around to be sassy. They're cowards, like I was before I met Asher. I wonder if this bold and brave person is who I am now that I'm done running. I like it. Sassy Lucy is fearless, standing up for the man she likes one minute and kissing him the next.

"Sorry for interrupting," Madeline says, and it sounds like her goodbye. She glances at Asher and then back to me. She's talking to me when she says, "I'll talk to Owen. I know the vote isn't coming up for a couple of weeks, but I'll talk to him as soon as I get home." She gives me a pointed look. "I like you. I'm not sure about Chatty Cathy over here." Her head nods towards Asher, who remains silent. "But I like you, and I'd hate to see you gone." She grimaces. "Then, I'd have to sit with Viola at all of these shindigs."

She leaves after giving me a side hug, which is awkward because I still haven't let go of Asher.

"You're kind of unexpected," Asher says when she's gone.

I look up at him. "Yeah, I've been thinking the same thing lately."

Then, I grip his tie and tug, pulling his lips down to mine.

CHAPTER TWENTY-FIVE

We don't develop courage by being happy every day. We develop it by surviving difficult times and challenging adversity.
Barbara de Angelis

I let go of him, reluctantly, while he goes to the restroom. I wait in the car with Xavier, unsurprised that Maybe Dominic went with Asher. He is *his* personal guard, after all.

I'm stunned when the car door opens, and I'm abruptly pulled into a hug.

"You're amazing," Asher says. He flusters me again by giving me a kiss as soon as he enters the town car.

It's over before I realize it even happened. I look around, almost expecting there to be cameras in the car. There aren't.

Ashton Kutcher? Where are you?

This is the first time since the night in Rogue's alleyway that he's initiated a kiss without having to. It makes my heart swell.

"What was that for?" I ask, breathlessly.

"That was a thank you." There are conflicting levels of tenderness and rage in his eyes. The anger wins over, and the result looks feral. "I cannot believe they said those things about me, and I just stood there like a goddamn idiot."

"Wait," I begin, disbelief coloring my voice. "You knew what they were saying?"

"Not when they were saying it, but I do now."

"How?"

"Translator app."

"How'd you know how to spell their words?"

"I didn't. I spoke them using the dictation feature."

"All of them?!"

"Yes." At my disbelieving look, he adds, "Photographic memory."

"Wow. No kidding." I hesitate. "What did they say? Before I got there."

His eyes darken. "I'd rather not repeat it."

I understand that. I didn't hear a lot of it, but what I did hear would have pissed anyone off. René called Asher, a man who built a billion dollar empire by the age of 25, one that René's livelihood depends on, an incompetent fool.

Doesn't René know who he's messing with?

Is he so clouded by greed for money and power that he doesn't realize what a worthy opponent Asher is?

I study Asher's expression. He doesn't just look furious. He also looks embarrassed.

I hate the look on his face, so I say, "Kiss me again, please."

It's reckless. Stupid. Emotionally driven.

But I don't regret it, because the embarrassment and anger on his face is replaced with exquisite heat.

And he kisses me again and again until my lips are red and chapped, and we're unaware that we've been sitting in the car, parked in his personal garage for almost an hour, while Xavier and Maybe Dominic sit awkwardly in the front seat, listening to the beautiful symphony that is our lips pressed together.

When we finally make it into our home, I hightail it to the kitchen. It's just us. Asher sent Maybe Dominic and Xavier home as soon as we exited the car. I rummage through the pantry to the musical soundtrack of Asher's laughter. It's at my expense, of course. My stomach has been making obnoxious growling noises since we exited the car. It's why we had to stop making out in the first place.

I open a packet of Famous Amos™ cookies and pour myself a glass of water.

Asher stops laughing. "Don't do it."

I smirk as I dip a cookie into my water in slow motion then pop it into my mouth.

He groans. "That is so gross. I can't believe I kiss that mouth."

My heart skips a beat at the word "kiss" coming out of his lips.

I kiss that mouth.

I kiss that mouth.

I kiss that mouth.

I wish I recorded him saying that, so I could listen to it all day long. I'd set it as my alarm tone if I could.

"I think it's delicious." I take another bite.

He's had several months to get used to my cookie eating habits. It's not my fault that it takes him a long time to adapt to awesomeness.

"That's because this," he points to the cookies and water, "is like dipping cookies into milk for you." He grimaces. "You drink fat free, lactose free milk. That stuff tastes like water."

"No, it does not!" I say, indignantly. To prove my point, I hop off my stool and pour a tall glass of fat free, lactose free milk for him. I hold it out to him. "Try it. I promise it doesn't!"

He eyes it in disgust. "No, thanks."

"Please."

He sighs, but there's a small smile on his face… until he takes a sip of it. His smile morphs into a grimace, but he still downs the whole cup quickly. "It tastes like water, you liar."

I shrug. "No, it doesn't." There's mock outrage in my voice.

But I'm smiling ear to ear, because he drank the whole thing even though he hated it.

He studies my smile. "Lucy?"

"Asher?"

"Thank you."

"You already said that."

"I don't think I can say it enough."

I flush. "It's not that big of a deal."

"Stop. It was."

"Maybe a little."

"Maybe a lot."

"You're welcome."

He's silent for a little while. "It was wrong of me to coerce you into this," he says, shocking the Hell out of me, "but I'm lucky I did. Still, I shouldn't have done it, and if you want to, we can stop this charade. No more favors. No more faking."

I gasp. This is it. My opportunity to get away from this scot free. I should want to take it, but I don't. I'm enjoying myself. I'm in *like* with Asher. I don't know if he feels the same way, but I know he wants me physically. I felt that desire pressed against me in the car when I straddled him during our kisses.

But is that enough?

Can I give up my freedom—my way out—without knowing if he wants me?

I would be stupid to.

But stupid feels so good.

He remains silent for a few more minutes. "Lucy? I'm giving you an out. No strings attached."

"Hold on," I say, pressing my fingers to my temples. The headache is rapidly brewing. "I'm thinking."

I know what Aimee would say. She'd advise me to say no, then run to his bed and demand that he ravage me. Which is why I know I should do the exact opposite of that. After all, Asher is giving me an *out* not an in.

Gosh.

Why do I want his offer to be an in?

An invitation to make this real.

"You can keep the clothes. I can get you your room back in Vaserley Hall. You won't even have to pay for it. I'll still write your letter of recommendation, too, and give you everything we agreed on."

I stare at him. He's really selling this. It's almost as if he wants me gone.

"Do you want me gone?" There's an unsurprising amount of hurt in my voice.

"What? No." He exhales heavily, frowning at my face. "I don't know."

I wasn't expecting that, but at least he's being honest like always. "What does that mean?"

"It means I want you to stay, but I also want you to go."

"Why do you want me to stay?"

"Because I like you."

"Why do you want me to go?"

"Because I like you."

"Oh."

"Oh."

He likes me.

He likes me.

He likes me.

I'm silent for a minute, but my heart is pounding loudly. I can hear the thundering sound in my head. "I have no idea what that means."

"You and me both," he mutters.

Gone is the fixer, the self-assured, dangerous man the world wishes to know, and in his place is the real Asher, vulnerable and honest to a fault. I just didn't realize that this is the real him until now.

"Asher?"

"Lucy?"

"Right now I'm finding it hard to believe you've ever killed anyone."

His eyes widen in surprise, but he remains grimly silent. That's answer enough.

"Why?" I ask.

"You can't un-kn—"

I interrupt firmly, "I can't un-know it. I know. Tell me, please."

"The first time—" I wince. That means there's more than one time. "—I was 18." He sighs at my look of incredulity, which is still there despite the fact that I've heard the rumors and remember what he said at L'Oscurità. "I learned to fight at a UFC gym, and Vincent decided that it was important to continue my training when I moved in with him. Except his training was more intense. I didn't just learn hand to hand combat. I learned tactical training, weapons training, strategizing..."

I try to reconcile this Asher with the 18 year old fighter. I can't.

"I never thought I would have the chance to use it, and Vincent never wanted me to. It was just a precaution. But then one night, there was an attack on our house. It was coordinated, planned to a T, but what they hadn't planned for was me. Vincent kept me out of the spotlight. Only the family elders knew about our bond, so no one knew I was living there.

"The attackers killed all of our guards. They lost some of their own, but they still had sixteen men. They thought they had this in the bag. Sixteen men against the great Vincent Romano. That was a fair fight. They didn't know I existed let alone lived in that house. I took them out before they even got to Vincent's room."

"Sixteen men. You took out sixteen men? How?"

"The first few were slit throats. I got in a few well-placed stabs, too. They didn't even know what was happening. The rest were confused. They thought it was Vincent, though they couldn't be sure in the dark, but suddenly, there was only nine of them left.

"They had their night vision goggles on in the darkness, so their peripherals were useless. I made sure they couldn't see me. And then, I turned on the lights and shot the rest before they could take off their night gear." He makes it sound so easy. "When Vince woke up, it was to a house full of dead bodies."

"He slept through the whole thing?"

Asher nods. "He used to take sleeping pills. It's why he had to have so many guards. Just in case." He gives a sordid laugh. "He doesn't take the pills anymore."

I exhale loudly. "And you killed all of those men?" I study him. "And more," I guess.

He nods, and I wonder why he's trusting me with this. "The Romano elders caught wind of what happened. There were too many dead guards. Vince couldn't cover it up. Plus, the Andretti family was responsible for the hit."

The Andretti are one of the five families. Their territory is in the South of the U.S. The northern area of their territory brushes against the southern area of the Romano's territory, causing a lot of territorial disputes over the years.

Pure hatred crosses Asher's face. "They killed our men and tried to kill Vince. It had to be retaliated. They gave me a team and sent me off to do it."

I gasp. "At 18?"

He nods. "And I was successful, too. It was actually pretty poetic. I never learned who specifically ordered the hit, but I went after someone with the same rank as Vince. I did it the same way they planned Vince's hit, too. In his sleep. An eye for an eye."

I don't want to ask, but I have to know. "Did he have a family?"

"Yes, but I don't kill innocents."

"But you still kill people."

"Killed," he corrects. "I don't do it anymore."

I believe him, but that doesn't change the fact that he used to. It's different suspecting that he's a killer through rumors and internet gossip, but having it confirmed in such detail, straight from his mouth, a mouth that I recently kissed, is sickening.

I run to the bathroom and dry heave into the toilet. I can sense Asher hovering at the door.

"I can't do it. I can't be with you when I know this," I whisper.

I don't know if this is a cheap way to fight the intense feelings he brings out of me or if I'm really this disgusted by him defending someone he loves. But killing people is wrong. I believe this with absolute certainty. Killing the assassins in self-defense is impregnable.

But going into Andretti territory and killing a *capo* and his men?

He didn't have to do that.

That's premeditated.

That's *murder*.

What type of person would I be if I know this and continue to pine after him? If I like him despite all of the blood on his hands?

His words mock me.

You can't un-know it.

I should have listened to him. Maybe then would we have our what-could-have-been back.

His mouth tightens, but he nods. "I'll have Xavier help you with your stuff."

"Wait!" I falter, knowing that what I'm about to say is so stupid, so reckless, and so emotional. I shouldn't, but I continue anyway, "I can't be with you romantically, but I'll still honor our deal."

I don't know why I say it.

Okay, I do.

But it's foolish, and nothing good can come from this. Nevertheless, I can't let down the Asher I've gotten to know over the past few months. The playful guy. The zealous kisser. The man who was strong enough to accept my help just hours ago and thanked me for it with delicious kisses.

How can I deny him my help when he still needs it?

And if I'm being honest, I'm not ready to let him go.

I like him.

My thoughts are so conflicting, I can't figure them out. I like him, but I don't think I can morally be with him if he's killed, but I still am choosing to help him, yet isn't that just as wrong, since it means that I'm helping a kil— I don't know.

I don't know.

I don't know.

I don't know.

I cut my tumultuous thoughts off and wait for him to speak.

He does. "Why would you do this for me?"

I didn't know the answer to that a second ago, but looking at the honesty in his face, I know it now. The truth sticks in my throat, but I force it out.

It tastes bitter. Raw. Exposed.

"I don't run from you."

I can't.

CHAPTER TWENTY-SIX

*Courage is being scared to death
but saddling up anyway.*
John Wayne

We have a hesitant truce. Well, truce isn't the right word for it. That implies that we've been fighting, but we haven't. The only things fighting between us are the could-have-beens and the shouldn't-bes. They're constantly at war with one another, rarely adhering to the truce that we outlined when Asher thankfully agreed to forget my words.

I don't run from you.

It was stupid to say, but he needed to know why I'm staying. At least I was able to give him a half-truth. No way can I tell him that I'm not ready to let him go.

I feel the could-have-beens at night when the space on the bed between Asher and me settles over us like an unnavigable fog. He's been sleeping on the bed with me since the nightmare, and I still can't bring myself to ask him not to.

I feel the shouldn't-bes when he gives me sweet little kisses for the paparazzi. After the charity match, we've been making more public appearances together, but we're still wary about the threat against my life. The police don't have any leads and neither does Asher's private investigator. So, Asher has ramped up security. I have two personal guards at all times, Xavier and whoever is assigned to me that day.

I'm half delusional and half realistic. I know that what we had wasn't actually something deep, but I also know that it could have been if I let it. But as it is, it was just a brief moment when two people that shouldn't be together realized they want to be.

And then it was over.

Quick but painful.

Oh, so painful.

And I find myself pretending that it didn't happen.

Asher, bless his soul, is playing along with me, helping fight the awkwardness together with me by pretending it doesn't exist until it actually doesn't. We pretend there are no reasons for it to be there, and after a few weeks, it isn't. So, in many ways, we're back to how we started before he barged into his room the morning of the polo match and revealed his insecurities about depending on others.

That was the moment I realized that he's vulnerable. The moment that had me questioning the killer side of him. If there isn't that moment, there isn't the next tender moment and the next and the next. So, I fought to forget that memory, and when I finally did, it was easier to forget the kisses that came after

and the intimate handholding

and the conversations we have just by squeezing each other's hands

and the looks we still steal from one another

and how angry it made me when those people spoke poorly of him

and how great it felt to defend a man that I admire deeply

and how time is just a construct when we kiss

and how he knows that I dip my cookies in water

and—

I shake my head.

I'm supposed to be forgetting about him not thinking about him more. Asher is on a flight to Italy. This is a rare break for me. Since Monica's screw up with not knowing about the polo charity match until last minute, Asher has been around more. About a month has passed since the event, and a new school semester has even begun, but until now, Asher hasn't left the state once.

He spends most of his time in the Black Enterprises office building, which still means I have the penthouse to myself for most of the day, but at night, I feel him slither into the bed beside me. It's the bane and highlight of my day all at once.

Even with Asher in the city, we don't talk much. I won't go out of my way to avoid him, though I want to. I refuse to put in the effort to avoid him, because it means acknowledging that there's something between us to avoid. I can't do that yet. Everything is still too raw.

So, I upped my coursework to twenty units and am always losing myself in mindless tasks. When I'm not doing schoolwork, which I still do in the penthouse, I'm physically wearing myself out, whether in the gym or Asher's shooting range.

That's where I am now, taking out my emotions on a piece of paper with the outline of a man on it. The loud bangs of the gunfire are being drowned out by pop music. I have Bluetooth headphones on underneath the soundproof ear muffs I wear when I'm on the range. A playlist I got from Rogue is blaring into my ears, so loud I can't even hear my own thoughts.

I press the button beside me, and the target paper moves forward. Once I unclip it, I study the holes. I've gotten a lot better, but I doubt I'd be able to do this to a person. In a real life situation, I probably won't even have the guts to pull the trigger let alone do so with accuracy.

Not that I need to.

That's what Xavier's for.

Entering the attached armory, I put away the hand gun I'm using and exit into the hallway. Xavier is standing beside the door, his eyes scanning the wide hall. He stays out here whenever I'm messing around in the armory, because he won't be able to hear any threats beyond the armory's soundproof walls.

If there is a threat, he presses a button on the door, and an alarm will sound off in the range and armory, which can only be entered through the range. When that happens, I'm supposed to enter the armory, which doubles as a panic room. There, I'm to press a sequence of numbers, and the doors will lock in a way that can only be opened from the inside.

Monitors of what's happening outside will slide down from the ceiling. They'll be high definition, live, and equipped with audio. Protocol also has me putting on full body bulletproof gear that covers my arms and legs and calling the police if I don't hear from Asher within fifteen minutes.

I've said it before, and I'll say it again: the security is overkill.

Even after the two shootings, I still think this.

When he sees me, I hand Xavier the target paper I've annihilated. He grins and says something that looks like, "Better," but I have my headphones on still and can't hear a thing. I tell him I'm going to take a bath, so he stays outside the bedroom door when I enter the room.

I strip my clothes off, leaving a trail of fabric on the floor until I'm completely naked. I'll clean it up later, before Asher returns. I'm dancing to the beat of the music, enjoying the freedom of having this place to myself again, when I enter the bathroom and see Asher.

I freeze. He's in the shower, completely bare. He has a hand on the marbled wall and the other on his hardened cock. With his eyes closed and his head under the running water, he hasn't spotted me yet, so I don't leave.

If you ever happen upon someone like Asher stroking himself as water drips down his muscular chest... well, you'd be lying to yourself if you say you wouldn't stop to stare.

I stand, rooted to the floor, as his hand strokes up and down the length of his enlarged cock. I feel myself gasp, but I don't hear it past the sound of the music coming from my headphones. Asher stills, his hand stopping midway up his cock, and lifts his head up.

When his eyes lock on mine, I thought he'd stop, but he doesn't.

He takes in my naked form, his eyes journeying up and down the length of me, gleaming in lust and appreciation. Then, he continues to stroke himself while looking at my body. His lips part, and I think a groan comes out of them, but I can't hear.

And Holy Hell, do I want to hear.

I rip the headphones out of my ears, tossing them carelessly onto the floor with the rest of my dignity. The magnetic pull that's always existed between us tugs me until I'm right in front of the shower, and the glass door is the only thing that separates us.

When I place one hand on the glass, his does the same, right over mine, shifting himself so he's face to face with me. I can open the door, and I'll be in there with him in a second. This isn't like that first night when we didn't know each other. He knows me, and I know him. He won't leave me this time.

But I can't.

I'm a coward.

Or maybe I'm brave?

I don't know.

But I'm not brave enough to leave him, and I'm too cowardly to join him.

Instead, I'm frozen in lust, watching him stroke his cock slowly. My mouth waters at the sight of a vein, running down his generous length. His clenched fist moves slowly up, stopping at the head of his cock and twisting before moving back down to the base.

Water from the shower head descends down his face, past his eyes, causing them to close. When he opens them, he catches sight of my fingers, which have dipped past the slickness of my slit and into my aching pussy. I finger myself, pumping two digits into my wetness and using the palm of my hand to ease my throbbing clit.

His eyes connect with mine, and when he speaks, it comes out as a growl. "Come for me, Lucy. Come *with* me."

My body succumbs to his demand immediately, submitting to the pleasure, submitting to him. Not even a second after, he joins me, and my eyes can barely stay open through the pleasure, but I force them open, refusing to miss the sight of him coming for me. Coming *with* me.

When we're done, panting and just barely satiated, our hands are still pressed against one another, separated by the glass door. It's clear and thin, but it might as well be The Great Wall.

I'm swimming on the roof when I realize that Xavier's not with me. I glance around, a frown tugging on my lips when I don't see him anywhere, and exit the pool. Water drips down my bikini clad body, but I wipe myself off with a plush towel.

After Caroline got shot and we decided on keeping me on lockdown at the penthouse again, Asher had the roof converted into a pool deck. Instead of railings or a waist-high wall to prevent me from falling off the edge of the tower, he had bulletproof glass installed all around the edges of the roof. It's clear, fifteen feet high, and can withstand repeated fire from any sniper's rifle.

The whole set up was installed at an impossible speed, and it was all done for me.

By Asher.

Who likes me.

Who came in front of me.

Who came *with* me.

Who I'm so confused about.

Who I realize is right in front of me.

"Where's Xavier?" I ask, breaking the silence between us.

It's been a week since I watched Asher come. Since I came with him. And I've been doing a great job of avoiding him. Whenever he's home, I lock myself in the theater room and fall asleep on one of the comfy seats. I don't even return to the bedroom until after he's left for work the next morning.

"I sent him home for the day."

I eye him warily. If he sent Xavier home for the day, it means he's planning on guarding me himself until the night shift comes. Or maybe even past then.

"You've been avoiding me," he says.

"I have."

He nods, accepting my truth with little fanfare. "Have dinner with me tonight."

"We're leaving the penthouse?"

We haven't been seen in public in a while. Maybe he has an event I need to be seen at?

"No, I'll cook for you."

"You'll cook for me?"

The image of Asher naked underneath an apron crosses my mind, no doubt a side effect of having seen him come. I flush, pushing the notion out of my head. I can't think about that.

"Yes, I'll make your favorite dish."

"Which is?"

I have a lot of favorite dishes. *Food* is my favorite dish. And it can't be narrowed down to one item.

"*Lomo saltado.*"

Oh. He's right. That *is* my absolute favorite.

"You'll make me *lomo saltado*?"

Do I sound as stupid as I think I sound repeating all his words?

I can't help my dubiousness, though. We haven't spoken in a week, and he wants to have dinner with me and make me my favorite food? And it's *lomo saltado*. It's an art form trying to get French fries crispy while sautéing them in a sauce. *I* can't even do it, and I'm a pretty darn talented home cook, especially now, after hours of practice on the Lucy's Kitchen app on my VR console.

"Yes. Now, if you're done playing Repeat After Me, I have a dress I'd like you to wear."

He pulls a garment bag off of one of the lounge chairs and hands it to me. The bag is black, the same color of the chair, so I didn't even notice it there. I don't open it.

"So, you're making dinner for me, and you have a dress for me to wear, even though we're eating at home… Asher, what is this?"

"It's a date." He says it so casually, so matter-of-factly, but it still flusters me.

A date?

"I told you I can't be with you romantically."

"You also came with your pussy wrapped around your fingers while you watched me stroke my cock. A cock that got hard thinking about your face, your body. A cock that came at the sight of you finger fucking your own pussy."

I shiver at the memories his brash words conjure. "So?"

"So, it changes things."

"And if we came together in the alleyway outside of Rogue, would that have changed things, too? Would I have gotten a date, too?"

I wouldn't have. We both know that. But I need him to say it. To say anything I won't like. I'm stalling, because I want to let him cook for me, to go on this date with him. But I'm afraid of what it'll mean about me if I do.

He's a killer.

He's killed a lot of people.

Remember that, Lucy.

"If you came as beautifully as you did a week ago, yes, that would have changed things."

The smile slips past my lips before I can trample it like the traitor it is. "You're a liar."

"So are you, Lucy. You lied when you said you can't be with me romantically. You can, but you're scared."

"Do you blame me?"

"Depends on what you're scared of."

"You tell me, since you seem to know all the answers," I mutter, crossing my arms bitterly.

He takes a step closer, causing me to tug the towel tighter around my chest. "You're afraid of my reputation. You're afraid of the mobster side of me, yet you haven't seen me do anything related to it. It's the predator that's been hiding you from the world that you should be afraid of. That's the man that went after the Andretti family, a warning for them to think twice before they go after his family again. That's the man that will do *anything* to protect the ones he loves."

I stagger backward, disbelief written all over my face. "You love me?"

"No," he says, dismissing the thought quickly. "But I *will*. That's where this is going. Don't you see that? I care about you, Lucy. We already care about each other so much. If we didn't, I wouldn't have jumped in front of a bullet for you, and you wouldn't have defended me at the polo match. But I did, and you did. Don't you see what that means?"

I do.

It means he's right. I care about him, and he cares about me. I know this. I've known this for a while now... but I'm still fighting with his past.

With the disturbing body count he's left in his wake.

At my look, he says vehemently, "I didn't kill those men for the Romano family, Lucy. I killed those men for *Vince*. Because he took me in. Because he gave me a home. Because he may as well be my dad. Because I love him, and he loves me. I did it for him, and I would do it for you, too. I don't regret it. Even if it means I'll never be the man you give yourself to, I'll always do anything to protect you, and I'll always do anything to protect my family."

I take in the earnest expression on his face, etching the way he just bared his soul to me in my mind, hoping that I'll never forget his words.

Even if it means I'll never be the man you give yourself to, I'll always do anything to protect you...

I'll always do anything to protect you.

I'll always do anything to protect you.

I'll always do anything to protect you.

It feels too soon to say something of that magnitude, but it also feels right. Like no other declaration can be made for what we have than "always." And that scares me, but I need to fight past that fear, because no matter what, I won't run from Asher.

But that doesn't mean we can't slow it down.

"If we do this," I begin, "we have to take it slowly."

A smile tugs on Asher's lips, and I know why it's there. We hooked up just after meeting, and we moved in together after barely knowing each other. We also recently came together. The time for slow has long passed.

But I don't mean physically.

I can handle that.

I mean emotionally. Because if we keep moving at this pace, my like will turn into love, and I won't be ready for it. And I need to be ready for this, for him. This feels too real and too special to mess up.

"We can do slow," Asher agrees, causing me to sag in relief. He leans in to kiss me, and I let him brush his lips against mine. When I try to tug him closer, he backs away from me and says with a smirk, "Slow enough for you?"

"I hate you."

He laughs and heads to the door. Over his back, he calls out, "Dinner. One hour. Wear the dress. I had Tommy sew in a bulletproof lining for you."

When he's gone, I open the garment bag, wondering what he picked out for me.

It's *the* dress.

My little black dress.

The one I bought in Morocco. The one I wore to Rogue. The one I thought Tommy donated.

Asher saved it for me.

CHAPTER TWENTY-SEVEN

Efforts and courage are not enough without purpose and direction.
John F. Kennedy

"I still **can't** believe you like me," I say, cringing as soon as the words escape my lips.

Asher studies me, a hint of a smirk gracing his features. "Why else do you think I asked you to be my fiancée?"

"You had no other choice!"

"I always have a choice."

"Well, you *chose* to ask Nicole, too."

"*She* asked me."

"Oh."

"Oh," he mocks, but it's playful.

I kick him under the table, but he traps my leg in between his and reaches down to pull it onto his lap. I'm glad we're home and not at a public restaurant, though I don't think that would stop Asher from touching me like this.

"Dance with me," Asher commands softly, releasing my leg.

"There's no music."

"Music!" Asher commands to the room, and a soft melody begins to play.

I let him pull me into his arms, a few feet away from the dining room, where we just had dinner. I'm still able to move lithely, though I'm stuffed from his *lomo saltado*, which was delicious and perfectly cooked. After a few minutes of swaying loosely in his arms, Asher pulls me dangerously closer. I tilt my head up, so my face won't be smashed against his collarbone.

He's quiet, but I hear him say, "You're clean."

I'm confused. "Sexually?" I blurt out, mortified by my lack of tact.

He laughs, and I feel it vibrate across his chest. And what a chest it is. I find myself pressing closer to him, so I can count how many ab packs he has across his stomach. I've done this before, but I will never get enough of it

"Your background, Lucy. Your background is clean. You intrigued me, and you had a clean background, so I picked you. I won't lie and tell you I wanted to be with you back then, but I did like what I saw."

"Oh." I breathe out sharply and back up slightly.

I'm teetering on the edge of uncertainty, not knowing whether or not I should feel guilty about my past. He thinks I have a clean background, but he doesn't know about Steve. It's not like I did anything wrong, but it *is* a lot of baggage. Baggage that I haven't mentioned once.

What happens if he asks me to go to Los Angeles for his hotel's grand opening, and I say no? Because no way will I be able to be in the same state as Steve. Not happening. The thought causes my legs to tremble, and Asher picks up on it.

"Are you thinking of running right now? Am I moving too fast?" he asks.

I know it's wrong to deceive him, but I still nod. I can't tell him about Steve now. Too much time has passed, and I'm trapped by my decision.

He looks me straight in the eyes as he says, "I'll slow down. But whenever you think about running, please, remember that you didn't run from me when I was the big bad wolf. You're braver than you think you are."

My face flushes red, and I mumble, "You still are the big, bad wolf."

"Oh, Lucy." He sighs. "Never to you. Never to you."

True to his word, Asher slowed down. I almost wish I hadn't nodded when he asked if he was moving too fast. That I would have told him the truth instead. But I didn't, and now I'm suffering the consequences.

It's been two days, and the most action I've gotten from him are a few closed mouth kisses on the lips. I've been going crazy, trying to turn every kiss into a make out session that I hope will turn into sex. But what I lack in willpower, he possesses in spades. And now, I'm in desperate need of a release, however I can get it.

I eye the clock on the nightstand, noting that Asher should be home soon. I reach down between my legs, running my finger down my slit anyways. I don't care. I almost hope he'll catch me. I dip a finger into myself, pumping slowly until my wetness spreads all over my walls. I drag my moist finger back out and circle my clit with it before plunging back into myself.

It's not enough. I grab a random pillow and tuck it between my thighs, pressing myself into it. I rock against the plush pillow until I can feel the delicious friction against my clit. One of my fingers pinches a nipple, and the other hand massages a breast. I can feel my wetness, dripping out of me and onto the pillow, but I don't care.

I'm panting, so close to ecstasy, when I hear Asher outside. He's greeting my night guard, and I know it's just a matter of time before he enters the room. I quickly grab the pillow from between my legs and throw it to the top of the bed before shuffling under the covers.

When he enters the room, I'm casually tossing birds at pigs on my iPhone.

"Don't you knock?" I ask, grateful that I'm able to keep my breathing steady.

"It's my room."

"Oh. Right."

He winks at me. "You know who should knock?"

"Monica."

He laughs as he enters the bathroom to take a shower. I relax my body, patting myself on the back for playing it cool. But when he finishes his shower and gets into bed, his head connects with the pillow I was grinding against, the one I almost came on, and he takes a deep breath.

His eyes connect with mine, the lust clearly there, but then he closes them before anything happens.

Before he touches me.

And all I can think is I don't want to go slow anymore.

CHAPTER TWENTY-EIGHT

It is only through labor and painful effort,
by grim energy and resolute courage
that we move on to better things.
Theodore Roosevelt

*A*sher's gone when I wake up the next morning, but there's a single black rose on the bedside table, accompanied by a note. My fingers brush lightly against the black rose, amazed by the deep ebony color. I've never seen a black rose before now, and it's beautiful.

It's sitting in a clear vase filled with a black liquid, probably water mixed with black dye to turn the white rose black. I pull the note out from beneath the vase gently, being careful not to tear it. It's typed on a fancy black card stock, and the text is in a pretty, bold white font that stands out against the black.

LOOKING FORWARD TO SEEING YOU TONIGHT.

I smile brightly. The note is unsigned, but it's safe to assume that it's from Asher. I mean, we see each other every night, but tonight, we'll both be dressed to impress at a Black Enterprises event. He may be looking forward to seeing me, but I'm also looking forward to seeing him, too. I've already caught a peek at the tux he set aside for tonight, and my mouth waters at the thought of him in it.

Before I move to get ready, I set the black rose carefully down in the vase. A few drops of the black water hits the table, and when I go to wipe it off with my finger, the dye smudges onto my hands. I glance down at my palms, staring at the inky blackness.

It looks ominous against my pale skin.

𝒜sher sends me a concerned glance when he hears my feet tapping anxiously against the ballroom floor.

Tap.

Tap.

Tap.

Tap. Tap. Tap.

I'm helpless to stop it. The nerves have invaded my body, and I'm no longer in control of my actions.

"It'll be okay," Asher whispers gently into my ear.

I nod and pull myself together, because I have to.

Asher and I are at Il Nero, one of his newest hotels in New York, where a Black Enterprises employee event is being held. According to him, Black Enterprises holds these shindigs four times a year to celebrate the end of each quarter. Normally, I'd have nerves, sure, but this isn't normal.

My stomach is churning like it's been hit by an F5 tornado, and I feel like I'm about to vomit. On one hand, the entire board and CEO of IllumaGen are here, and Asher is about to introduce me to them. On the other hand, this is the last day of the business quarter. That means that Asher's vote before the Black Enterprises board is set for a week from now, and this is the last day we have to impress them.

And I just happened to stick my nose so far into Owen and Madeline's business last time I saw them, I can still smell the stench. I hope Madeline made good on her word and talked to Owen on behalf of Asher. I guess I'll find out soon enough, because they're both standing with the men from IllumaGen.

Oh, and *what's up with that?*

Why do all these companies only put men in positions of power? Fuck that.

When she sees me, Madeline's eyes light up, and I'm immediately relieved. I allow some of my stress to escape, glad that at least one of my concerns is partially eased.

"Lucy!" Madeline hobbles over to me, her heavily pregnant belly preventing her from moving any faster. "I'm so glad you're here!"

My arms wrap around her waist in an awkward embrace given the growing thing in her. "So you don't hate me?"

She rolls her eyes and says, "How can I hate you when we've been having sex, like, twice a day?! Seriously. I thank you. Owen thanks you. My vagina thanks you."

I curtsy dramatically in my evening gown, causing the high slit to expose even more skin. Madeline shakes her head in mocking disapproval when Asher eyes the visible flesh, sending a jolt of lust soaring through my blood.

It's only been a few days since my dinner date with Asher and about a week and a half since I walked in on Asher showering, but I can still remember how long and thick he was in the palm of his hands, how great it felt to come undone before him. For the sake of taking things slowly, we've been skirting around what happened, and I'm glad for it... because if he ever brings it up, I won't be able to hold myself back.

"You two are like a bunch of horny teenagers." Madeline tuts at us and shakes her head, though her lips are turned up in a smile.

I hip check her. "Says the woman with a vagina that thanks me."

We're laughing when Owen approaches us, a relaxed smile on his face. He looks a lot friendlier than the last time we met, so maybe he actually isn't mad at me. "You look lovely, Lucy." He kisses my cheek then shakes Asher's hands. "Asher."

The four of us head toward the IllumaGen board, where I'm introduced to the C-level officers of the company and a few key shareholders. After the introductions are done, they immediately cut back to their conversation. I frown as they only work to engage Owen and Asher into the discussion, leaving Madeline and I to stand there as mere accessories.

"I propose cutting the research lab in transposable elements. It's a drain on our resources with little to no gain," says the CEO.

He's met with nods from the rest of his board.

Asher turns to me. "What do you think, Lucy?"

My eyes widen, alarmed by the sudden attention on me. I feel like the kid that's been called on in class because she's not paying attention. But when I look at Asher, I see that he's genuinely curious. He wants my opinion on this.

"I-I think it would be foolish to cut off TE research."

Well, from a limited business standpoint, I suppose I understand why the CEO would suggest this without truly understanding TEs. TE research is still rudimentary, having only been discovered in the 80s. But once more discoveries are made, the possibilities are endless.

I continue, "Hemophilia A and B, predisposition to cancer, severe combined immunodeficiency, and porphyria are just some of the diseases TEs are known to cause. Research in TEs will be vital to curing these diseases."

When I look at the IllumaGen board, I realize that I'm not

convincing them. They make money off of temporary cures, drugs that need to be used over and over again. I need to speak to Illuma-Gen's biggest moneymaker—antibiotics.

Holding back a grimace, I say, "Already, we know that transposons in bacteria often carry a gene for antibiotic resistance. Imagine if we can figure out a way to prevent these transposons from transposing."

"Antibiotics would be able to be used more often, resulting in an increase in sales for us," the COO finishes for me.

I hate that these men see groundbreaking, potentially lifesaving research as an avenue for profit, but if it means the research will continue, I can't complain. Science saves lives, but there's no science without money. It's irritating, but there's a reason grant writing is a job.

The CEO studies me for a moment, an odd look on his face, before he says, "So, we'll have to make budget cuts elsewhere."

"Not necessarily," I say, earning his interest. "From what I'm hearing, you treat each field of research as a separate division, but if you treat them as interdisciplinary"—I think of Dr. Dennis Slamon, who developed the breast cancer drug Herceptin on the back of birth control research— "you'll be able to cut out a lot of iterative work. Less work, less chemicals, and less time equals—"

"Money saved," interrupts the CFO.

I nod. "Exactly."

When the conversation continues, Madeline leans into my ear and whispers, "That was amazing!" At my furrowed brows, she explains, "These guys are misogynistic assholes. They've never once talked to me other than to say hi. It's like my opinion doesn't matter, never mind the fact that I graduated Summa Cum Laude at Wharton while their CFO only graduated Cum Laude."

I squeeze her hand sympathetically and nod, taking the opportunity to lean into Asher's side. Business and STEM fields are both male dominated fields, but combine the two, and you've got guys like these—assholes that don't even stop to consider if a woman's mind has merit. I've seen it before, and I'll see it again.

Asher is surrounded by these type of men through work, yet he's always been respectful to me. He asked for my opinion, and he's always valued what I have to say.

How am I just realizing how amazing Asher is? Or have I just been in denial?

CHAPTER TWENTY-NINE

*Courage and perseverance have a
magical talisman, before which difficulties
disappear and obstacles vanish into air.*
John Quincy Adams

***I**t's nearing dinner* time when Asher, Owen, Madeline, and I approach the head table. It's raised above all of the others, like it's meant for royalty. And I suppose, in this company, the board and CEO are.

We take our assigned seats, and when we settle down, I notice the seat beside René is empty. I haven't seen Viola around, but I just assumed that she was off somewhere, rating poor girls on their appearances.

One look at René and my stomach is in knots. He has an eager look on his face, which can't mean anything good is coming. I look away immediately, but he speaks up.

"Lucy, what a wonderful surprise to see you here."

"Is it?" Asher asks, a warning in his voice. "This is a company event, and we always bring our spouses to events. Lucy will soon be my wife. Her presence shouldn't be a surprise to any of us." He narrows his eyes. "But I see your wife isn't here. Having trouble at home, René?"

"Not at all." René's grin spreads wider, his face the unsettling picture of anticipation. "She was feeling under the weather, but luckily, another friend of mine happens to be in town. So, I decided to invite him instead."

Asher's eyes are narrowed in suspicion. "Anyone we know?"

René's grin is so wide right now that it has to be hurting his face.

"I don't think you two have had the pleasure of meeting, but your dear Lucy should know him well."

I freeze.

It's someone I know?

I don't really know anyone.

Aimee? Tommy? Eduardo? Minka? Her lackeys?

They all already live "in town," and no one from my past has the money to vacation in New York City. So, who else can it be? Asher's hand grips mine under the table, but I can't reassure him. Or is he reassuring me? I don't know. I don't know anything right now. I have no idea who René might have brought.

My mind briefly considers Steve before I dismiss the ridiculous notion. No one knows about him, and I've changed my name. There's no way René could've found him.

But I have a sinking feeling about this, even as I open my mouth and casually say, "Oh? What's this person's name?"

"Now that would ruin the surprise, wouldn't it?"

And for the next fifteen minutes, René has that stupid look plastered all over his face. Even Martin, who is to René what Nella is to Minka, looks uneasy.

"There you are!" René says jovially, just as I'm shoveling lobster bisque into my mouth.

I nearly choke, knowing this has to be his secret guest, but I force myself to swallow. When I lift my head to see who it is, I almost choke again.

Because it's *Steve*.

I distantly hear René introduce him to the other executives and their wives, but I'm not paying attention. Asher swings his head to face me, the concern evident, and I can't give him the reassurance he needs.

He clearly doesn't know who this is.

No one does, except René, who's swiveling his head between me and Steve like the only thing that would make this better is a bag of buttery popcorn to contribute to his gut.

My first instinct is to run. To put as much distance between Steve and me as I can.

But then I remember Asher's words.

Whenever you think about running, please, remember that you didn't run from me when I was the big bad wolf. You're braver than you think you are.

Is he right?

Am I brave?

Sitting here, trembling and completely silent, I certainly don't feel brave.

Asher leans closer to me, his breath light against my ear, and says, "What's wrong?"

I can't answer him. I can't even appreciate his proximity. I'm shaking. I've been underplaying my history with Steve in my own mind, mentally denying that I have been the victim of anyone let alone a low life like Steve.

I wore the clothes he had given me like a badge of survival only I recognized, but one look at Steve, and I know that I'm wrong. I haven't surviv*ed* anything. I'm *still* trying to survive. It's an ongoing process that is quickly approaching its end.

I can wear the clothes and pretend I'm okay. I can brush off a nightmare and say it's not a big deal. I can convince myself that I'm over it, that I don't wonder if anything more happened that night and other nights. If he's touched me before.

But I'd be lying to myself.

Those are all lies I've compounded in my head. I haven't healed. Instead, I ran.

When I catch sight of Asher, who is leaning forward, a scowl on his lips, I know I can't run any more. He doesn't know who Steve is, but he knows I'm scared and doesn't like it. I can see that he's about to do something about this even if he's in front of Black Enterprises' board, and while I want to let him, I can't allow Asher to sacrifice his company for me.

Not when there's an alternative.

Not when I can be the person he believes I am.

It's time to face my past.

My hand automatically reaches for Asher's knee, squeezing it until he stills.

I inventory the situation, knowing I need to do so as quickly as possible. Too much time has already passed since Steve arrived, and he's standing there awkwardly, his fanatical eyes on me. Clearly, this is the reaction René expected, because he's currently leaning back in his seat, allowing the situation to run its course.

As I consider my options, I realize why René brought Steve here. If he knows about Steve, he knows what happened. He knows that I ran. He thinks I'll run again, and if I run, there goes Asher's stability.

It's a gamble on René's part, and he looks so certain that I'm not sure if he realizes that he's gambling.

He doesn't know me well enough to know I'll run. He's just assuming it based on my past decisions, but I'm not that girl anymore. I have a future that I refuse to part with. I have Aimee and Tommy and Xavier and even Eduardo.

I also have Asher.

So, I grip Asher's hand for strength and say to René, "What is this?"

Now that I'm no longer shaking, Asher straightens himself and his hand lands on my thigh. He squeezes it. It may be a warning or it may be a question. Either way, I ignore it. I need to do this. René wanted to catch me off guard, and it worked. But I'm not about to let him win.

I want to ruin him.

He let my demons back into my life, and he did it to hurt Asher.

That's not something I'll ever let him get away with.

"What do you mean?" René is grinning widely now. "Is there a problem? I thought you'd be happy to see your dad. I mean, you were an orphan, and this kind man took you in. You could at least be a little more grateful."

Beside him, Steve nods enthusiastically, but I can't stomach the sight of him, so I quickly avert my eyes. That only makes René smile wider. He thinks he's winning.

I narrow my eyes, but keep my voice level. It takes a lot of effort, but I manage. "Steve is not my dad. He fostered me for two years before my social worker removed me from his home. The government even allowed me to change my name."

There's no better way to take René down than with the truth, even if I have to sacrifice my heart, my dignity and my pride in exchange.

I'm satisfied when René begins to pale. He expected me to be weak, to cower in the face of a man that I allowed to hurt me. But I'm done being weak. Sitting next to me is one of the strongest men I know. I feel empowered by the knowledge that, in the short time I've known him, I've stood up to him on multiple occasions and even stood up *for* him on one.

So, I persist. "But if you were able to track Steve down, then you know what happened when I was just seventeen years old."

There are some gasps around the table from those who have picked up on my insinuation, but I ignore them. I even ignore how tense Asher has gotten beside me.

I lean forward and go in for the kill. "What kind of man brings a pedophile and possible rapist to a party when he knows the victim will be in attendance?"

Then, I take a moment to accept what just happened. I just sacrificed my secrets, my sanity, and my dignity for Asher. I want to say it was for me, but I know it wasn't. I didn't have to do this. I could have fled, like I'm so damn good at. I could have done this privately.

But instead, I did this here, in front of his board, so they can see who René is. So, come next week, they will choose Asher's side. I aired my dirty secrets and made myself vulnerable. For Asher. And I would do it again in a heartbeat.

Amidst the ensuing silence, I make a show of eyeing René up and down, scrutinizing him carefully for theatrical emphasis. "What kind of man are you, René? Because you certainly don't seem like one fit to sit on the board." I turn to the men at the table and ask, "What do you guys think?"

I'm putting them on the spot. Those in René's corner don't have time to come up with excuses for him. And if they disagree now, there will be a stronger rift within the board, and they'd be on the losing side. I see the defeat in Martin and his wife's faces, and it almost makes sitting in Steve's presence worth it.

Before they can speak, René, white-faced and fury-eyed, turns to his coworkers and says, "She's lying."

His words reek of desperation. He can't refute any of my claims. I have the truth on my side. But he doesn't care, because if he doesn't say something now, he'll be over. Hell, his career at Black Enterprises is already over. But he's not the type to go down without a fight.

It turns out that neither am I.

I admit aloud for the first time since I told my social worker, "Steve targeted me. I was underage at the time. That's no lie."

From the seat beside me, Madeline gasps, her hand reaching for my hand that's on her side. I let her, but I do it to make her feel better, not because I need her comfort. I don't need it when I have Asher. When I have myself.

René jerks forward. His mouth opens and closes and opens and closes. He's at a loss for words, so I know he's still flustered. But it also means he's still trying to find a way out of this. And I won't let him. The only way to show the board that I'm telling the truth is another confirmation straight from the other source.

I finally turn to Steve, whose eyes are still riveted by me. "My last night living with you... was that the only time you snuck into my room?"

It's a loaded question, and only the two of us know what I'm really asking—did you *just* touch yourself? Or did you touch me, too?

I make sure we're making eye contact, because I have to see if he's telling the truth. I have to look him in the eyes for this.

His cheeks are red, and his eyes look warily around the table at everyone else but me, until they finally return to me. "That was the only time."

Oh, God.

I hear a whimper, and I think it's mine, but I'm too busy absorbing everything to care.

Relief like I've never known floods through me. I sag in my chair, wondering how to process this, whether or not I should believe him. Maybe it's wishful thinking, but for some reason, I do.

And then, I see a blur of movement, and in front of his whole company, the board, and IllumaGen's board, Asher punches Steve across the face, sending him flying onto the floor.

CHAPTER THIRTY

Wisdom, compassion, and courage are the three universally recognized moral qualities of men.
Contucius

The entire ballroom is eerily silent. When I look on the floor, I see Steve, sprawled out on the dark hardwood planks with his eyes cemented shut.

Holy shit.

Asher knocked him out.

When I finally manage to glance at Asher, he's shaking. I don't know if it's from rage or not, but it's hitting me harder than seeing Steve again.

A screech of a chair is the first sound to break the silence, and everyone turns to watch as René hauls himself out of his chair and heads my way. Asher immediately springs into action and cuts him off before he reaches me, but René still manages to lean deeply to the right and jab a finger in my direction.

"You," he seethes. "You ruined everything."

I'm not sure why he's complimenting me like that, but I am sure that his behavior is extremely unprofessional and public, for his whole company to see.

But then again, so was Asher's.

Oh, God.

The vote.

I don't believe René will still be with Black Enterprises after tonight, but I also don't know if Asher will either. He punched a guy in front of his company's board, his employees, and the IllumaGen board. That's not something a CEO fit to lead a billion dollar company does. If it happened any other way, this would certainly have been the victory René was looking for—Asher, acting violently, fueling the mafia rumors.

But it didn't happen another way.

It happened for me.

And Asher might suffer for it.

It dawns on me what a sacrifice this is. I may have pushed aside my dignity and confronted my demons for Asher, but I didn't lose anything that I can't gain back. Asher, on the other hand, risked his company for me. A company he loves enough to ask a complete stranger to marry him. He jeopardized that for *me*.

You don't do something that big for a woman you like. You do that for a woman you *love*.

Oh, my God.

I think Asher loves me.

My hand instinctively reaches for his back. He's still standing in front of me, shielding me from René, but at my touch, he leans back, pressing himself into my hand. The movement is so natural, I feel it inside of me, like he's an extension of myself.

With my hand still on his back, I approach his side, so we're standing next to each other.

I'm staring René straight in the eye when I say, "I'll be getting a restraining order."

I know nothing about law, so I don't know if I have any legal grounds for it, but it felt like the right thing to say. Like one final jab to René in front of everyone. And then I take Asher's hand and leave, nodding in goodbye to everyone else at the table.

I can feel thousands of eyes on us until we're out of the room. As soon as we're in the hallway, Xavier and Dominic appear out of nowhere. They walk us to the car, where Asher and I sit in silence until we're back in the penthouse.

It isn't until we're alone in his room that Asher finally speaks.

"Why isn't he in jail?"

"There was never any hard evidence. It was my word against his. I asked my social worker to help me leave, and she did."

"I'll take care of Steve."

"Okay."

I don't really care anymore. I've risen above the pain and uncertainty Steve has caused, and I finally feel like I'm healing. But it'll be nice to know that Steve will be taken care of and can't hurt anyone else.

"Legally," I add, just in case.

Asher smothers his small smile with a kiss to my forehead.

I let us simmer in silence for a moment before I say, "You love me."

His eyes widen, but he doesn't deny it.

So, I ask, "Why?"

When he takes a seat on the bed and gestures for me to join him, I do.

"Remember when I drove you home for the first time?" After I nod, he continues, "You were so scared of me, yet you managed to demand something in return for this arrangement. I couldn't believe it."

"And you loved me then?" I ask, dubiously.

He shakes his head. "No, but I'd be lying if I say I didn't like what I saw. I started paying better attention to you after that, noticing your random bouts of bravery. Despite your fears, and there are a lot of them,"—I snort—"you're able to overcome everything. I've never seen true courage like that before.

"Don't get me wrong. I've seen Romano soldiers go into battle knowing they're as good as dead, but those men aren't afraid. They don't have to overcome their fears in order to get the job done. But you have to, and it's beautiful.

"And when you stuck up for me, you didn't even have to stop and consider it. You just acted. There was something so pure about your instinct to protect me that I couldn't help but give you a piece of my heart that day. After that, I was pretty much a goner. I fell in love with your compassion and your courage and your strength and yo—"

I cut him off with a kiss, pressing my lips against his with surprising urgency. When I pull back and say, "I don't want to go slow anymore," I might as well have said, "I love you."

Because I do.

My God, I really do.

Asher is looking at me like he's about to demand everything of me. And right now, I'd do just about anything he asks of me if it means he'll push me onto the bed and press his lips against mine. Break my dry spell. Bare himself to me.

"Kneel," he says, his demanding voice causing my nipples to pucker under my shirt.

"Okay, Mr. Grey," I say, teasing him, but I do so anyway.

"Don't. I don't do romance novels," he replies, and I know I'm about to be fucked.

Roughly. Passionately. Brutally.

The warning is loud and clear, but I know better. Asher may not "do" romance novels, but he *is* a romance novel.

I wink at him, glad to push aside the stress of the evening with playfulness, if only just for a moment. "But you would for me."

He doesn't deny it. "Good thing you'd never ask. For me."

And then he stands up, my face eye level with his thighs, and walks around me, so he's facing my back. I shiver as he trails a lone finger from my shoulder to my neck and down my spine. When he reaches the zipper of my evening gown, he tugs it downward and slides the straps of my dress off of my shoulders. The fabric slides off me, pooling around my knees in a circle of red, baring me to him completely.

He groans in appreciation when he sees that I'm not wearing a bra nor panties. The sound goes straight to my clit, and I jerk forward, humping the empty air desperately. He chuckles lightly at my eagerness and walks around me until I'm facing him.

I watch intently as he strips the jacket of his tuxedo off and begins removing his button down, each pop of a button revealing smooth, tan skin. When he slides the shirt off his shoulders, letting it fall to the floor, I admire the hard planes of his chest and abdomen, eyeing the light smattering of hair that dips past the V of his hipbones and down into his pants.

Unable to stop myself, I reach forward to remove his pants. My fingers fumble on his belt, barely able to slide it off in my rush. Too eager to wait, I pull his boxer briefs and pants down at once, revealing a thick, long erection that has my mouth watering in anticipation.

Asher threads his fingers through my hair until his hand is resting on the back of my head. "Open."

As soon as my lips part, he jerks his cock forward and into my mouth. We both groan the instant my lips make contact with the head of his cock. I place my hands on his thighs in an attempt to steady myself as he fucks my face, taking what he wants from me without remorse.

He takes what he wants, but I use him right back. As he fucks my face, I inch my body closer to him until my clit is brushing against his leg. My hips shift up and down, and my body revels in the friction until I'm dripping down his leg.

Asher pulls back abruptly and grabs my arms until I'm standing. I crawl onto the bed and remain on all fours. Behind me, he runs his palm against my ass in a teasing touch before giving it a firm spank. His fingers burn a trail down to my pussy, and I let out a long moan when he traces my slit, stopping to massage my clit.

After plunging two fingers inside of me, he asks, "Would you like a safe word?"

His gruff voice betrays his lust. He's on the edge of losing it, but so am I.

I moan at his words, barely able to let out a "no" before his fingers leave me and are quickly replaced by his cock, sinking deep into me from behind. I meet his violent thrusts with my own, grinding my ass roughly against him. My fingers grip the black sheets tightly, struggling to keep my body grounded as each solid pump of his cock pushes me forward.

I sweep my hair over one shoulder and twist it into an untied ponytail, forming a thick leash. When I hand it to him, he growls and pulls on my hair until my back arches and the pain hurts so good.

After he tugs my hair back, forcing my head to turn, and kisses me roughly, biting down on my bottom lip, I come hard and uncontrollably, helplessly convulsing around his cock.

My arms wobble, weak from the intense orgasm. I put them behind my back and press them against one another, as if they're bound by invisible cuffs. Asher groans at the sight. My face rests on the mattress, while he continues to fuck me from behind, each thrust pushing my face harder into the sheets. I can feel a second orgasm approaching, but before it reaches me, Asher pulls out and flips me over, so I'm on my back.

He sinks back into me, his eyes so dark with lust, I don't even recognize their color. I can't help but close my eyes at the feel of him from a new position.

"Open your eyes," he demands. "Look at me when you come again."

When I open my eyes, our eyes lock, the connection so intense and so intimate, it's at odds with the brutal pounding of his body into mine.

A throaty moan tears out of my lips, and I pant, "I'm so close."

Asher leans forward, so our entire fronts are pressed together, and quickens his pace, chasing my orgasm into fruition. When my walls begin to shake around his cock, I feel his fingers wrap around my throat, lightly squeezing until the vulnerable feeling of being dominated has me coming even harder.

Not a second later, his come spills into me, and I can't help but wish he had taken me bare. The thought of his skin against mine with no barriers has my walls gripping his cock tighter.

Asher chuckles knowingly and says, "We need to get you on birth control first."

"I have an IUD," I say, as he pulls out of me. "And I'm clean."

He smirks. "I know. I am, too."

I nod, though I already knew that. He's too cautious to contract an STD. Asher treats his body like a temple, working out often and eating well. The only times I've seen him eating poorly is when he indulges me, but even then, he never eats junk food.

Asher goes to the bathroom and comes back with a warm, wet hand towel. I relax into the mattress as he wipes me down. When he stops abruptly, I open my eyes and glance at his face. He's eyeing my neck, where the reddish beginnings of a bruise have undoubtedly begun to form.

When he speaks, it's soft. "I'm sorry."

A devious smirk crosses my lips. "I'm not."

And then I grab his arms and pull him against me, claiming his lips with mine.

Earlier today, I thought I was at the beginning of like, but I realize that I'm on the opposite edge—the hazy territory, where the lips of like and love kiss, and lines get blurry. And when Asher slips into me again that night, sliding slowly in and out of me, our hands clasped together and his eyes locked on mine, I slip closer into love, dangerously past the cusp of falling into forever.

CHAPTER THIRTY-ONE

The best protection any woman can have... is courage.
Elizabeth Cady Stanton

I wake up to a flash of light. It's quick and over by the time I open my eyes, but it was bright enough to wake me from my slumber.

"Asher?" I ask, groggily. "What was that?"

"The panic alarm," he replies calmly from across the room. "It's a bright light that shines once, followed by three quick and successive rings at a high enough frequency to wake us from a deep sleep."

I shoot up in alarm. When I glance at him, he's already fully dressed and putting two magnets attached to a keychain on random parts of the full body mirror beside the door. It pops open, and inside of it is a safe built into the wall. There are weapons, ranging from an assault rifle to a samurai sword, in the safe.

"Put some clothes on. Something that shows as little skin as possible," he says. His voice is still relaxed, as if he didn't just tell me the panic alarm was sounded and isn't currently loading his body with enough weapons to fight a small army.

I force myself to calm down, trying to exhibit the same cool Asher is. If he isn't worried, I shouldn't be either. By the time I'm dressed in black socks, black leggings and a black turtleneck, my hands are no longer trembling. I notice that Asher is dressed similarly and take the time to appreciate Asher's command. Covered like this, we'll both be fully protected from bullets everywhere but our heads.

I follow Asher into the armory, both of us moving silently across the hardwood floor. It's so silent in the halls, I almost don't believe there's a credible threat. When we reach the armory, Asher loads up on some more ammo, placing it on some strap that winds across his chest.

He turns to me and says, "If I don't return in 15 minutes, call the police and ask for a Detective Jameson. He's with me."

And then he presses his lips to mine and leaves before I can say, "What?"

A few seconds after he's gone, the armory doors begin to shut and flat screens descend from the ceiling. I realize that Asher initiated the panic room protocol. When the screens are fully lowered, I focus on studying the images on them, ignoring the pit in my gut that forms at the thought of Asher in danger.

I immediately recognize Asher's security team. There are about thirteen of them outside the penthouse doors. Two of them are by the elevators, two are stationed in front of the stairs, and the rest of them are looking at some device attached to the door that separates the hallway from the penthouse. When I zoom in on the device, I realize that it has a bunch of wires on it and freeze.

Is that a *bomb*?!

The idea is so ludicrous, so absurd that frantic laughter bubbles in my throat. I turn away from that screen, because I can't focus on that without freaking out. All of the rooms are empty, except the open area downstairs, where the living room, dining room and kitchen converge in one large open space.

There are some men sprawled across the floor. I don't recognize any of them, so I know they're the attackers. The three guards that normally stay in the security room are joined by Asher's night guard and mine. Even with the five of them alive and several of the enemies down, our guards are still outnumbered three to one.

It worries me that I don't see Asher anywhere, but I can't focus on that or I'll lose my cool. A glance at the clock tells me less than a minute has passed since Asher left, though it feels like an hour. I'll give him his 15 minutes before I call the cops but not a second more.

I observe from the safety of the panic room as my night guard fires two shots, the sound silent thanks to the silencer attached to the barrel of his gun. One hits an attacker in the neck, and the other hits one in between the eyes with unnerving accuracy. Two down, thirteen to go. My heart stops as one of the guards is hit in the chest with a bullet. He falls down and doesn't get back up. There are only four guards left, and I still have thirteen minutes and fifty-two seconds before I can call the cops.

The countdown reads thirteen minutes and eighteen seconds by the time I see Asher slithering his way down the stairwell. There are nine attackers left and only one of Asher's guards standing. The rest have fallen on the floor, their bodies lifelessly still. My heart mourns for the loss of these men, but I force myself to push these feelings aside until the threat is eliminated.

Asher stills at the last step, his body hidden behind the bend of the stairwell. While he stays there, the last guard is shot in the heart.

It's only Asher and the nine men now.

I watch as the men separate into three groups of three. One group clears the left hall and the other clears the right hall. I still, my hand hovering over the panic room's sat phone, when the last group silently approaches the stairwell, where Asher is hiding.

But in one quick moment, Asher has thrown knives into two of them and has the last one in a head lock. When the guy passes out, Asher binds his wrists with a zip tie. Everything was done so quickly, so efficiently, that the only sound emitted was a soft thump from the knifed bodies hitting the floor.

I watch as Asher enters the left hall, where one of the groups of three is still checking the rooms. He attaches a silencer onto a handgun, then slides into the office and shoots two of the attackers in the back of the head before they even realize he's there.

The third one is just now entering the hall from the theater room he just cleared. He passes the open office door and freezes. He and Asher make eye contact, and Asher springs into action, snapping the guy's neck before he can even lift the gun in his shocked hands.

There are only three attackers left and about ten minutes on my timer to spare. A few minutes ago, I would have thought it was an impossible task, but now I know better. Asher was born for this. I can see that now, in the way he moves, calm and self-assured. Each step he takes has such purpose and beauty, it makes these deaths seem almost stunning.

That thought sickens me so much, I have trouble watching Asher kill the other three with ease. I move to turn away from the screen, but when I see Asher approaching the door to the outside hallway, I leap into action, running to the intercom and pressing a button.

"Don't!" I shout.

Asher pauses on the screen as the sound of my voice echoes through the speakers, and I watch as his eyes lock onto the camera, a brow arched.

"There's a device on the other side. I think it's a bomb," I say. "Xavier and some other guards are out there dealing with it."

He nods and gestures for me to stay in the room, so I do. I watch as he clears the rest of the house by himself. I'm calm as he does this, because I can see from the security cameras that there's no one alive but him, but I let him continue anyway. Better safe than sorry.

When he's done clearing the penthouse, he approaches the panic room. I press a button, and the door opens, the screens slide back into place, and the sat phone retreats back into the wall. As soon as Asher sees me, he open his arms, and I move to hug him.

He leads me downstairs, and my brows furrow in confusion when he says, "*The Walking Dead.*"

There's humor laced in his voice, which booms loudly into the room. I jump in fright when I see the five guards rising. My night guard even stretches his hands out in front of him and poorly mimics a zombie's walk. He isn't winning any Oscars anytime soon.

I breathe out, my voice just a whisper. "What the fuck?"

Asher's night guard hears me and grins. "Bulletproof clothes."

Understanding dawns on me immediately. This is why the bulletproof clothes are only divulged on a need-to-know basis. For situations like this, where the guards are outnumbered and might get shot. They pretended to be dead, while Asher remained hidden and waited for an opportunity to strike. The foresight necessary to have such a precaution in place is genius, and I find myself appreciating Asher even more.

But I can't help the jab I throw his way. "*The Walking Dead*? You couldn't come up with something better?"

Asher shrugs, a smirk gracing his lips. "I thought it was funny."

There's a groan on the floor. I watch as the zip tied attacker blinks his eyes a few times before shooting upright. He freezes when he sees me, Asher and the five very much alive guards. Then, he turns around and runs towards the door, his hands still bound behind his back.

I remember the bomb on the door and stick my leg out, tripping him. It's an elementary school move, but it works. He face plants onto the hardwood and slides a little across the floor before one of the guards steps on his back, stopping his movement.

"Nice," says Asher, a grin on his lips.

I roll my eyes, but I'm smiling, too, because this is weird. I just tripped a guy sent to kill us.

After the guards cut off the guy's zip tie and cuff each of his hands to separate arms on one of the dining room chairs, Asher says to him, "I'm going to ask you a series of questions, and you're going to answer them."

The guy nods warily.

"You're not mafia," he says, though I have no idea how he knows this, but I trust that he's right. "So, you have no loyalties. No reason to lie. Keep that in mind."

The guy nods again but remains silent.

Asher flips the butterfly knife he's holding into the air and catches it. "Who hired you?"

The guy doesn't even hesitate when he says, "No names, but he was about 5'10", middle age, and wearing a suit. Dark hair, dark eyes, and a round gut. Looked corporate."

Asher pulls out his phone, types something in, and shows it to the guy. "Is this him?"

When the guy nods, I lean over to peak at the image. It's René's company picture.

Asher continues his interrogation, "How did you get in here?"

"Some lady gave us a key and helped us get through the biometrics. The client also gave us a file with all of your security protocols." He eyes the guards' clothing. "Well, I guess not all of them."

Asher nods, and then, in a movement too quick for me to track, slits the guy's throat. He turns to his night guard and says, "Stage it and erase the security footage from tonight. Make it look like they did it."

The guards nod at Asher, and I watch in shock as the guy is untied and sprawled on the floor, so it looks like he was killed during the fight. He's still faintly alive on the floor, but he's losing so much blood. It's pooling around him in a crimson halo.

The sight is so gory, I lean over and throw up onto the floor. Half of it lands on one of the dead attackers, and I grimace before throwing up again. I run to the closest bathroom, and thankfully, Asher doesn't follow.

CHAPTER THIRTY-TWO

Fate loves the fearless.
James Russell Lowell

"**D**id you have to kill him?" I ask Asher, my arms crossed and eyes narrowed.

We're in the office, standing disturbingly close to the three bodies Asher killed in here.

"Yes." At my disgusted look, he explains, "He knew about the bulletproof clothes. He had to go. It's us or h—"

"Him," I finish.

Asher's right. I can't fault that logic. I've seen firsthand how effective the clothes are and the potential they have for tricking enemies. But if people were to find out about them, they'd be prepared. They'd go for headshots and make sure that those who are down are dead.

It's us or them, and I'll always choose us.

That's just the way this world operates.

"So, it was René?" I ask, even though I know the answer to that. I just need him to confirm it, to make it real.

Asher nods and pulls out his phone. When I glance at it, I see an email from Owen.

To: a.black@blackenterprises.com
Fr: o.carter@blackenterprises.com

Subject: Emergency Board Meeting

Dear Mr. Black,

I am writing to inform you that the board has convened an emergency meeting in response to Mr. Toussaint's actions tonight. In a unanimous vote, the board has decided to dismiss Mr. Toussaint from his position at Black Enterprises, effective immediately. He will receive no pension nor severance pay, given his actions against your fiancée.

On a second note, we have also decided to cancel the upcoming vote regarding your position as CEO at Black Enterprises. We feel that you have suffered enough at the hands of Mr. Toussaint, and his claims against your competency are little more than a personal vendetta against you that has already been allowed to manifest itself long enough.

Mr. Toussaint has just been sent a similar email, informing him about our decision to let him go effective immediately. He has also been made aware of the cancellation of the upcoming vote concerning your position at Black Enterprises.

We suspect Mr. Toussaint will not take too kindly to his dismissal and will apprise you of the situation as it develops further. Until then, we suggest you brief your security detail on Mr. Toussaint, and we will do the same with the company's security team.

Thank you for your time. If you have any questions or concerns, feel free to email me at any time.

Very Best,

Owen Carter, COO

>When I'm done reading, I say, "It was revenge."
>Asher nods. "It looks that way."
>"And Monica?" I ask, remembering what the guy said about a

woman letting the attackers in. As far as I know, she's the only other woman with access to the penthouse.

"She'll be taken care of."

"How involved in this do you think she is?"

"She let them in and probably gave René access to the security detail."

I remember the late warning she gave Asher about the polo match. "And the polo match?"

Asher winces. "She probably thought I wouldn't reroute my flight to Dubai."

"But you did, and she was pissed off."

He nods. "I'm not sure why she's doing this, though. I was under the impression that she likes me. I had no idea that she wants me dead."

I cringe. "Maybe you're not the target for tonight either? I was the target for the last two shootings, after all."

I eye the dead bodies guiltily. It's their fault they chose this line of work, but it's also my fault they're dead. All this death for me. It hardly makes any sense.

"I know what you're thinking," Asher says, his eyes intently on my face.

"Of course, you do."

"This isn't your fault."

"Not entirely. It's also René's."

"And mine."

I nod, because he's right, but it doesn't make me love him any less. "So, what are we going to do about this?" I gesture a hand toward all of the dead bodies.

There are over two dozen in total.

"I've called Vince, and we'll g—"

"No."

"Excuse me?"

"No, you'll call the cops."

"I can't. If I call the cops, I have to do this their way."

"Exactly. Do this by the book. You have enough evidence."

"Do I?" He eyes René's men. "They're dead. They can't exactly testify against René."

He's right, but I'm sure there's something connecting them. "If that guy met him in person, then there has to be something to connect him and the rest of these guys to René. Footage of the meet? Wire transfers?"

"Are you willing to risk everything for that?"

I'm okay with René being free if it means Asher keeps his company. I've seen how much he loves Black Enterprises, and I refuse to stand idly by while he risks his position there again. This isn't like punching Steve in front of the whole company.

This is, judging by what Asher's capable of, killing René. If he does this, there's no going back, and I can't let that happen.

"Yes, I am."

"Well, I'm not."

"Think this through, Asher." I take a step forward and wrap my arms around his waist, tilting my head up to look at his face. "If you do this, there's no going back. René isn't part of the underworld. He was on the board for your company, a company that only just cancelled their meeting to vote on whether or not you're a risk to its wellbeing. You do this, and you're as good as done at Black Enterprises."

"I don't care." There's a stubborn expression on his face. "I have to do this, Lucy."

"Why?"

"Because they went after you."

My heart warms, realizing yet again how much this man is willing to risk for me.

But I can't let him.

"They went after you, too, so I get a say in this. And I don't want him dead. I want him to rot in jail." I grab his hand, unclench his fist, and intertwine our fingers together. "Please, do this for me, Asher."

There's a long stretch of silence before he nods, and I sag in relief, my body swaying onto his.

He catches my weight and smirks. "Was that our first couple's fight?"

Rolling my eyes, I pull back and smack him playfully on the arm. Then, I walk towards the kitchen with Asher trailing behind me. When I enter the kitchen, more of Asher's security team is there, surrounding the kitchen island. Even Xavier is standing here, which I assume means the bomb has been disarmed.

"The rest of the guards are calling contacts and setting up in a perimeter around the building," Xavier says to Asher, who nods.

I eye the countertops. A few bottles of tequila lay strewn across the marble, along with at least a dozen shot glasses. Xavier pours me a shot and hands it to me.

I grab it. "What are we drinking to?"

"The fact that we still can."

I down the shot.

CHAPTER THIRTY-THREE

The opposite of courage in our society is not cowardice. It is conformity.
Rollo May

It's all sorts of wrong, but I find myself laughing under my breath when the cops come and some of their eyes bulge at the ridiculous amount of bodies that lay strewn around the building.

Apparently, Asher's perimeter guards killed fifteen of their men in the garage. Along with the fourteen I watched die on the security cameras, the thirteen that were already dead before that, and the guard whose throat was slit, the body count is a mind boggling forty-three.

René didn't just hire a few men.

He hired a small army.

And they failed.

I learned that Xavier and the other twelve men that were in the hallway with them were able to get to us so quickly because they live on the floor below ours, which is another security measure that's need-to-know. They didn't even explain that to the cops.

Nor did they discuss their bulletproof clothes.

Instead, Asher and the entire security team put on clunky bulletproof vests over their shirts before the cops arrived, then put on a convincing show of explaining how the attackers only hit their vests. They even had all the bullets that were shot at them tucked away in a Ziploc evidence bag before the police arrived.

"So, none of these cameras picked up a thing?" a female detective asks Asher.

Again.

He sighs, clearly irritated. "They wiped them and shut them off before I killed them all."

"Okay," she says, but she clearly doesn't believe him. "And all these weapons?"

"Legally owned. I have licenses, if you would like to see them."

"You can forward copies to the email listed on my card."

Asher nods, his arms crossed. He's undoubtedly over this interview already, and I can't blame him. I would be, too, if I endured the same level of scrutiny. Instead, when they arrived, the officers took one look at the throw up on the floor, which Xavier rudely pointed out is mine, and inched further away from me.

Because the panic room is also need-to-know, I told them I hid under the bed and didn't see anything until Asher called me down when it was over. After eyeing the vomit again, they didn't question my story. Xavier thought it was hilarious, of course.

The cop finally nods for Asher to leave, and he joins me on the couch, where I've been not so subtly eavesdropping.

I lean my head on his shoulder and breathe in his familiar scent. "What do we do now?"

"I'm taking you to Vince's."

I immediately sit up straight. "No. Absolutely not."

"Why not? He can protect you."

"While you do what, exactly?"

"The cops went to René's house to bring him in for questioning, but he's gone. It's only Viola there with their kids. I'm going to track him down."

"And when you catch him?"

"I'll hand him over to the police." It's supposed to be a statement, but he says it like it's a question.

"You will?" I ask, dubiously.

"Yes," he says with more certainty. "I'm leaving to find him. That's nonnegotiable. You won't be safe until he's dead or behind bars." His eyes glint dangerously under the light. "While I would prefer him dead, I know you don't want that. I'll compromise on that, but I won't compromise on this. I'm going after him."

"Fine. But I'm not going to Vince's."

"Why not? His house is the safest place for you right now. You can't stay here. It's an active crime scene. Xavier will come with you."

"I'm not going to the Romano family, Asher."

"Vince isn't just a Romano. He's my family, too."

"I know that, and I have nothing against him, but it doesn't change the fact that he's a Romano. And turning to a Romano after an attack like this will look bad to the board."

"Fuck the damn board, Lucy. It's you I care about."

"But you care about your company, too."

"Not as much as I love you."

I don't think I'll ever get sick of those three words.

And it's because I feel the same way that I notice what he's feeling right now.

"Asher... Are you scared?" I ask, surprised.

"No, I'm rationally concerned."

I sigh, because that's as close as I'll ever get to an admittance. "I'll be safe with Xavier wherever we go. It doesn't have to be Vince's place. René's too busy on the run to come after me again."

"You don't know that."

"Then, I'll hide out until you find him, but it won't be at Vince's. It won't be at the expense of your future at Black Enterprises."

"Where else would you go?"

"Vaserley."

He scoffs. "That's too obvious. You've lived there before."

"There aren't any records of that, thanks to you. And the only people there that know I lived there live in my hall. I'll sneak in, and they won't even know I'm there."

"And you'll stay in the dorm despite the chance that René might have interviewed your hall mates in the past and found out you've lived there?"

I consider it. "If he was going around asking about me, Aimee would have told me. Half of the girls in the hall are Team Aimee. She has informants everywhere."

"It's still a risk."

"It's my risk to take."

"No, it's not. Not when I love you."

I sigh happily at his words but still manage to say what needs to be said, "Fine, but that means going after René isn't your risk to take, because," I mumble quickly, "Iloveyou,too."

"What?"

I groan and say louder, "I love you."

This isn't how I pictured my first time saying those words would be like, and judging by the shocked look on Asher's face, he didn't either.

"You love me?"

When I nod, he closes the gap between us and kisses me roughly.

He pulls back and demands, "Say it again."

"I love you." My voice is stronger this time, confident.

He rests his forehead against mine, stares into my eyes, and says, "Fine. You can stay at Vaserley, but I'll have three guards on you at all times. I'll have a security team access security footage from Vince's, and there will always be one breach team and one extraction team less than sixty seconds away. Your three guards will be Xavier, your night guard and Bastian."

"Bu—"

"Nonnegotiable. I compromised, so you'll have to, too."

I sigh but say, "You know, you're really hot when you speak to me in your boardroom voice."

Asher throws his head back in a carefree laugh, and despite the gravity of the situation, my heart races and my soul warms.

We take about a dozen cars, and when each of the cars exit the garage, they split up into different directions. If René is tracking us, he'll have to guess where we're going. One of the cars is headed to Jersey, another upstate, and the rest to random motels and Romano businesses.

I lift a questioning brow when our car stops at a red light and Asher opens the door for me. He gestures for me to get out, and I notice that we're surrounded mostly by giant trucks, so no one can see us. One of the trucks is actually a massive moving truck, and I'm ushered into the back of it, with Xavier, my night guard, and Asher following closely behind me.

There's no light in the back of the truck, but I can make out the outline of several boxes. I tap on one of them, testing it for sturdiness, before I take a seat on top of it. Someone turns on a light, and the back of the truck becomes dimly lit.

There's an amused look on Asher's face when he says, "You did well on your first bait and switch."

"Second," I correct. "Technically, the whole Caroline and Damien thing was a bait and switch, too."

Asher nods. "You did well, then, too."

I grin and shrug, remembering Asher's accusation a few months ago. "I've been told I'm one part mafia spy and one part corporate spy."

"You forgot honeypot."

"That, too."

"Well, aren't you guys cute?" a deep voice says.

I screech, almost falling off of my perch on the box when a figure emerges from the shadowed corner.

So much for being a spy...

Asher reaches out to steady me, and I let him, my body tense. When the car lurches forward, the light no longer red, I'm able to lean on Asher to prevent another fall. His body doesn't even sway with the jerky movements of the vehicle.

"Don't worry," Asher murmurs. "He's with us."

"My name is Niccolaio, but you may call me Nick," the man introduces himself.

I look at him, taking in his tan skin, dark hair, and dark brown eyes. He's dressed in all black—black sweats, black shoes, and a tight black shirt that hugs his trim, muscular frame quite closely. There's something about him that looks dangerous, lethal. It's the same something Asher has, except I don't trust it on Nick.

I press closer to Asher and hope my voice doesn't betray my wariness when I say, "I'm Lucy."

"I know. Lucy Ives," he says, a brief smile flashing across his face.

A frown tugs heavily on my lips. "Yet, I don't know you."

It's bothering me that he knows my last name, and I don't know his... even though my last—and entire—name is fake. Speaking of which, I should tell Asher my real name sometime.

There's a rumble of laughter before Asher wraps an arm around my shoulders, squeezing me against him in an openly affectionate side hug. "That's Niccolaio Andretti."

My jaw drops, practically unhinging itself from the normalcy of its socket. "Andretti?"

"Yes. I spared his life when I took his uncle's," says Asher, casually, and I think he's referring to the *capo* he went into Andretti territory to kill. "We're... friends."

Niccolaio scowls, "We won't continue to be if you keep spilling my secrets to everyone you know."

Asher rolls his eyes. "Don't be dramatic, Nick. Lucy isn't everyone.

She's one of mine." He turns to me. "Nick will be with me while I track down René."

I'm immediately relieved to learn that he has back up. Even though I neither know nor trust Nick, Asher seems to, and I trust Asher with my life... until the car screeches to a halt, and Nick gestures to the box I'm sitting on and says, "Get in."

CHAPTER THIRTY-FOUR

*Faced with what is right, to leave
it undone shows a lack of courage.*
Confucius

"Excuse me?" My arms are crossed, and I'm glaring at Nick. "You want me to get in the box?"

He ignores me, reaches inside a gym bag, pulls out some clothes, and hands it to Asher and the guards. The three of them strip, and I can't even enjoy a shirtless Asher, because I was just asked by an Andretti to stuff myself into a cardboard moving box.

When the guys are done dressing, they're in some sort of work uniform of jeans, a t-shirt, a baseball cap, and heavy worker boots. The caps read, "Donato's Moving Company," while the t-shirts have the company's logo sprawled across the front. The caps are pulled low enough that, if they keep their heads down, Asher and the guards will be unrecognizable.

I see what's happening.

Wherever we're going, they'll be disguised as movers, and I'll be hidden in a box they'll move. Lucky me.

"Fine," I say, hopping down from the box and lifting its lid.

The box may look like it's made of cardboard on the outside, but the inside is sturdy and made of plush leather. Asher stops me for a moment and presses a button, causing wheels to descend from the bottom of the box. A handle even pops up, which I assume is to help move me easier. The whole set up is fancy, and it leaves me to conclude that this isn't the first time they've moved people this way.

Asher helps me into the tall, rectangular box. I sit down, shifting until I'm comfortable. When Asher leans in to kiss me, I glare at him but let him anyway. He's smirking when he closes the lid on me.

My fingers latch onto the wall to steady myself as I'm rolled down a plank. There's less than a minute of darkness before the lid of the box opens, and I'm standing inside a fashionable brownstone.

"Where are we?" I ask Nick, as Asher and the guards head back out to bring in more moving boxes, which are actually just empty.

"Wouldn't you like to know?"

I roll my eyes but don't ask again. The drive didn't take very long, so given the New York City traffic, we're probably still pretty close to Asher's. My guess, considering how fancy this place is, is that we're in one of those expensive brownstones by Central Park.

When Asher returns, he hands me the bag I packed. I packed light with only the bare essentials—a phone charger, toiletries and two changes of clothes. Asher, on the other hand, stuffed his bag with an insane amount of weapons and ammo and all black clothing. He only has two changes of clothes in there, too, which gives me hope that he doesn't think this will take too long.

We're led into a room with a bunch of high tech computers and screens, and until nightfall, I watch as Asher, Nick and the guards sift through René's life, unveiling everything from the semi-fascist article he wrote for his high school paper to the pregnant mistress he paid off a few years ago. She walked away with a sizable chunk of his net worth and still receives a massive monthly check, which might explain René's desire to acquire Black Enterprises for himself. There's even a deleted email on René's private server, connecting him to my invitation to the Wilton networking event.

I'm unable to look away as the guys sift through all of René's secrets, hardened and horrified by the violating realization that René must have done the same to me at one point.

The moon is in clear view again by the time Asher informs me that it's time to leave for Vaserley. Instead of leaving in the moving truck again, we take a town car that's sitting in the garage. As we get in the back and Nick draws the curtains on the black tinted windows, I realize that it's for us.

Or maybe it's just me he doesn't want to know where he lives.

Either way, I can't see the road as we drive out of the garage and onto the street. In some ways, it's like being moved in the box again, except I have Asher sitting beside me this time. About half an hour passes before we pull up to Vaserley, which doesn't make a lot of sense, since Asher's place is less than a minute from Vaserley, and the drive to Nick's place yesterday only lasted ten minutes at the most.

I assume the driver must have taken a long route or driven in circles. I'm not sure whether that's to confuse me or someone that may be trailing us. Regardless, I'm extra wary of Nick's cloak and dagger routine, though to some extent, I recognize these moves as similar to the protocols Asher has put into place.

When I get out of the car, I notice that we're in the private parking lot for Vaserley employees only. The cars that usually park in this lot mostly belong to the dining hall staff, housekeepers, R.A.s, P.C.s, and resident living administrators. So, it's pretty empty right now, considering it's a weekend and the only staff that sleep at Vaserley are R.A.s and P.C.s.

There's a door to enter the staff area of the hall, but it's guarded by a fairly young campus security guard. He looks to be about in his mid-twenties. I'm surprised when Asher approaches the guy, and they bump fists.

"Ash, long time no see!" the guy greets with an easy smile.

"Hey, Mark." Asher gestures to me. "This is my fiancée, Lucy." He turns to me. "Lucy, this is Mark. We used to train together at my neighborhood's UFC gym."

Mark adds, "That was before Princess Asher got swept away by Prince Charming and pushed into a life of prep schools and Ivy leagues."

Asher rolls his eyes. "He's still bitter that he's never won a fight against me."

"Yeah, yeah." Mark becomes serious, his eyes cutting to Nick and the guards before returning to Asher. "I let Bastian up a few minutes ago. Is everything good?"

"Yeah, Lucy's hiding out here for a few days with these two," he gestures to the guards, "and Bastian. We have surveillance on Vaserley, but I'd also appreciate your eyes and ears, too."

"Of course. Same phone number?"

Asher nods, then Mark opens the door, and we're ushered inside through the back entrance. Vaserley is a ghost town as we make our way to my old hall, which makes sense given the late hour. We stay quiet, though, being sure not to wake anyone up.

One of Asher's guards sent a message to Aimee ahead of time to find somewhere else to stay, so we won't be waking her up by going inside the room. Using my old key, I open the door into my former dorm room and turn on the lights. I roll my eyes when I see that Aimee's mess has found its way onto my old bed. Typical.

Even Asher's brows raise when he takes in the scene. "Was it ransacked?"

I'm not sure if he's joking or not, so I answer anyway, "This is 100% Aimee."

"Huh."

No kidding.

Before I can reply, there's a knock on the door. Asher opens it slightly, his gun ready in one hand, before relaxing his trigger finger and opening the door all the way. I see Bastian first and relax, but when Minka enters my line of sight, I'm instantly tense again.

"What do you want?" I ask, bluntly.

Bastian answers instead, "She's offering to give you her room. Sounds legit."

Minka rolls her eyes at the suspicion in mine. "I owe you for saving me from the spiked drink. We're even after this."

"I vetted her electronics history and did a full sweep of her room. Everything checks out," Bastian continues, ignoring us. "It's a better option than Lucy's old room."

Asher turns to me and lifts a questioning brow. I sigh and nod, because Bastian is right. It makes more sense to hide out in Minka's room than one that I'm known to have stayed in.

"We'll take it," Asher says.

Minka crosses her arms and adds, "Just to be clear, I still don't like you, but I respect you for what you did for me."

I don't reply, because honestly, I don't give a fuck. I just want this whole thing to be done, so I can have Asher back safely already.

CHAPTER THIRTY-FIVE

She was warned. She was given an explanation. Nevertheless, she persisted.
Mitch McConnell on Elizabeth Warren

Three days. That's how long it's been since Asher left. In those three days, I have paced and tossed and turned and paced again, hardly sleeping at all. I'm certain that, if another day passes without any word from Asher, Bastian will leave me here—I'm getting on his last nerve.

Hell, I got on Minka's last nerve an hour into my stay, when she and Nella, who shares her dorm room, got up to sleep in one of her lackeys' room instead. My night guard followed after her until another of Asher's guards could take his place. None of us trust Minka and Nella to keep their mouths shut, so they have to be watched.

When there's a knock on the door, I shoot upward from the desk chair and head straight to the door. To my irritation, Xavier cuts me off, and Bastian opens the door in my stead. There's a moment of tense silence before I see Asher walking through the threshold. A small cut lines his forehead, and his lip is busted, but other than that, he looks okay.

Not caring who sees, I run up to him and jump into his arms, making him stumble slightly into the crowded hallway until he carries us back into the room. He winces, and I immediately untangle myself from him, but he pulls me back into his arms. I slither my fingers under his shirt, pressing gently around his abdomen, pausing when he hisses in pain.

"What happened?" I ask.

"Probably a broken rib."

"You need to see a doctor."

He gives me an awe-shucks-aren't-you-so-cute? smile that pisses me off. "No need. It'll heal."

I don't press the issue. I won't win, and I need to pick my battles. "What happened?" I ask again, though this time, I'm referring to what happened while he was gone.

"Nick and I were ambushed by René's men."

"How many?"

"Nineteen at a warehouse in Jersey."

Nineteen. After the showdown at the penthouse, I have no doubt Asher can handle nineteen men—with or without Nick's help. Clearly, Asher is fine. He's here, after all.

So, I ask, "Nick?"

"He's fine. He blew out of town to lay low."

I don't ask about that, because I don't give a damn about why Nick needs to lay low so long as he's okay. "And René?"

"We found him at a motel a mile away from the warehouse."

"What'd you do?"

He narrows his eyes at my accusatory tone. "We didn't kill him, Lucy."

"Then, what'd you do?"

"We called the police."

"And they arrested him? With what evidence?"

Asher smirks. "He didn't have any evidence with him, but we may have planted some for the police to find when they search the room."

"Asher... that's illegal."

"So? It's only illegal if the police finds out, and they won't."

I should be worried that he broke the law, but I'm not. I'm just relieved he's here, and this is all over. "And Monica?"

"Fired with a lawsuit pending for breaking the NDA. We're also gathering evidence against her as we speak for a criminal suit. We have the security log showing her entering the building right before the attack. We handed that over to the cops. She should be in jail soon if she isn't already."

"But you don't know if she's in jail yet."

"It's only a matter of time."

"Oh."

"Lucy?"

"Yes?"

His eyes darken. "The black rose..." he begins.

My mind races, confused. "What about it?"

"René sent it to you. We were able to track the purchase."

My eyes widen. "I thought you gave it to me."

Asher places a finger under my chin and tilts my face up, so I'm looking into his eyes. "For future reference, if I send you roses, it'll be a whole damn bouquet."

I smile and lean forward to kiss him. When I pull back, I ask, "So what now?"

"Whatever you want, Lucy."

*T*urns out that what I really want after all of this is to have a normal day with Asher, and that includes going to my only class today. I'm taking another course with Dr. Rolland this semester, one on the applications of physics in biology. I haven't actually physically gone to it, thanks to the threat on my life, but I'm excited to now.

"We're going to be late." I frown.

Asher lifts his brow, as if to say, "So what?"

"Splash zone."

I laugh when he quickens his pace, but it dies immediately at the sight of Monica. She's hovering outside the entrance of Vaserley just as we exit. In her designer getup and perfect blow out, she reminds me of the third world cuisine I was accustomed to eating during my travels—seasoned to death to hide the rotten meat underneath.

When she sees me, she snarls. "You!"

I approach her as Xavier and my night guard grab her arms. "What about me? You're the one that tried to kill Asher."

"I'd never hurt Asher. It was supposed to be you!"

I laugh at her naïveté. "Is that how he got you to go along with this? He promised to kill off your competition?" I know I'm right when she freezes in her struggle against Xavier's hold.

She opens her mouth to say something, but it doesn't matter. I'm already walking past her with Asher by my side. Xavier stays behind and waits for the cops to come, but I don't.

I move forward, and I move on.

And when Asher and I enter the lecture hall and see that the only free seats are in the splash zone, we sit down anyway. I giggle a little when a speck of Dr. Rolland's spit lands on Asher's cheek, and he rolls his eyes at me. When he pulls the handkerchief out of his suit pocket to wipe it off, I take the time to admire him.

Asher's a killer. He's a genius. He's loyal. He's my kind of perfect. He's the type of man a girl would sit in the splash zone for. And most importantly, he's mine.

EPILOGUE

The wooden floor is cold beneath my bare feet as I make my way towards Asher's office. I leave the lights off, not needing the light to guide me through a home I already know like the back of my hand. Hell, the only true home I've ever known.

By the time I open the door to Asher's office, my body is shivering, and I'm surprised my feet haven't turned blue.

Asher looks up at me from his desk, smiles that panty-dropping smile of his, and takes in my body from head to toe. When his eyes settle on my freezing feet, he says with a self-assured smirk, "Cold feet?"

"Ha. Ha," I deadpan. "I could say the same about you." I make my way towards him, glancing at the clock on the wall before perching myself on the edge of his desk, my entire body facing his. "It's three A.M. on the morning of our wedding, and you're up five hours early. Is this the part where the bride-to-be is supposed to be worried?"

"Just going over logistics." He waves his hands toward the sheet of paper beside me, which has the words "Wedding Security Detail" typed across the top of it in Times New Roman font, before handing me his glass of sparkling water. He arches a brow when I take the glass and set it down beside me without drinking from it.

I laugh, unable to help myself. About a month ago, Aimee reminded me of our conversation the day Asher first visited me on campus. The one where we had joked about my wedding with Asher, only back then, we said I'd get shot and poisoned.

I didn't think either of those things were going to happen, but I hadn't thought I'd have a hit out on me either, and that happened. So, I started taking precautions, leaving the wedding security up to Asher and only eating and drinking things that I prepared myself.

I thought I was being sly about it, but obviously I wasn't, because the whole ordeal ended with Asher confronting me and threatening to withhold any future orgasms until I finally confessed my fears.

I didn't even last 24 hours.

I reposition myself so I'm at the center of the desk, in between Asher's legs. "You know I was just joking, right? I don't actually think you or anyone else would poison me." Truthfully, I just want this—him, *us*—so badly that I'm willing to do anything to make it happen. "I just... I didn't want to risk anything coming between us."

My breath hitches when his fingers touch my hip, leaving a teasing trail downwards until his fingers reach my foot. He grabs it and brings it onto his lap, rubbing it between his palms until his body heat transfers onto my cold toes.

When he's done with my right foot, he switches it out for my left foot, replicating his previous movements while maintaining eye contact with me. "I'd never let anything happen to you, Lucy. We could be on opposite ends of the world eighty years from now, divorced and pissed the fuck off at each other, and I still wouldn't let anything happen to you. Because you're mine. Always will be."

"And you?"

He tugs my leg until I slide off the desk and onto his lap, our faces barely an inch apart. "I've always been yours, Lucy."

I sigh, snuggling against his body and resting my chin on his shoulder. "You know, you just painted a future of us, where we're 1) physically separated, 2) divorced, and 3) pissed the fuck off at each other. On our wedding day, no less. Are you sure you're going to say *I do* today?"

"Yes, Smart Ass." He leans back, forcing me to look him in the eye, because I can't not. Asher is *everything*, and trying to look away from him is like trying to avoid death. Or taxes. Damn impossible. "But even if we don't have today, if we don't have this wedding, you'll still be the woman I'm spending the rest of my life with. We don't need to be married to validate that. Being able to call you Mrs. Black is just a bonus."

"I know, but just so *you* know, Asher Aaron Black, *I do*. Eighty years from now, *I do*. Across the world from you, *I do*. Pissed the fuck off at you, *I do*. *I do* a million times."

ACKNOWLEDGMENTS

Goodness, I have so many people to thank! First and foremost, thank you to my family—my German Shepherd, Bauer; my husky/lab mix, Chloe; and my amazing boyfriend, L. I love you guys so much! Thank you for being there when I needed you guys and leaving when I didn't. (Y'all know how cranky I can be when I write!)

Elan—thank you for finding the time to text me every single day, even as I write this now, and you're gallivanting around Europe, surely with better things to do than talking to little ole me.

Another thanks to my professors from UCR and Harvard, all of whom have worked hard to shape my writing. I wouldn't be who I am today without you guys! A special shout out to Derrick, who was instrumental in completely changing my career path.

Last but not least, thank you to everyone reading this, along with the author community. I've never even met most of you guys, yet many of you took the time to help me out. In this regard, a special thanks to author Kat Mizera is much deserved.

ABOUT PARKER

Parker S. Huntington hates talking about herself, so bear with her as she awkwardly toots her own horn for a few sentences and then bids her readers adieu.

Parker S. Huntington is from Orange County, California. She graduated pre-med with a Bachelor's of Arts in Creative Writing from the University of California, Riverside. As of August 2018, the 21-years-old novelist is still pursuing a Master's in Liberal Arts (ALM) in Literature and Creative Writing from Harvard University. *Go Crimson!*

She was the proud mom of Chloe and will always look back on her moments with Chlo as the best moments of her life. She has 2 puppies—a Carolina dog named Bauer and a Dutch Shepherd and lab mix named Rose. She also lives with her boyfriend of five (going on six!) years—a real life alpha male, book boyfriend worthy hunk of a man.

For more information:
www.parkershuntington.com
parkershuntington@gmail.com